The Pendant Cross

Emma Batten

First published in Great Britain by Emma Batten.

ISBN 978-1-9995820-6-7

Printed and bound in the UK.

A catalogue record of this book can be found in the British Library.

Edited by Maud Matley.

Proofread by Amanda Giles.

Cover painting by Kate Western.

Cover graphic design by Aaron Birks at Bluebirch Creative.

For my son, Kim, with love and thanks for your interest in my writing adventures.

Many thanks to artist Kate Western who produced my gorgeous cover painting.

Thank you to Phil and Joan Castle who have advised me on small details to make the era authentic in this novel. I would not have been brave enough to set off on a Saxon journey without your support.

Also, thanks to Anne Petrie for reading this and giving valuable feedback before it was printed.

And special thanks to Maud Matley who has given me so much encouragement and shared her knowledge of the Catholic Church, as well as working with me to create Elder-Modor's song about Queen Ethelburga.

About the book

This time I am taking my readers back to the late 7th century. The book was inspired by an area called Sandtun (now West Hythe) on the eastern edge of Romney Marsh. In Anglo-Saxon times there was a shingle spit, roughly where the Dymchurch seawall and Hythe ranges lie, and behind it was a sheltered lagoon. The surrounding land was beginning to dry out and our present-day Romney Marsh was forming. Archaeological digs on the Sandtun have led to suggestions that this was a seasonal trading camp and an area where people would fish. People gathered there for a few days a year to trade with men who sailed across from mainland Europe.

As I began to explore the area and immerse myself in the Anglo-Saxon era, I learned about the story behind Botolph's Bridge pub sign. It shows four monks carrying a coffin with a golden light showing the way across a plank bridge. I will not say any more — it may spoil the book.

I then looked for a village within a few hours walking distance from Romney Marsh and with Anglo-Saxon connections. Knowing nothing about Lyminge and its status in those times, I stumbled across information about the royal feasting hall discovered on Tayne Field and discovered the site was used by royalty during the

5th to 7th centuries. I was fortunate to find the 633 AD Saxon church uncovered as part of a dig. I also learned about Queen Ethelburga, the church and minster founded by her at Lyminge. Her story is told in the form of a song within this book, a common method of passing down stories in those times.

I have chosen to keep to modern place names for local villages, and to use names in keeping with the period for ancient roads, areas of the country and the sea.

It was the book *Romney Marsh: Survival on a Frontier,* by Jill Eddison, which first told me about the Sandtun and, as always, has been a valuable resource. The website www.regia.org has been frequently visited as I search for information on-line.

With thanks to Amanda Giles and Maud Matley for proofreading and editing, and to Anne Petrie and Michelle Jeffery who read the novel before it was printed and checked for any mistakes which had slipped past earlier checks. Thanks to Lucie Bolton from Kent Wildlife Trust's Fifth Continent, for allowing me to be a part of training sessions and to experience some of the work an archaeologist does, while we hunt for the remains of the Saxon port at Old Romney. As always, I am truly grateful to my readers who are such amazing supporters, and to local stockists of my novels.

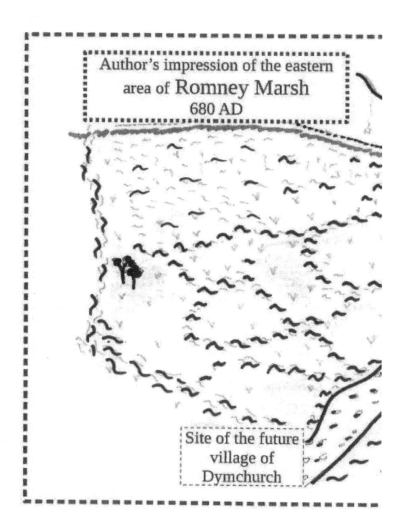

Author's impression of the eastern area of **Romney Marsh** 680 AD

Site of the future village of Dymchurch

6

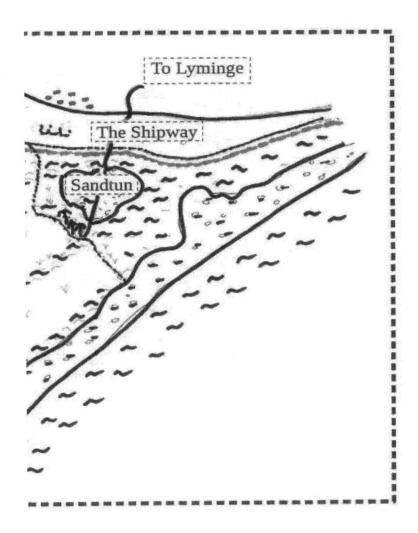

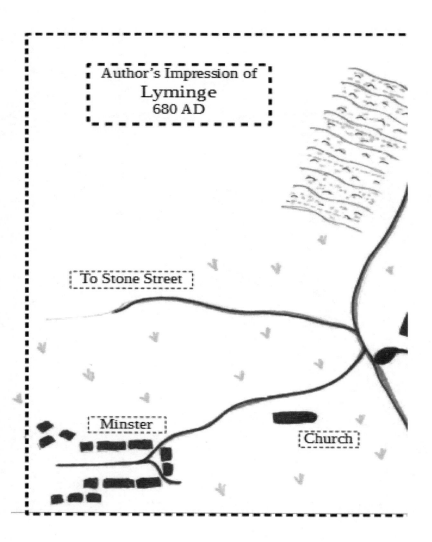

Author's Impression of
Lyminge
680 AD

To Stone Street

Minster

Church

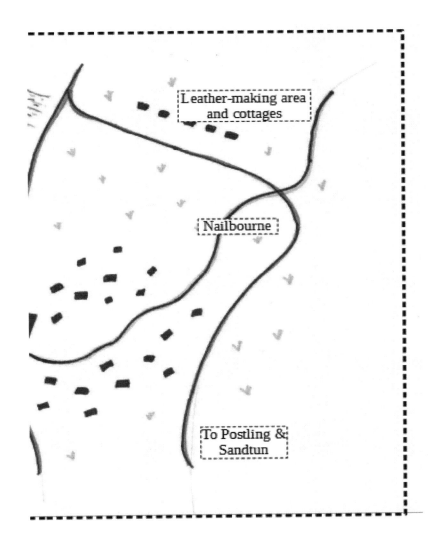

Leather-making area and cottages

Nailbourne

To Postling & Sandtun

Chapter One
Somewhere in Middle England
680 AD

"What sort of place is this Romney Marsh?" the monk asked. The words did not come easily: his lips only knew prayer; his tongue only knew to move in the gentle rhythm of the psalms.

"There's nothing to speak of," Brother Halig replied, his voice low and monotone. "It is as bleak as one could imagine and will serve our purpose well."

There was silence for a moment as this news was digested by the first monk, who perched with two others on a fallen log in a woodland clearing. Brother Halig sat just a few feet away from them, his woollen tunic resting on the skeletons of last autumn's leaves, and the bag with its treasures at his feet. Dusk was now well established and the four of them had just eaten some of the coarse bread and rich cheese they had carried with them since leaving the monastery the evening before. The sounds about them were muted: the scuffle of a small mammal, the distant grunt of a boar, the rustle of leaves in the trees. The air was rich with the smell of damp moss and decaying vegetation; it was moist as evening settled upon them.

"Shall we move onwards?" the first monk asked. He glanced towards the shrouded figure on the ground and already felt the burden of their journey. It was only the beginning though; they expected to be on the road for many nights.

"It is time," replied Brother Halig, the one who would lead them on this journey. It was he who knew of the land he called bleak and assured them Romney Marsh would provide the solitude they needed.

They had already formed a pattern of working in pairs and, as Brother Halig gave his approval, the two other monks moved to take the wooden handles of the stretcher. The body lurched a little but settled within the woven sling as it was lifted. Then, with Brother Halig taking the lead, they stepped forward, their toes kicking aside any debris on the track.

Within a few minutes the woodland had ended and, in the light of the half-moon, the wide Roman road named Earninga Street was a soft grey ribbon before them. The four of them paused for a moment and listened. There was no sound to indicate other men on the road and a slight wave of Brother Halig's hand indicated it was safe to move on.

They now marched in single file: first Brother Halig, whose eyes were alert to any man upon the road at night, then Brother Edwen, who still wondered about their destination. Finally, the two young monks with the shrouded figure slung between them. They would move onward in this fashion for a time, keeping an even pace and holding their thoughts in their own minds. It was already apparent that Brother Halig would encourage no idle chatter.

After a while, the sling was lowered to the ground and Brother Edwen took his turn at the front. He lifted the prone figure with ease; his muscles were strong from labouring in the grounds of the monastery. All three of the younger monks had been chosen with

12

their strength and resilience in mind. But with the weight pulling down on him, Edwen's upper arms were soon feeling the strain and, with darkness all around them, there was little to distract him as one foot after the other moved him forward through the area of middle England known as Mercia.

A moment of relief came when the body was again lowered, but this time Edwen was not released from the task. He sighed, flexed his arms, rubbed his back, and wrapped his hands around the handles of the sling once more. The ground was unforgiving, with only the leather of his shoe between the sole of his foot and the rough stones topping a road kept busy with a large volume of horses, carts and men travelling on it during the daylight hours. Edwen looked towards the silver moon and its beauty gave him some pleasure; he breathed deep, filling his lungs with the damp air of the night, and appreciating the scent from flowers in the hedgerows.

Another hour passed and this time they paused on the roadside to drink weak ale. Brother Edwen rubbed his hands together and moved his arms to and fro to prevent them from stiffening. A leather sack was opened, and they snacked on seeds, soft apples and cheese. Then Brother Halig looked towards the road and no words were exchanged as the sling was again lifted between two of the monks.

As they walked, Brother Edwen, now free of the burden – not that he should think of it in such a way – broached the subject of their destination again. "What makes the land bleak?" he wondered. "Has no one ever settled there?"

"They settled on the islands risen from the marsh," Brother Halig replied. "But that is no concern of ours.

No man has bothered about the area we are bound for, not since the Romans were driven away."

"Three hundred years or so," Brother Edwen murmured. He refrained from asking any more: it was enough for now.

Leading the way, Brother Halig kept his eyes on the road and his fingers fretted at the leather holding his pendant cross. Had the other three men been able to see his face, perhaps they would have noticed that his lips moved and words flowed without sound. But he walked ahead of them and they knew nothing of his constant prayers.

As the first streaks of pink were cast across the sky, Edwen was again carrying the sling. He felt his heart lighten a little and his pace quickened. Brother Halig now searched on either side of the wide road and the three who laboured knew there would soon be some respite and, God willing, a comfortable place to rest their aching bodies.

Chapter Two
Lyminge, Kent
680 AD

"Word has come; we must make haste to leave."

Eadlyn looked up at her husband who had entered the weaving shed: he stood behind her as she worked at the loom. A smile broke across her face, and she turned to him. "I'll fetch the children and some food, and..." She reached out to touch his arm, clad in the woollen sleeve of his tunic, then continued, "Blankets, we must remember the blankets and a bucket for water... We forgot it last year"

"We've known this day was coming." Todd placed a kiss on her forehead. "It will be as we planned. I'll fetch the horse."

"Of course," Eadlyn said. She could feel the fluttering in her stomach and tried to calm it. "We have planned for this and all will be well. I'll ask my sister to finish the cloth and it will not matter if I go now." She watched Todd leave through the open doorway.

It was dark in the weaving shed, even with the wide doors open; much of the work was done by touch. Finishing the section she was working on came easily to Eadlyn, while her thoughts were all on the adventure ahead. Eadlyn had been working the drop spindle and weaving the thread since she was not much older than her own young daughter. She moved away from the loom and approached her sister.

"I saw Todd was here," Janna spoke first. "You want me to finish the weaving?"

"Please," Eadlyn replied, trying to hide her excitement. "We have to leave."

"I know." Janna stood, pushed the stool back and dropped the yarn she was teasing from a bundle of wool. "But Eadlyn... take care. It's a strange place, that Romney Marsh. They say things happen there, and it holds mysteries, unexplained happenings."

"It's done me no harm." Eadlyn flashed a smile.

"No." Janna paused. "Let's hope it stays that way."

"And I'll see you again within the week," Eadlyn said.

"You will. Then it will be over for another year."

Stepping out of the shed, Eadlyn paused for just a few seconds to allow the summer sun to warm her skin. She took the scarf off her head and shook it to release dust particles which had settled on it as she worked. Then she removed the hair comb and untied the string holding her hair in a knot at the base of her neck. Thick waves of hair, the colour of ripened wheat, tumbled onto her shoulders: she ran her fingers through it and retied the knot, before replacing the scarf. It felt good to have her hair loose and the fresh air around her scalp, if only for a moment. Then, holding her dress free from the ground, Eadlyn raced across the worn grass, past the bakehouse and the thane's hall, to her own home on the edge of the village of Lyminge.

Like all the other buildings in the village, Todd and Eadlyn's home was constructed of vertical plank walls with a roof of thatched straw. It was no longer than

16

fifteen paces, and half as wide. The door stayed open all day in the summer and now, at the threshold, there was a small pile of their belongings. Todd appeared with the cooking pan. He placed it beside a box containing their wooden bowls, spoons and a sack of dried beans, peas and grain. "I'm off to get the horse," he called out.

Eadlyn raised her hand to acknowledge his words and, walking past their home, she went in search of the children. They were by the pig pens; two-year-old Cym was fascinated with the animals. Clover had a wicker basket in her hand.

"Clover, go and tell Elder-Modor we are leaving for Romney Marsh," Eadlyn said to her daughter as the children ran up to her. Reaching in her purse for a coin, she pressed it into Clover's hand, "And can you buy some cheese; I'll take the eggs." Glancing in the basket, she saw there were six of them, brown and warm from the sunshine. "Cym must come with me, as I must change his tunic before we leave."

Scooping up the little boy, Eadlyn perched him on her hip. Cym was fair-haired like herself and his sister. His limbs were still chubby and browned by the sun. He wrapped his arms around her, and she kissed the top of his head; he smelt of chickens and pigs and straw. Back in their one room home, the fire had been left to go out and the air was thick with smoke from smouldering ashes. Eadlyn lay Cym down on a bench and removed his muddied tunic, singing to the little boy as she replaced it, hoping to distract him before he tried to wriggle away.

"I've got the cheese." Clover skipped through the doorway.

"Thank you, dearling." Eadlyn looked up at her daughter, who was silhouetted by the sun. "Can you

17

put it in the box with the grain and cooking pot? Your faeder will be back in a minute; he has gone to fetch a horse." She allowed Cym to scramble off the bench. "Let's see if we have everything we need."

Outside the home, the cart was laden with leatherwork, all crafted by Todd. There were blankets, shawls and Todd's cloak. Eadlyn added the cooking pot and box of food, then removed the pot stand from its place over the fire. Scanning the contents, she frowned.

"Modor, we have no bread," Clover pointed out.

"I thank you," Eadlyn grinned; already Clover was showing what a fine young woman she would grow up to be. "It's still cooling by the bread oven. I'll get it." She turned and walked down the hillside to the bread oven in the centre of the village, unable to keep the skip out of her step.

The oven was domed, built of clay, then clad with turfs. A woman was on her knees in front of it, one hand shielding her face from the heat, the other manoeuvring a long-handled wooden spatula, so as to scoop her loaf from the rack above the glowing embers. A shelter nearby had a long central table where the women mixed and kneaded the dough every morning, and on shelves to one side, the freshly cooked bread cooled before being collected. Eadlyn took her bread and turned on her heel, then headed back to the family home.

Todd was there, with a horse loaned to him by the thane. The exchange was a fair one. They were lucky this master of their village, and his father before him, were good to the people. Just the month before, Todd had presented the thane with two good leather bridles and now he could borrow one of his horses for the duration of his time away from the village. Eadlyn grinned to see her husband harnessing the horse to the cart; they would be leaving within minutes and the summer adventure would begin.

Sitting on the cart, the children nestled amongst the blankets, their eyes bright. They looked about, wanting to attract the attention of their friends who were sure to be envious of them. Todd held the horse's halter at its neck, while Eadlyn walked beside the cart, nervous of how full it was, ready to catch anything that might topple. It was mid-afternoon and they expected to reach the Romney Marsh before sunset. The sky was bright, the roads dry after several weeks of good weather, and if the clouds gathered to the south, then they were soft and white, bringing no threat of bad weather.

The village of Lyminge, with its cluster of plank and thatch homes, its pens of animals and neat rows of crops, was soon behind them. The road they took was narrow and often banked with woodland or high hedgerows; it ran steadily downhill. They passed the occasional farm labourer and a couple of young men with handcarts. The children, pleased with their high viewpoint, chattered away and pointed this way and that, at whatever took their interest. After an hour, the distinctive rounded hill of Tolsford could be seen to their left and the land opened up, with far-reaching scenes across acres of pasture.

"Let's stop here for a while," Eadlyn suggested, as views to the great sea, the *Oceanus Britannicus*, were revealed in the distance. "Isn't it beautiful?" she said to the children. "Can you see the sea?"

"Boats?" Cym asked, reaching out to be lifted from the cart.

"Boats coming all the way from Francia," Clover informed, as she crawled over the blankets and tipped herself out of the cart.

"And fishing boats, bringing food for our bellies," Todd added.

"Fish. For us?" Cym asked.

"If we give them a coin," Todd replied. "Then we'll fry the fish in our pan."

"But now a little bread and some cheese." Eadlyn broke pieces from the loaf and cut chunks of cheese with the knife which hung from her belt.

Todd passed around a beaker of weak ale. After a short time, they decided to move on, eager to be settled long before dusk.

The road levelled out a little and soon all views of the sea were lost as they passed through woodland; oak and beech trees formed a canopy above their heads and there was a chill in the air. When the trees gave way to open land again, the family were approaching the Shipway crossroads and even young Cym was silent as he marvelled at the view set out below.

The sea was before them again, and across its sparkling depths were the grey mounds of Francia's coastline. Romney Marsh was spread out to the south-west: a vast tract of flat land and tidal creeks, stretching into a hazy distance. Waterways were fringed with swathes of reeds and the occasional cluster of bent willows. The traders saw little clue of man having put down any permanent habitation.

The seawater had retreated over the centuries since the Romans first discovered this sheltered haven. Areas of water-logged land had dried a little and, as they did so, soil was revealed, rich from the sediment left by the sea. These were the stories passed through the family: tales of a place once covered by a shallow sea, and of the marshland emerging over time. It was a new land and one that already held a reputation of concealing mysteries. The mists hung low over tidal creeks, and waters gurgled as the sea surged in and found its way amongst the reeds. The mud shifted and belched, still unsure of its final resting place.

Parts of this low-lying area were being tamed by man. The signs were there: some areas of grass had cattle and sheep grazing; and there were salt pans, where the incoming sea was channelled. It was said that way beyond the view from the Shipway track and wooded escarpment, there were settlements forming. Eadlyn searched the scene with her eyes, but she couldn't see the roof of a house or the spiral of smoke from a fire. Messengers had come to her home in Lyminge and told of the people who were making their homes in the new land and encouraging the traders to bring their boats ashore in their haven. There was a place named Romney and another was Lydd, both on land newly risen from the sea.

What was is it like to live on the Romney Marsh, perhaps at the mercy of the sea? Eadlyn thought of the gentle hills and woodland, and the village where they lived, with the thane's hall at the centre, and the church on a gentle slope overlooking the village. It was all very well to visit this place, but not to live there with the harsh sea winds and nothing but flatness all around her. Eadlyn shook her head a little; she would be content to return home to the hills.

"Are you ready?" Todd's voice broke into her thoughts.

"Aye." Eadlyn looked at the steep track leading down to the Sandtun. "I forgot how treacherous it is."

The Shipway track went almost straight down the hillside; it was narrow, with deep ruts and stones scattered about.

"Nay, treacherous is when the rains come and we're slipping to the bottom," Todd grinned at her. He offered the horse's leading rein and said, "You take his head and I'll hold the cart back as best I can. We don't want him being pushed along faster than he can manage."

"And the children?" Eadlyn questioned.

"Clover can take her brother's hand. And they'll walk behind the cart."

So the small family started to walk down the hillside to the Sandtun, an area they had not been able to see from their position on top of the hill. They took small steps, their posture awkward and limbs tense, and Todd used all his strength to hold back the laden cart. The trees grew high on either side of them and their roots held tight to the earth banks at the side of the track. Eadlyn looked back at the children, seeing the concentration on their young faces. Despite the awkward path down the hillside, her heart felt light – they were almost there.

They reached the bottom and crossed a wide plank bridge spanning a tidal creek. The trees gave way and another view was before them: they had finally reached the Sandtun and all it offered.

"We are here, at the Sandtun," Clover screeched. "Look Cym, look. Do you remember?"

He didn't remember of course, as he had been just a year and a half when the family had last made their summer journey to the coastal camp. But Cym was a cheerful little boy; he felt the happiness in his mother and wanted to please his big sister. "Aye. Aye,

Sandtun," he cried out, releasing his hand from Clover's grip and running ahead along the track.

"Some of them are already here – the wood-turner and metalworker and..." Eadlyn said, looking back at Todd, wanting him to be sharing her joy. "And a boat; there's a boat pulled up on the beach!"

"I can see, my dearling," Todd replied. "Let's hope there is money to be made and good trade."

"There will be," Eadlyn answered. "I am sure of it."

The track took them along the edge of a beach within a sheltered tidal inlet. The sand sloped gently to the water's edge. Clover looked at her mother, and Eadlyn nodded her approval; the girl pulled off her leather shoes and then helped Cym with his own. Hand in hand they ran to where the water rippled against the sand and dipped their toes in the sea.

"It's cold!" Clover shrieked.

"Of course it is, sweeting," Eadlyn called back. She longed to feel the damp sand and gentle waves on her own feet, but there was work to be done first.

The Sandtun was a small area of raised land; it would take no longer than five minutes to walk across from one side to the other. The ground seemed thick with debris cast upon it by the sea; the plants were a mixture of wiry grasses and creeping succulents with a strong salty taste to their leaves. For most of the year, only the fishermen crept down the hillside from the nearby village and fished from the shallow inlet. The land was not suited to house a small community in permanent homes; to live on the hillside above was preferable, for stagnant ditches in nearby marshland oozed bad air over the Sandtun, and the sea was a constant threat.

23

"Who is going to help me set up camp?" Todd called to the children. They turned their backs to the sea and scampered up the beach.

"Me."

"Me."

"We'll need firewood," Eadlyn looked over the Sandtun, where only a few stunted bushes grew.

"I'll send Clover back to the woods," Todd nodded towards the lower hillside.

"Aye, there will be plenty lying about," Eadlyn agreed.

They followed the beach-front track a little further, then led the horse and cart onto the scrubby grassland to the driest patch, raised a little above sea-level. Six tents were already set up and a couple of fires smouldered. Looking back, Eadlyn saw another cart had followed them down the Shipway and reached the beach. There would be twenty tents pitched by nightfall, and as many traders waiting to sell their wares.

The tent frame was a simple design of strong ash poles: two standing tall and one ridge pole. Clover held one upright, with Cym and Eadlyn at the other. The children squealed as Todd draped a homespun cloth over the poles and, with wooden pegs, began to pull it into place. Their temporary home took shape – walls were stretched outwards and another cloth was placed over the ridge. The doorway was tied open and another cloth was spread on the hard ground. Blankets were brought in, along with the box of food.

"Can we collect wood for the fire?" Clover asked.

"Of course, a good fire will keep the marsh insects at bay," Todd replied. "They like to nibble at young children!" Clover and Cym squealed with both fear and excitement.

"Will you go with the children?" Eadlyn asked her husband. "It's too far for them to carry the wood, and we need stones to circle the fire."

"Aye, I will, but Clover is growing up strong and her brother isn't going to be left behind. A couple more like them and we'll be well looked after."

"There will be more soon enough," Eadlyn said, grateful the babies were not coming as often as they did for some women. "I'll go and buy some fish." They walked together back toward the beach. While Eadlyn walked onto the golden sands, the others stayed on the track leading to the base of the hill.

There were a couple of small boats pulled up beyond where the sea flooded in. The fishermen were well-known faces, there at the Sandtun year after year. They walked down the Shipway every day when the weather was fair and caught fish to sell in their home village of Lympne. But the best money was to be made when the Sandtun came to life with the annual traders. These families had coins in their purses and paid well. And if a foreign trinket could be bought when the boats came in from Francia, then it kept the fishermen's wives and sweethearts happy.

"Good afternoon, wife of Todd leathermaker," the fishermen greeted Eadlyn. "What news do you have from Lyminge?"

"All is well," Eadlyn responded. "The thane treats us well, Christianity thrives as we have both church and minster, and the crops look healthy this year."

"Indeed, all is well in Lyminge," the fisherman agreed.

"And what news from you this past year?" Eadlyn asked.

"My eldest son is wed," The fisherman told her, and as he did so he stood a little taller. "We expect his son to be born any day now. We also have the foundations of a church, ours is to be built in wood." They both gazed up at the heavily wooded escarpment. "God treats us well in both Lympne and Lyminge."

"He does," Eadlyn agreed. "And now we need some fish to fill our bellies."

"I put a couple of nice ones aside for you." He took a knife from his belt. "And as I like to see your pretty smile, I'll gut them for you." With a few strokes the innards were gone and thrown to the circling gulls.

Eadlyn handed him a coin and he placed the fish in the pan she carried. "They'll fry up nicely," she said.

By dusk quite a settlement of tents grew on the Sandtun. There was plenty of fish to satisfy their appetites and two or three families shared a fire, sitting around in companionable groups. Most of the faces were known: traders from nearby villages who came together once a year to sell their wares at the Sandtun. Children grew up, young men came with new wives, and tales were told of family members lost within the last year. An air of celebration or festival filled the place as the families greeted one another, and newcomers were welcomed.

Chapter Three
Somewhere in Kent

Brother Edwen opened his eyes and looked across at the shrouded body. It basked in soft rays of light filtered by sturdy oak trees. He turned away. When he woke an hour later, Edwen's throat was parched and he thought of the pretty stream winding through the woodland. Easing himself up from a bed of dry fern, he saw two of his companions still slept and Brother Halig was sitting on a fallen trunk, his head resting in his hands.

As he stood, the monk's tunic and hooded scapular fell into place and he brushed his hand over the woollen material, smoothing it further and removing small pieces of leaf and twig. Edwen tightened his belt a little and allowed his hood to stay resting at the nape of his neck, liking the feeling of the slight breeze running over his head of cropped hair. His tonsure was newly cut by Brother Halig, who had taken his blade to all three young monks just the day before and removed several weeks of growth from their scalps. Glancing back at Brother Halig, Brother Edwen moved down the woodland slope and onto an area of mossy earth. He knelt and reached down, hands cupped for water.

"Ah." Brother Edwen could not help showing his appreciation. "Thank you, Lord." The first of the water he scooped up cleansed his mouth, the second was splashed over his face in a manner which almost seemed reckless. Leaning down again, he took more and drank again, relishing its earthy taste.

The afternoon was long, it now being midsummer. Brother Edwen was bored; his eagerness to see their final destination made him restless. Once the sun had set, they would take the Shipway track, pass by a village named Lympne and then move down onto Romney Marsh.

Although embalmed with sweet-smelling spices and ointments, the body on the stretcher had flies settling on the linen shroud. *God forgive me for thinking such a thing: I'll be glad to be rid of him,* Brother Edwen thought. *May Romney Marsh be worth this tiresome journey.*

At the edge of the escarpment Brother Edwen broke from the line and stood beside Brother Halig. He breathed deeply through his nostrils, savouring the rich scent of the sea. In the distance the *Oceanus Britannicus* shimmered, mystical and blending into the night sky. The coastline was indistinct and perhaps a mile or two from the hillside. The moon was a bright crescent, but the clouds heavy and fast encroaching upon the only source of light.

The monks had just a moment to take in the landscape below. It was almost flat, the undulations barely perceptible, and it appeared to be empty of settlements. The sea was on the rise and a million silver sparkles flowed with the tide, filling creeks and flooding low-lying land.

"Romney Marsh," Brother Edwen said, allowing the words to roll slowly around his tongue. And then it was gone. The moon, obliterated by thick clouds, gave no light to the land. But already Edwen was drawn to this vista below him; he felt it held mysteries, untold stories he was destined to learn.

"Romney Marsh," Brother Halig repeated. "We have arrived!"

"It is indeed a lonely place," Brother Edwen observed. There was nothing much to see of it, just a hint of land and sea.

"It is as I remembered," Brother Halig said.

What had brought him here before? Brother Edwen wondered. *I will not ask, for he will not be inclined to tell. Perhaps I will find out when I see more of this place.*

The body on the stretcher now lay slumped on the thick grass at the roadside and the other two monks stood looking into the nothingness. "The hillside is steep," one commented.

Glancing back at the stretcher, Brother Halig said, "We have brought him this far safely and will take care on the track." The others nodded their agreement.

Brother Edwen looked upwards to the sky and inhaled deeply once more. Frowning, he turned to their leader and said, "I smell smoke." He breathed in the night air once more. It was rich with salt and seaweed, but was there a hint of something else – wood-smoke?

"The Romans are long gone," Brother Halig stated. That was true enough. They had left Britannia three hundred years beforehand.

Had others settled here? The words remained on Brother Edwen's lips. *If it were good enough for the Romans then why not for the Jutes, who had come from Denmark to live here in the Kingdom of Kent?* He sniffed the air once more – salt and seaweed. Brother

Halig was right of course: if he said this land was deserted then it must be the truth.

The descent was slow, with the body on the sling now being carried in a sideways crab-like motion down the hillside track. On reaching the bottom Brother Halig gestured that they were to follow the line of the hills at their base, taking a narrow track through the trees, which were the last before the marshland. Now the air had a peaty smell, still laced with salt. Brother Edwen could almost see the water bubbling up through the reeds as the saltwater oozed its way through on the tide. He longed to be free of the trees and set foot on the Romney Marsh.

Chapter Four

The evening sun was setting the sky ablaze with streaks of orange and red. The willow trees became black silhouettes, and the feather-topped reeds whispered the secrets of the marsh. Those sitting around the fires wrapped their capes around them as the night chill set in, and swiped at flying insects longing to suck on sweet human flesh.

News had been exchanged, old friends greeted and new traders welcomed. They had shared food around the firesides and now the families who had journeyed to the Sandtun were drowsy, their talk less frantic.

"There's curious things happening on the marsh tonight, and I don't know I understand it." These words came from an old woman; a newcomer to the Sandtun. Her name was Hlappa and she wore her old age for all to see, in her skin that was wrinkled like a dried apple, and her wisp of dull brown hair. Her voice was hoarse; she coughed a little, then reached for her mug of weak ale, before closing her eyes.

Her son, the clay-worker, gave a sigh. "She's always worrying over one thing or the other."

"That's how it is with the elders," Eadlyn smiled at him. She ran her fingers through Cym's hair. The little boy dozed on her lap.

"I get these feelings and they play in my head," Hlappa opened her eyes again and looked at those

31

gathered nearby. "We are not the only ones on the marsh tonight."

"Perchance there's a farmer out with the cattle?" The clay-worker's tone was irritable. "That's enough of your talk."

"A farmer is an innocent man, or so we would hope," she raised her voice a little, disturbing the children, causing the mothers to draw them closer. "The folk on the marsh tonight move in secret. Why else do they travel by dark?"

"Travel by dark?" her son repeated. "You're being foolish, you've lived beyond the years our Lord intended. I should have left you behind and would have done if anyone would care for you."

"They have more chance by night," Hlappa persisted.

"Keep your wambly words to yourself," her son snapped. "I've been hearing enough of your nonsense these past seasons."

Eadlyn frowned and held Cym tight; she noted that Clover had sidled up to Todd. These people, the clay-worker and his mother were new faces at the Sandtun, and she didn't like the way he spoke to his elder. Hlappa had lived to a good age and she deserved his respect.

"I have wise words, son, as you well know," Hlappa continued. "Listen to my words; there's dark happenings here tonight."

But her son ignored her, and the traders spoke of other matters, although the woman's words rang in their minds. They were all just visitors to this land which sat below sea-level and they knew when they lay quietly in their tents at night, they would hear the water approaching on the incoming tide. It would slide along the creeks, and slither amongst the reeds. The

Sandtun would almost be surrounded at a high tide, with the sheltered beach and tidal inlet to the east and the low-lying marsh all around it. The nearby hills were steep and dark with trees. Any number of wild dogs or boar could be roaming on the escarpment, adding to the unease of those who camped out.

"I'll make the fire safe," Todd said. "Time for bed I think." Cym was asleep in his mother's arms and Clover was struggling to stay awake. He stood and offered Eadlyn his hand; she took it, allowing him to help pull her up.

The last rays of the sun's light still gave a red glow to the west, while the great flaming ball had already sunk below the horizon. The campfires were smouldering and one-by-one the visitors to the Sandtun were retiring to their canvas shelters.

"They'll sleep well," Eadlyn said as she shuffled into the tent on her knees.

"Go on, dearling," Todd kissed his daughter on her golden curls. Clover crawled in and straight to her blanket. "I'll see you all at first light."

"Take your blanket," Eadlyn said, offering it to him.

"I'll need that," he grinned. There was a chill in the air now and they already wore their cloaks, despite the warmth from the fire.

Todd slung the blanket by the cart. He always slept under it when they stayed at the Sandtun; who knew how many thieves might descend the Shipway and take a chance at stealing some of the fine goods on offer? The leatherwork he had for sale represented many months of hard work.

"Good evening, cousin!" A low voice attracted Todd's attention. He looked up from the fire, which he was covering in turf in order to keep it smouldering overnight. The tall figure of his cousin stood there in the darkness. All light from the sun had now gone.

"Fremund!" Todd stood and stepped towards the other man. They clasped each other's forearms in a gesture of joy. Then stepping back, Todd continued, "We were talking about you. Hoping all was well. You're late."

"Aye, my son was born this morning and I waited to see him come into the world."

"A son!" Todd exclaimed. "Well done, my friend. And your wife, is she well?"

"A little weary, but she has her mother and sisters. I have to come to the Sandtun, you know that." Fremund shrugged his shoulders. "I put my cart beside yours and I'll sleep beneath my metalwork, with you under your leather. But first, I have a bottle of mead. We must drink to my son's good health and much trading at the Sandtun."

Todd pushed aside any thoughts of wrapping up in his blanket and closing his eyes. He settled back down on the rough grass and reached out for the noggin of mead. He took a sip, savouring the rich honeyed taste as he rolled it around his mouth, feeling it burn as it trickled down his throat. It tasted good; he took another sip.

The cousins spoke quietly about their lives: their families, village life and tales heard of places further afield. Across the Sandtun, a few others still crouched around their fires; their voices were nothing but murmurs carried across on the sea breeze. Most were sleeping under the canvas. Not far from the tents, ponies jingled their harnesses, snorted and stamped on the sandy ground. Two tiny lights moved with the rhythm of the waves. Two boats with men of Francia

34

were anchored in the bay. In the morning, they would pull up on the sands.

After three noggins of mead, Todd's thoughts were swimming about in his mind. He had to concentrate on each word as it left his lips, taking care to construct them properly. After the fourth noggin, he said to Fremund, "Enough, my friend. I'll sleep well tonight but tomorrow my head will suffer if I take another sip."

"I could enjoy another..." Fremund began to push aside his tunic in order to relieve himself. "But first..."

"Not here where the children play," Todd admonished his cousin. "Come to the creek where the tide will wash it away."

Fremund gave a grunt and followed. The two men moved from the camp to the beach track and followed it to the bottom of the hill. Here they met with the plank bridge they had crossed after descending the Shipway track earlier the same day. They didn't step on the bridge but walked to the edge of the soft mud. The tide was pouring in, filling the creek and forcing its water to move against its natural flow. The air was salty. Todd breathed deeply and licked his lips, tasting the salt on them. Side by side, the men emptied their bladders and their waters mixed with those in the creek.

They were about to turn back to the camp when a noise caught Todd's attention and he put his finger to his lips. Both men stood still for a moment, listening to the gentle breeze amongst the trees and the soft swish of the incoming tide moving through the reeds. A stone rattled its way down the Shipway track.

"Latecomers?" Fremund questioned.

"Perchance someone was delayed," Todd replied in a low whisper. "It's late to set up camp."

They continued to listen. Another stone tumbled down the Shipway, and a low cough confirmed it was humans rather than animals on the track.

"Let's see who comes our way," Todd suggested.

"Aye, the mead has made my mind lively and I'm not ready to sleep yet," Fremund agreed.

A few minutes passed and the sounds of a group descending the track continued with the occasional chink of stone on stone, a repeated cough and some indistinct voices. The cloud passed from the face of the waxing moon and the cousins expected to see the newcomers on the bridge. No one appeared.

"Where else could they be going but the Sandtun?" Todd murmured.

"There's a track towards the old Roman Fort," Fremund suggested. Nothing to see but a pile of stones.

"What would take them there?" Todd wondered. "Perchance they've taken the wrong path and meant to come to the Sandtun?"

"Perchance they have reason to skulk about at night and I'm curious to know where they're heading," Fremund said. "There's nothing but marsh and pasture and waterways."

The men, who still stood by the side of the creek, turned and walked back to the beach track. With silent agreement, they stepped onto the bridge and crossed the water. Now trees loomed tall in front of them and the moonlight would help no one who chose to walk under the cover of the trees. Todd strained his eyes to see the path he knew was ahead of him, searching for the narrow track leading away from the Sandtun and towards the ruins of the Roman fort. He tried to shake away the mead, which befuddled his mind. There was a mystery here, Todd was sure of it, and he would need his wits about him.

"This way," Fremund tugged at Todd's arm and pulled him towards the track. "Take it easy."

Todd placed a protective arm across his face; the track was barely used, and branches grew across it at all angles. A slim young sapling whipped at his hip and brambles lashed his ankles. He could barely see his hand in front of him. The darkness was a thick smoke around him and the tree tops a blanket between him and the night sky. Their shoes brushed on wild garlic causing a pungent scent to rise from the leaves.

The cousins moved on slowly, Fremund taking the lead, feeling the way and muttering every time a branch caught the wool of his tunic or the skin on his face. Todd, a step behind, was at least warned of the dangers ahead.

"Do you see them?" Todd whispered, frustrated by the darkness.

"Nay, but we are not far behind." Fremund paused and sniffed the air. "I smell their sweat in the air, and a scent – something from a foreign land." If Todd could have seen his cousin's face, he would have seen the lines of Fremund's forehead deep in concentration. "And something else, it lingers in the air. I can't say what it is."

Todd caught a whiff of some odour. It was stale and yet scented too. "I'd say these men have no wives or mothers to wash their tunics, or no fresh water to bathe in," he said. "Do we really want to move any closer?"

"Not really," Fremund replied. "But I'm curious to see, and if the woods were to thin a little, then I have a feeling we would have our curiosity satisfied."

Feeling their way with the toes of their boots and outstretched hands, the cousins moved onwards. Trees thinned a little and the stone walls of an abandoned Roman fort shone a soft grey in the weak moonlight. Fremund put his hand up and Todd stopped, his attention on the walls which slumped on the lower reaches of the hillside. His gaze turned to the path ahead of them and his heart thudded awkwardly in his chest.

"Monks?" they whispered in unison.

"Hell's flames, what brings monks wandering here?" Todd murmured.

There were four of them, standing in a row, all looking towards the ruins. The hoods of their scapulars were thrown back on their shoulders, revealing freshly shaved tonsures and so, even in the darkness, the soft light of the moon gave away their vocation as it fell upon the bare skin. Unaware they were being watched, one of the monks indicated that it was time to move onward and they turned.

The monks moved on the track, preparing to change direction and turn away from the hills, and it was at that moment it became clear to the onlookers that the monks had something slung between them. They stooped as if burdened by the weight of whatever they carried and shuffled awkwardly in order to turn themselves in the wooded area. Then they moved onward, led by one who stood taller than the others. They crossed a low bridge under which the incoming tide slid inland and moved out of sight.

"What *does* bring monks wandering about on the marsh?" Fremund echoed Todd's words. "I see no reason for it."

"These tracks lead nowhere." Todd was sure of that. He had often explored the area when the trading was done. There was some pasture with cattle and sheep, but nothing to attract a band of monks. He stepped forward; the scent of the monks still lingered in the air. "Let's move to the edge of the trees."

"Whatever they carry, that's the answer," Fremund suggested. "Did you see it? Did you see the shape of it, hanging long and low in the sling?"

"Aye, I saw it," Todd frowned, trying to make sense of it.

"It was a body." There was an urgency to Fremund's voice. "It was a body and I'd not like to say if it was dead or alive."

The two men stood on the edge of the woodland and before them was the open land of Romney Marsh. The moon had slipped behind one of many clouds in the vast sky; it emitted only a faint glow, giving little light to the land. All they could see was the indistinct images of four men and the sling they carried as they made their way along the path.

"I'm not following them any further," Todd stated. "Even in this poor light, they could turn and see us at any moment. They may be monks, but they're up to no good and I'd not like to get mixed up in it."

It was time to turn back to the camp at the Sandtun, but the men were loath to take their eyes from the monks. Just then, the metal edge of a pick or spade, caught a little of the moonlight and shone for a moment.

"May the Lord save us," Fremund breathed. "Those monks carry tools. I swear they are to bury the body out on the marsh."

"They have much to hide," Todd responded. "For who would find it in a place such as this?"

"I'm not done with this mystery," Fremund stated.

"I agree," Todd replied. "But for now we must return to camp." His thoughts strayed to Eadlyn sleeping with the children. He had left them alone and perhaps vulnerable to danger. *What are we doing?* Todd asked himself. *What foolishness is this, when we should be in our beds and the leatherwork has been left unattended?*

The cousins turned around and retraced their steps through the wood. Their minds were still thinking of the monks and the precious cargo they carried, while their bodies were becoming weary and ready for their beds.

Chapter Five

It was only a matter of minutes before a collection of pale stone walls could be seen midway up the hillside. Fear gripped Brother Edwen – a settlement. They were not alone: there would be men roaming the hill, tending their cattle.

"The Romans," Brother Halig stated. "It is their abandoned fort. I told you no man has used the Romney Marsh for centuries."

Brother Edwen relaxed.

The track turned and now the monks faced away from the steep hillside. Finally, they stepped free from the trees. Brother Edwen felt the need to pause and breathe in the sights and scents of this new land, but his duty was to keep moving forward. Besides, there was nothing to see in the darkness. He had a feeling the land around them was open, not hemmed in by settlements, woodland or further hills. The air was still sharp with salt and there was also a strong earthy smell. He became aware that the track was almost a causeway, at least it was raised a little and occasionally a pool of water glittered in the weak moonlight. A gust of wind came suddenly and with it the rustle of long grasses, or most likely reeds. This was indeed the bleak land promised to them.

And so the four monks continued in the manner to which they had become accustomed: in single file with

Brother Halig leading, then the three others, two of them carrying the stretcher and the other resting.

"How will we know...?" Brother Edwen began, but then faltered, not wanting to question the wisdom of the older monk.

But Brother Halig heard his words and replied, "A divine light will lead us to the spot."

Brother Edwen looked up to the sky and the moon which was almost smothered by thick cloud. He felt his body slump a little; the journey was not over yet. The pace of the monks slowed; the track was narrow and every footstep needed to be taken with care, lest they should slip and their precious cargo launch into the gurgling marshland. The very thought of it caused Brother Edwen's stomach to lurch. Reeds brushed against his ankles and there was an occasional rustle as if a water-rat or wading bird had been disturbed by the nocturnal humans. In the half-light of a cloud-covered moon, Romney Marsh gave away none of its secrets.

Their leader came to an abrupt halt and the others stood...waiting. Brother Edwen strained his eyes, searching for something, for a clue. Why here? He stepped forward, standing at the older monk's shoulder. Something shone, a dull metallic-like glow, similar to the gloss on a piece of polished metal plate. Water. There was a stream, or inlet of some kind. It was not wide, as far as Brother Edwen could ascertain, but would thwart their journey, for the land around it was likely to be boggy. It seemed as if the causeway they walked upon had come to an abrupt end. The three younger monks said nothing, knowing it best to wait for Brother Halig to announce the next move.

Brother Edwen closed his eyes for a moment and breathed deeply. The air flowed through his nostrils and he savoured the scents of the sea and marsh. He felt a warmth settle on his face; it was the loving glow of a summer sun caressing his skin, yet there was no sun. He opened his eyes and gasped, knowing that something truly miraculous had come about. The monk felt his body relax and he basked as a heavenly light washed over him.

The ray of light came from directly above them: a golden beam, the colour of a harvest moon, bringing with it the scent of ripened wheat and the heat of the midday sun. It shone down upon the waterway, bringing to life the pale green of the reeds and the bright green of the creeping plants, which spread along the edges of the water and clung to the strong upright stems of the reeds. The light-beam showed the water swirling inland, finding its way, searching out new channels as it swept in on the tide. It touched on the tails of wildfowl as they fussed and scattered into the shadows.

The monks looked down upon a sturdy wooden bridge, three planks wide. It was as robust as any they could hope to find on this land. In fact, its being there raised thoughts in Brother Edwen's curious mind. Was the Romney Marsh not as desolate as he had been led to believe? Who had taken the time and care to create this?

"The light!" Brother Halig announced with bravado. His back straightened a little and his chest expanded. "We are truly on the right path." He moved forwards paying little heed to where he placed his leather-clad feet, as if trusting all would be well.

The two stretcher-bearing monks followed, with less abandon. Their boots nudged at the reeds and they made sure each step was placed onto firm ground. Soon they were on the bridge, which almost glowed as if it took light from the heavenly beam. And then Brother Edwen was on the planks, feeling how firm they were, how they barely flexed under his weight. He took a few steps and then he was scrambling up the bank. As he reached the top, a chill breeze licked around the monk's shoulders. The golden shaft of light had gone.

The ground underfoot was firm, with rough grass, and Brother Halig strode forward with confidence: the other three followed, their eyes adjusting to the darkness again. As the soft light of the moon once again broke free from the clouds, a row of stunted willow trees was revealed, and Brother Halig expressed his pleasure. "This is the place. Abbot Botolph can rest undisturbed here on Romney Marsh."

The day before, silver coins had been exchanged for a pickaxe and a couple of shovels, all forged by a blacksmith in a village named Aldington. Brother Edwen had been the one chosen to leave their day-time hideaway and venture out to buy the necessary tools. Now he placed the sharp end of the pickaxe on the ground and prodded the earth; it was baked hard by the summer sun. *He will have to lie as deep as his height,* the Monk reflected. *I pray he looks down on us and recognises the endeavours we'll go to in order to save his holy body.*

"We'll start with the axe," Brother Halig ordered. "This ground will resist our efforts to open it. We must share the burden of the task."

Brother Edwen swung the tool over his shoulder. The three others stepped clear. Using all his strength, the monk moved the pickaxe in an arc and placed a blow on the earth. The blade dug in and a crack opened. He repeated the move ten times, then passed the tool to the next monk. When the three younger monks had taken their turns, Brother Halig had moved further away and was examining the contents of his sack.

He has no thoughts of taking his turn, Brother Edwen scowled and reached out for the pickaxe. The ground became loose with chunks of clay-earth. Needing no orders from Brother Halig, the monks now pushed the clods aside and then started the process again. Each time the cycle began, the earth became softer. Before long they worked, one at a time, from within the pit. Their shoes became soiled with sticky clay and the hems of their tunics discoloured by the earth. Their scapulars were thrown on the ground, and sweat ran freely down their bodies, soaking into their tunics.

A couple of hours passed. Brother Halig knelt at the side of the body on the ground, his head bowed and fingers fretting at his holy cross. Prayers flowed from his lips, unheard by the three who laboured hard. It became more difficult to pull out the monk whose turn it was to dig from within the grave. Damp soil crumbled and the sides were beginning to break away.

"We are done," Brother Edwen informed his elder. "Any deeper and we will be buried with him. The soil is very wet, and the sides now fall into the pit."

Brother Halig acknowledged this with a gentle incline of his head and got up to inspect the hole, as best he could in the darkness. He returned to the body. Reaching into the sack which lay beside it, the monk took St Botolph's only possessions and placed them within the shroud – a gold pendant cross and a book of offices.

The wooden poles were removed from the sling. All four monks took a corner of the material, which had held the body for several weeks as it journeyed from Middle England to the Romney Marsh in the farthest corner of Kent. They shuffled sideways to the grave and lowered the body into it. Brother Halig prayed, and as he did so the body of Abbot Botolph made a light thud on reaching the ground.

The sky was lightening to the east when the monks turned away and set off back across the field. But just as he bent to adjust the strap on his shoe, Brother Edwen spotted a golden cross lying in the early morning dew. He reached down, picked it up and placed it in the leather pouch hanging from his belt.

Chapter Six

The sun had risen over the shingle bank separating the marsh and harbour from the sea, when Eadlyn and the children crawled out of the tent the next morning. The rough grass was thick with dew and she wet her hands in it, then used it to freshen her face. It smelt both sweet and a little salty.

"Look at your faeder, still sleeping under the cart," she said to the children. "I thought he'd have risen with the sun."

Clover looked towards the sun and then back to Todd. "He'll wake when it shines in his face."

Todd stirred and opened his eyes. "Hello, my sweetings. How was your sleep?" He closed his eyes again, only opening them when the children were under the cart with him and disturbing his bed.

"A little restless; I miss my straw mattress," Eadlyn admitted. "But the little ones slept soundly."

"They were tired out with all the excitement, weren't you?" Todd said, as he rolled out from under the cart, before pulling himself to his feet. He yawned and rubbed his eyes.

"I wasn't tired," Clover replied. "But Cym was. He's only little."

"I wasn't," Cym said, pulling his hand from his big sister's grasp.

"What ails you?" Eadlyn asked, noting his sallow complexion. Her husband's skin was darker than hers, his hair and eyes a glossy brown. He usually looked so healthy.

"Fremund arrived late," Todd said.

"Oh, did he?" Eadlyn raised her eyebrows. Now she knew the reason for Todd's heavy eyes and recurrent yawns, which he tried to hide with his hand.

Todd shrugged, and looked towards his cousin's cart.

Eadlyn's gaze followed her husband's. She saw the tousled red curls and Fremund's long lanky body under a blanket. "We're going to the creek," she said. "Come on Clover...Cym."

"I'm coming too," Todd scooped up his young son and tickled him. Cym squealed, loving the fun he had with his father.

There were already several families at the creek. The water was low, the banks sticky with mud. Eadlyn sighed; they could relieve their bladders there, but she would need to wash Cym in the sea. She moved down the bank towards the water, lifted her skirts and let the warm liquid trickle into the shallows. The children copied and then ran back out of the creek.

"Come along to the sea," Eadlyn called, and chasing after the children, she picked Cym up. "Come sweet, we must wash your bottom or the skin will be sore."

The little boy shrieked and squirmed as he was dipped into the cold sea. Then Eadlyn stood him where the water met the beach, and the whole family wriggled their toes in the water to wash away the mud from the creek. Their feet sank into the coarse sand and their toes squirmed amongst the shells.

The men from Francia could be seen on their boats, watching the activity on the shore. There was no hurry for the traders to bring their carts to the beach. It would be some time before the tide had risen enough for the boats to be pulled up on the sands.

Todd had walked on ahead and the fire was already burning when Eadlyn and the children reached their camp. Fremund was crouched on the ground by the fire. *He looks a mess,* Eadlyn thought. *I'd like to run a comb through his hair.* She gave a brief smile, knowing she could not hide her dislike of him. "Good morning, Fremund."

"Eadlyn, Good morning!" Fremund's reply was friendly.

"Fremund is a father," Todd informed. "His son was born yesterday!"

"Yesterday!" Eadlyn repeated. "A new life. I hope all is well."

"His lungs were healthy!" Fremund gave a shrug.

Eadlyn scowled and gathered their clay cups. "Would you like some hot rosemary? Did you bring a cup?"

"Aye, Brona packed the cart before the boy was born." Fremund pulled himself to his feet and stood tall. "I'll fetch it."

"She's a good woman," Eadlyn commented, and then to Todd, "I'll fetch more water after we've broken our fast and tidied the camp."

Breakfast that morning was porridge sweetened with coarsely chopped apples. When they had eaten, Eadlyn carried the bucket with the bowls, spoons and cups down to the beach. Clover took the pan in both hands and Cym scampered along with them. All three were barefoot; it was easier that way on the Sandtun and the beach. They stood ankle deep in the shallows and washed the sticky porridge from the utensils, the children shrieking as waves broke on their legs.

When they got back to the camp, Todd and Fremund were returning from the wooded area at the bottom of the escarpment. They carried dead branches for the fire and began to break them up. Everyone on the Sandtun was busy, whether it was tending the fire, cooking breakfast, checking on the horses or minding the children. Words flew from one family to another as news was exchanged and advice given.

Eadlyn, kneeling on the ground by the entrance to the tent, became aware of a gradual silence. Voices turned to whispers until finally there was just the cackle of gulls and the slap of the waves on the sand. Frowning, she turned and looked back across the Sandtun, her eyes following the beach track leading away towards the marshland.

Now she saw the reason for the quiet amongst the traders and their families. Four men walked the track. Their bodies were stooped, not through old age, but presumably they were weary. Three of them carried tools, yet they were not men who laboured on the land. These were monks, wearing muddied tunics and hooded scapulars. The hoods fell down their backs, so their bald tonsures shone in the morning light. With heads bowed, eyes on the track ahead, they moved along the beach track looking neither left nor right. It almost seemed as if they were unaware of the tents, the fires and the families camped there. And equally so, it seemed as if they had not noticed the sea or the boats from Francia, or even the two small fishing boats and the men who waited for the tide.

They did know. Eadlyn was sure of it. They chose not to look, not to be a part of all that happened on the Sandtun. It was as if they wanted to be loners on the path they trod. *Perhaps they didn't expect us to be here, on this sand dune which is deserted for all but a few days a year?* Eadlyn looked across the flat wastelands of the Romney Marsh. *Where had they come from? What reason did these monks have for being here?* Something was not quite right, Eadlyn could sense it. She stood with the others and watched them walk towards the Shipway track.

The men turned back to their work. Todd was hitching the pony to the cart in order to move it to the beach. Others were doing the same. Some were not as fortunate as Todd and Fremund: they had brought their wares in handcarts. At first there were whispers flowing amongst the people on the Sandtun, in deference to the monks who passed through. Then someone called out to a child, and the moment was broken; life on the camp between marsh and sea continued as before.

"I'm going to get a bucket of water," Eadlyn told Todd. "Clover can watch her brother." She took the bucket and a clay jug, and fastened her shoes.

The water in the ditches had bad air around it and was salty from the incoming tide. It was the same at the wider creek at the bottom of the hills: here the water flowed faster and appeared fresh but it was still tidal and too salty. With the bucket swinging at her knees, Eadlyn went to cross the plank bridge before searching for a hillside stream.

She paused on the bridge and looked down towards the sea. There was a lot of activity on the banks of the creek and in the water itself. Women squatted and men stood to pass water, which in turn would be carried out to sea. One woman was washing her baby's tunic and another scrubbing the porridge pot. A metalworker's daughter, now on the brink of womanhood, was laughing with a young woodworker. He reached out and touched her face; she pushed her pert young breasts forward; this was a place to find a beloved as well as sell wares to the men of Francia.

Eadlyn walked a short way up the Shipway before stepping onto the rugged hillside. She knew of a place where water sprang directly from the ground and gathered in a pool before trickling down the hill. But no sooner had she walked through the trees lining the track, than Eadlyn saw the four monks gathered about the very pool she wanted to use.

The monks had shrugged aside their scapulars and squatted around the pool in their habits. The arms, thighs and calves of these young men were muscular, the shape of their shoulders rippled under coarse wool. They plunged their hands into the water and scooped it up, either drinking it or sloshing it over their faces. Their tools and bags were strewn on the ground, and again Eadlyn wondered at the reason for the tools they carried. She sensed these monks were in a celebratory mood, as if they were released from their daily chores, or some other burden which was too great for her mind to understand.

They must have sensed her presence, as one by one the monks stilled and turned towards Eadlyn. She bowed her head, looking at the long grass and the toes of her shoes made by her husband, Todd the leatherworker. The bucket rested against her knees. She was about to turn and search out another spring she knew of, but Eadlyn heard the rustle of fabric, the grunts and sighs as the monks stretched to full height and prepared to leave.

One of them, he who appeared to be older and to have an air of being more learned, stepped forward and spoke: "Stay. The water is yours now."

"I thank you," Eadlyn replied, her voice grave. She looked up at them quickly, then diverted her gaze again.

She didn't expect him to speak again. "I wish to speak to one of the men in your settlement," the monk said.

"One of the men?" she repeated, with a frown. "I'll ask my husband or his cousin to meet you. On the Shipway?"

"The Shipway?" he repeated.

"Aye, the track."

"We'll wait there."

They walked away and Eadlyn put her jug to the silvery water as it trickled through the rocks. She filled the jug and poured the liquid into the bucket several times before retracing her steps across the grass and through the trees edging the Shipway. As she walked down the track, Eadlyn saw the four monks waiting amongst the trees; she averted her gaze and scurried along, the water slopping about inside the bucket.

"Todd," Eadlyn called. He looked up from where he stood in the cart amongst his leatherwork. "There's some monks on the Shipway, wanting to speak to someone. A man, they say."

"Oh." Todd frowned. The memories of the robed figures had moved to the back of his mind. Now his thoughts were focused on the day ahead.

"I don't know what they want, but they are just there." Eadlyn pointed to the line of trees, marking the track.

Todd looked at the two boats still anchored in the shallow haven and two more entering from the narrow inlet to the east. "They won't be able to beach for a while. If you can put the belts out – like this, over the side – then I'll go along to see them."

His curiosity was aroused, and Todd was soon crossing the bridge, then walking up the lower reaches of the Shipway. A monk stepped onto the track, causing Todd to start. The other three stood in the shadows of the oak trees. Suddenly the Shipway, with its dark ivy creeping up the tree trunks and muffled sounds of people and animals unseen, took on an eerie feel. These were the four who had carried a body and moved by night. What did they want with him?

"Good morning, friend," the monk spoke, his voice low. "We have travelled far, as is God's will, and are in need of food."

Todd merely nodded his understanding.

"We have tools to exchange for food. Are there men in your village who would trade?"

"This is no village." Todd looked towards the Sandtun. "We are merely here for a few days and have no spare food. We bring with us a bag of oats, wheat for our bread, and little more; there is none to spare."

"I see," the monk replied. He turned to the others, "It is a temporary camp."

"There will be fish and perchance a trade to be done," Todd suggested. "But the men are still waiting to push their boats out when the tide rises. The sun will be on its descent before there is fish to be had."

The monk slumped as he understood there was no food. Turning to the others he said, "We must walk on in search of a village."

"At the top of the hill, turn to the west," Todd said. "You will find a village."

"I thank you." The monk inclined his head.

54

Todd watched their retreating backs as the monks trudged up the steep track, their shoulders rounded and heads bowed. Their clothes were soiled and spirits low. They carried nothing more than the tools and small sacks. Whatever or whoever they had been moving about the night before, it seemed that it was now disposed of.

It had been thirsty work moving the cart to the beach, with the summer sun already beating down on them and no shade in the open landscape. Todd thought of the spring, just a few steps away from the Shipway. He stepped through the trees, saw the sparkle of water amongst rocks and the area of damp trodden grass around it. It only took a few strides to reach the pool and Todd sank to his knees, kneeling forward with cupped hands to drink some of the cool water. As he moved back to squat on his heels, Todd saw something glinting in the long grass. He reached out, his fingertips feeling their way through damp fronds. It was a gold cross on a cord, and one that was of fine workmanship. He slipped it into the leather pouch hanging from his belt, intending to examine it later.

Chapter Seven

Having accepted his coin, Eadlyn smiled her thanks to the man from foreign lands, and looked up to see Todd walking across the Sandtun. There were now four boats beached on the sand and another entering the sheltered inlet. She had already sold a couple of leather bags. It promised to be a good day and they exchanged smiles as Todd approached.

"The monks wanted food," Todd told her. "I said we had none."

The smile fell from Eadlyn's face. She thought of the monks and nuns who lived in the minster on the hill above their home in Lyminge. Although aloof from the villagers, they had their respect. In fact, she was a little in awe of them. To refuse them food – well, it seemed so wrong, almost sinful. "You're right," Eadlyn admitted. She looked out towards the fishing boats.

Todd followed her gaze. "They had tools to trade and didn't want to wait for the fish."

"Tools?" Eadlyn frowned.

"Aye." Todd turned his attention to the man from Francia who was holding out a silver coin and gesturing towards the belts and jerkins. But before he busied himself with trying to get the best price, a memory of the four monks walking at night flashed though his mind. Whatever, or most likely whoever, they had carried was now gone. Buried in the marsh.

Todd shook the thoughts away. The man before him had money to spend. The quality of Todd's leatherwork was well known and some men of Francia would brave the *Oceanus Britannicus* to buy as much as they could carry back to their own country. The royal connections with Lyminge lent value to the leather crafted there. Whoever bought a belt, a bag, shoes or a jerkin, was impressed by the tales that it came from the settlement where the King of Kent had once built royal palaces, and his daughter, Ethelburga, had founded both a church and minster.

Eadlyn walked away; she wanted to see what else was on offer from those who joined them at the Sandtun. Although there was rarely anything to lure her to spend their silver sceattas, as Lyminge was a thriving village, run by a fair thane, and it supplied all their needs. However, a brooch or hair comb from across the sea might tempt her.

Everyone was busy setting out their wares to attract the buyers. Although the traders on the Sandtun were friendly, each of them knew that they needed to go back to their own village with an empty cart. No one wanted to return without a pouch of silver coins. Eadlyn gave a friendly nod or smile but didn't bother those who were busy selling their work. Occasionally she moved closer to inspect something and was admiring a box with silver and bronze inlay when someone touched her arm.

"Eadlyn, I knew it must be you!" The woman was slight, with a beaky nose, bright eyes and wisps of red hair showing around her headscarf.

"Megan!" Eadlyn gave a broad smile and reached out to offer the other woman a brief hug. "I was wondering… We hadn't seen you."

"We arrived late," Megan told her. "We came this morning, just in time."

"And your family, are they well?" Eadlyn asked, as the two women moved away from the trading area.

"Aye, the children are strong, but my husband, Penton, was injured last winter. He broke his leg and it has healed badly." Megan shrugged her shoulders. "We live on his brother's charity now. Penton's brother is a good man, but life is hard."

"Is it his brother, here with you now?" Eadlyn asked. She looked across to a man who looked very much like Megan's husband.

"Aye, that is him – Arlo. They worked together. Now Penton does what he can, but his spirits are low. We all live together in our home."

"His brother has not married?" Eadlyn asked.

"Nay. At least no more: his wife died in childbirth some time ago, and the baby with her. Penton allowed us to come to the Sandtun with Arlo this year, but next year it may be different. He is a young man who will be seeking a new wife." They were now at the tented camp and Megan asked, "Shall we make bread together as before, and you can tell me your news?"

"Aye," Eadlyn smiled. She enjoyed the different ways of doing things in the camp; one of them being the new foods they tried and how they adapted to only having the fire and no bread oven.

"The children are together," Megan said. "Clover knew us of course, but Cym was a little uncertain."

"They'll have fun together." Eadlyn reached into her tent for the cooking pot. "We can mix our flour in here, but we need fresh water from the spring."

As the two women walked up the Shipway, Eadlyn told Megan about the monks she had seen earlier that morning.

"It sounds as if the tools they are looking to trade for food are the ones from my cousin in Aldington," Megan said, her freckled nose wrinkling up as she considered it. "It was only one monk, but he was there in the village yesterday, paying with silver for tools."

"One afternoon they buy tools and the next they are finished with them and need food," Eadlyn said. "It feels wrong saying it, but I'm certain there is a mystery there. I didn't like to pry, but their tunics were covered in mud."

And so the friends gossiped as they collected water and mixed the dough. It was as if they had never been apart in the last year. The sun rose to its highest point, the children returned to their mothers. They devoured the breads cooked on a flat pan, along with cheese and apples. The women took food to the men who were selling on the beach and, with the next meal never far from their minds, prepared a pot of beans and grain to simmer on the fire until suppertime.

That evening the families gathered around one fire. Megan came with her children, a boy and a girl. She introduced her husband's brother, Arlo.

"How did the men of Francia like your metalwork?" Todd asked.

"It sold well," Arlo replied. "I'll go back to Aldington a happy man."

"You have some pretty brooches and clasps," Eadlyn commented, as she prepared the fish to fry in the pan.

"Aye, the women like them." Arlo gave a smile and dimples showed in his cheeks, which were rough with blond hair. His eyes were a bright blue and he held Eadlyn's gaze. She blushed a little and looked away.

Before long, the stew of beans and grain was being spooned out of the pan. Wooden bowls were being offered and then filled by Megan.

Eadlyn walked around the group offering fried fish. "There's mussels at the far end of the beach," she said. "I might gather some tomorrow and we'll try them for our midday meal."

"We can forage for them with the children," Megan suggested.

"Aye, they'll enjoy that," Eadlyn said.

Spread out across the Sandtun, in a line between the tents and the beach, about six fires burned and above each fire was a metal frame supporting a pot. Families joined to share in the cooking and eating. The men and older children had gathered firewood and each person did their share. There was a festive atmosphere with the occasional song drifting along through the camp, a shout or burst of laughter causing everyone to turn and look. For most, it had been a good day and there were more days left to sell their wares. But for those sitting around the fire prepared by Eadlyn and Todd, a new arrival caused discomfort.

"We've fish to fry and add to our broth, if you're done with the fire..." Hlappa strolled over and all heads turned towards her.

"Aye, but you'll have to gather wood like the rest of us," Fremund countered; he had been slouching, but now he sat upright, his eyes narrowed.

"My son is in the trees gathering it now," Hlappa announced with relish.

"Very well," Fremund gave a shrug. "I'll go to fetch some water." He moved away with the bucket hanging against his knee.

The sun still glowed in the sky, and the air was warm against their skin. Their stomachs were full of pottage and fish. At the top of the beach, the children played happily. Yet something had changed, Eadlyn felt her body tense and she exchanged a glance with Todd. There was something about Hlappa and her son, the clay-worker, that disturbed her and it seemed as if the others on the Sandtun felt it too.

Bradwin was walking towards them now, with a bunch of thin branches under his arm, clasped against his scrawny body. Eadlyn watched as the two men passed, Hlappa's son and Fremund. She saw no greeting between the two men.

"How tall Fremund is," Megan remarked, watching his long strides.

"Aye," Eadlyn replied, "He does seem so, especially next to..." The clay-worker was now amongst them and Eadlyn realised she didn't want him to hear her words; she let them trail away.

The newcomer's expression was sour, as he began to break the wood, holding one end and stamping down on the branch. Small pieces of bark flew off in the direction of those who had been relaxing just minutes beforehand.

"Stand back, will you?" Arlo stood. "I'll give you a hand." He took a couple of branches and moved away from the families seated on the ground.

The other man stayed where he was and spoke to no one in particular, "Place the pot over the fire; it has been a long day with those goose-headed Frenchmen, who won't make a proper bargain. What's wrong with them?"

"Perchance you'll fair better tomorrow," Todd suggested.

"Aye, there are new boats sitting in the harbour as we speak," Arlo continued.

"Well, let's hope these men have some sense about them," Bradwin snarled.

Hlappa, her body bent and frail, leaned over the fire with a flat pan in one hand and turned the fish. It soon browned and she tipped it into her pan of broth. The pan was hung over the fire and now she stood and stirred it with a wooden spoon. Her son added wood to the fire. No one spoke for a while, until the old woman turned to face Todd and Fremund. "What were the two of you doing out of your beds last night?" she asked.

"Out of our beds?" Fremund snapped. "What makes you say that?"

"An old woman sleeps lightly," she responded. "Especially when the ground is hard and not even a thin straw mattress to give comfort. There's no other on the Sandtun with your red hair, is there?"

"What do I know?"

"There's young Megan here and her two children, all three of them with red hair, but don't tell me they were out wandering at night." Hlappa's lips curled and her face seemed to shrivel up more than ever. "The moon slipped out from under the clouds and the man I saw was tall, with his cousin, dark as this one here," she nodded towards Todd.

Eadlyn frowned. It seemed a strange thing to be making a fuss about. What did it matter to the old woman if Todd and Fremund stayed up and drank too many noggins of mead? A chill settled on her shoulders, and Eadlyn stood, gently rubbing warmth into her arms. She turned towards the tent; there was no reply from the men, or none that Eadlyn heard as she reached inside for her cloak.

On her return, the talk had turned to how many boats could be expected the next day. The clay-maker continued to fret about lack of trade, with most of his anger directed at Todd, "What difference does it make if the pots are made in Royal Lyminge and perchance a King has one by the same hand, or if they are made in Saltwood, up on the hill over there? What difference does it make to the pot or cup?"

"None at all," Todd shrugged.

"Let us hope it doesn't tomorrow," Bradwin snapped. "Or I'll be packing up and leaving here."

"That's your business," Fremund shrugged. "We all fare well here on the Sandtun. If you don't, then take your chance elsewhere."

"Perhaps I will."

Eadlyn and Megan exchanged glances. It wasn't like this on the Sandtun, not usually. They had never known unease amongst the summer traders; both the camp on the raised land and the selling on the beach had always run smoothly, with no bad feeling amongst the yearly visitors.

The sun was now lowering itself onto the gracefully curving tops of a group of willow trees. Their black silhouettes were bent away from the coast and the sky was ablaze with orange streaks. But it was an evening of two halves: to the east, hanging over the hills of Saltwood and distant Folkestone, the clouds were gathering in a dense mass of smoky purple. With the sun completing its journey for the day and the rain clouds steadily moving towards the escarpment, it was time to think about gathering the children for bed.

But Hlappa was not done with them: "I'd say there's gold to be made on the Sandtun if you are lucky enough."

"Gold?" Fremund scoffed. "Not one of those men of Francia carry gold in their purses."

"Gold for some who have the luck on their side." Again, Bradwin's sneer was cast in Todd's direction. Eadlyn felt her stomach churn, and she glanced at her husband. He chose to ignore the comment.

"Gold for someone who had the fortune to come by it," Hlappa continued. "I sense it and I'm telling you it will pass from hand to hand carrying bad luck with it. And when it settles, if he, or she, can hold it close their luck will change."

"What stories you tell." Bradwin reached for his ale. "Now take our plates down to the water and clean them up; I didn't bring you to sit around talking nonsense."

"Show some respect for your elder," Todd said. He kept his voice low and was not one to cause an argument. However, the old woman did not deserve to be spoken to in such a manner.

"She's an old witch and I'll speak as I want." Bradwin stood and leaned down, placing his hand on Hlappa's shoulder. "Get yourself up."

The old woman, seemingly unperturbed by her son's aggressive tone, began to pull herself upwards. Eadlyn stood and placed a hand under Hlappa's elbow. "I thank you," Hlappa said, offering a toothless grin in her wizened face. "These legs don't work so well nowadays."

"The mouth does," her son muttered, as he strode off, leaving her to take their dirty plates.

"We'll all go together and wash the pans before darkness falls," Megan suggested. "Come on little ones, come to the river before bedtime."

"Aye and we'll have a noggin of mead," Fremund suggested to Todd and Arlo. "What do you say?"

The three men sat close together near the fire. The cousins, Todd and Fremund, dark and red-headed, were hard-working, but whereas Todd was serious and deep-thinking, Fremund was care-free and eager for adventure. Both twenty-six years of age, they had grown up with the annual Sandtun gathering of craftsmen, at first trailing behind their fathers and later bringing their own carts. Arlo, with his thick head of blond curls and neat beard, was just a year younger. New to the Sandtun, he was quickly accepted. Cheerful and hard-working, Arlo had shown he was willing to help with the chores. With the noggins of spiced honey mead held in their rough hands, a friendship was soon formed. They were united in their dislike of Bradwin the clay-maker and in their feeling of unease when near Hlappa.

Neither Fremund nor Arlo knew of the golden cross snug in the bottom of Todd's pouch. That morning he had examined it: noting its weight, rubbing his finger on the rounded garnet in the centre and tracing the delicate curved pattern on it. Then he had wrapped it in a scrap of cloth and placed it back in his pouch where, hanging from his belt, it would always stay close. Only Todd knew how real Hlappa's talk of gold was, but he was not one to dwell on tales of bad luck. He had a good life, with his wife who was both fair and cheerful, and the two healthy children she had blessed him with. All was well and he expected to go home with a pouch of silver, as well as the pretty silver and copper patterned box he had bought for Eadlyn as a gift.

"There's no cloud to bother us yet." Fremund looked upwards to the moon, whose light was gathering strength every minute. "The paths will be well lit."

"No cloud?" Todd frowned, as he looked to the east and the bank of cloud hanging over the hills.

"No cloud covering the moon, and I reckon we have an hour before the rains start." Fremund continued, "I've a mind to follow the monks' path again."

"The monks' path?" Arlo questioned.

"Aye, we saw them last night and they were up to something," Fremund told him. "Four of them and it seemed like they had a body slung between them; if it was dead or alive, I couldn't say."

"So she was right, saying you were out at night!" Arlo grinned.

"Perchance she was, but I don't like her questions," Fremund replied. "I don't like the way her son treats her, but she's an old witch and I'll keep my distance as much as I can."

"Well, you're right, the rain's not coming yet, so I'm ready for a walk," Arlo rose to his feet.

"Aye, I'm curious," Todd agreed. "Because whatever those monks carried, it wasn't with them this morning and they are done with the tools, so it seems likely they buried the body."

Chapter Eight

Unbeknown to the monks, they had been trailed by an unseen observer since the first day they had entered the Kingdom of Kent. Now Abbot Botolph was safely interred under the willow trees, the person who had witnessed the burial skulked about in the ruins of the Roman fort on the hillside. He was waiting for darkness; the waxing moon still appeared full in shape, the sky was clear and stars were gaining in brilliance as the sun disappeared below the vast stretches of Romney Marsh. His path would still be well-lit.

He had no name that he knew of, although presumably his mother had given him one. No memories of her remained in his mind. She was probably dead. He had grown up with no family, sleeping in the corner of a home or barn belonging to one person or another in the village until they tired of him. They may have been cousins or uncles, and probably were, but no one admitted to being his kin. He did the lowliest jobs for them, ate food destined for the pigs or chickens, and stole from whoever did their best to help him.

By the time seven years of his life had passed, the boy left the village of his birth and lived wild in the hedgerows and woodlands. There was food to be found in the form of nuts and berries, but this boy became wily and could enter any village unseen. He stole freshly cooked bread, eggs newly laid, and dipped his beaker in pans of simmering pottage. The clothes he wore had been taken as they were laid out to dry. Knives hung from a good leather belt and a pouch contained three silver coins. He kept his hair neat and his clothes in good order. He did not know his age was twenty years, but he had learned how to look after himself very well.

It was when he was following the path of a stream through some woodland, that he came across four monks sleeping. At first he thought there were five asleep, but closer scrutiny showed the fifth inert body to be forever asleep. Curiosity was aroused. The sleeping monks were relieved of some cheese and dried fruit before the newcomer retreated into a thick evergreen bush and prepared to wait for them to wake.

Over the next five days, the nocturnal monks were followed through the wooded valleys of Kent and onto a ridge of hills. It was not in their nature to steal and scavenge and he could see they were reluctant to go into the villages. Their unseen companion had no such qualms and fed himself much better than they did. It was during the night they descended onto Romney Marsh, when two others joined the scene. As the monks paused before the ruins of the Roman fort, the man who watched them stood behind the ancient trunk of a sturdy oak tree and investigated the darkness. On hearing Todd and Fremund approaching, a grin had spread across his face as he wondered if their arrival would challenge the monks in any way.

He recalled his disappointment on seeing what happened when the monks left the shelter of the trees; the other men had stood and watched as best they could from a distance. Some of their whispers had drifted on the night air and the on-looker learned that these men were reluctant to follow any further. They retraced their steps, presumably returning to wherever they had come from.

Now dozing in the long dry grass growing against the grey stone of the ancient fort, the young man thought of what happened when the monks' journey came to an end. From his hiding place, the steep bank of a water-filled ditch, he had seen them bury the body. It had not come as a surprise; they couldn't carry it about for much longer. But why here on this flat land, where the air smelt of salt and the water crept along the ditches and between the reeds? His mind was alive with ideas: there could be all kinds of treasures buried with whom he presumed was another monk, and one of some importance. At the very least a gold cross of good quality.

After a while, and a pleasant dream in which he was strolling in a woodland glade and met a young woman bathing naked in a pool, the loner woke. He smiled, knowing in the summertime there would be plenty of opportunities to seduce someone. He often saw a woman picking berries or mushrooms, a basket under her arms, her figure deliciously tempting under a thin woollen dress, and her hair cascading down her back. He allowed himself to dwell on his dream for a while longer, then pushed the thoughts aside. There was work to be done first, and he needed tools.

Those monks had carried tools and now he scolded himself for letting them go their own way. He had thought he was done with them, but how easy it would have been to take a shovel while they were sleeping. Now he would have to find a village and steal one. There was a path leading straight down the hillside and, from the shelter of the Roman walls, he had seen the occasional shepherd or fisherman descend the rugged hillside. He knew there to be a settlement at the top of the hill, although he didn't know its name; this area of Kent was new to him.

Pulling himself to his feet, he ambled towards a stream and washed the lassitude away with cool water, which he splashed over his face before cupping his hands and drinking deeply. He sighed, readying himself to walk up the hillside and steal a tool. On his return, dusk would have settled over the land and he would be ready to retrace his steps from the evening before.

Chapter Nine

"Goodnight, my love." Kneeling in the tent, Todd kissed Eadlyn. Her lips were slightly salty. "I miss lying with you."

She wrapped her arms around his neck, pulling him closer. "You could stay for a while?"

He thought of the noggin of mead, and the men waiting for him by the fire. "The others... we..."

"You've not finished your mead?" she asked.

"Nay, it's not that. We were just talking of some business." He didn't want to tell her about the monks and the body. Not yet, anyway.

"Go on then." Eadlyn kissed him once more. "Go to your cousin and I'll see you in the morning. Sleep well."

Todd smiled down at her. Eadlyn's long curls were smoky dark in the tent, with no hint of their golden colour. He reached out and ran his hand through them, then trailed a finger across her cheek. Shuffling back on his knees, he moved through the doorway and left his family for the evening.

The other men looked up as Todd approached. "We thought you were planting your seed!" Fremund said, a grin on his face.

"I thought of it..." Todd shrugged his shoulders and reached out as Arlo offered the mead. "Are we off to find this monk then, or whoever they buried?"

"Aye, I'm curious to know where they put him to rest," Fremund replied. He drained his noggin and rose to his feet.

"And what brought them to the Romney Marsh?" Arlo mused. "Although a dead body can't tell us much."

"Let's say no more of it for now," Todd advised.

They walked to the top of the beach and followed the track to the bridge. To the west, there was still the last of the sun's light in the sky. To the east, the trees and escarpment were in darkness. In unspoken agreement, the three men paused for a moment on the plank bridge. The tide was rising and the water had swelled in the creek. It pressed against the fresh water from inland, and together they swirled, fighting against each other. The wind had increased a little and with it, the rhythmic pounding of waves on the beach became more vocal.

Todd inhaled deeply, liking the scents from the sea. "Let us go under the cover of the trees while there is no one else about."

"Aye," Fremund murmured his agreement.

The cousins led the way to the narrow track, with Arlo close behind. The light of the moon and the stars were of little use now. As before, the men walked with their hands shielding their faces, nervous of the thin branches. No words were exchanged, and their pace was slow; they needed to be alert to any other person or animal nearby.

After a while, the trees thinned a little and the grey stone of the slumped Roman walls could be seen shapeless in the moonlight. "This is where they turned," Todd said, his voice low.

The three men left the hillside and the trees behind them and took the track leading to the open land. It seemed now as if they were on a causeway: the track was raised a little, lifting them up from the marsh, and all around them tidal waters were oozing through boggy ground. Now they were free of the trees, the scents of the sea were once again strong.

Soon the land on either side became pasture and the moonlight picked out the fleece of dozing sheep. There were still the signs of the area being vulnerable to the sea, in the form of shining pools of water and clusters of spiky reeds. When the track ended abruptly, all three men stood looking down into the water-filled ditch and saw a wide plank bridge.

"It's a good bridge," Fremund said, placing his foot on it and pressing down.

"Aye, mayhap they drive the sheep across it?" Arlo suggested. The field on the far side was also good pasture and, once they had crossed the water, they saw the track led around the edge of it, following the line of the wandering ditch.

Todd, straining his eyes to look ahead, was the first to spot a dark figure against a line of willow trees. There was the clink of metal on stone and, as the figure moved, the light of the moon shone on the head of a tool.

"Drop down," Todd whispered, his heart slamming into his chest.

"What the devil...?" Fremund breathed. But he crouched on the ground beside the others.

"There's someone there," Todd said. "Under the trees, digging or something."

"Not the monks?" Arlo asked.

"Nay, the monks are gone, I'm sure of it," Todd replied. Already he was backing into the ditch, probing the rugged bank with his toes.

"Digging for the body!" Fremund said, his words tinged with both horror and anticipation.

The three men crouched, their legs amongst the reeds and their arms resting on the edge of the field. Their heads were turned and eyes narrowed as they concentrated on the figure of a man, whom they watched as he put all his effort into digging under the arching branches of the willow trees.

"He must have followed them too," Arlo suggested. "Perchance he knows who is buried there and of the treasures with the body."

"Treasures?" Todd questioned. He recalled the cross, still wrapped up and nestling at the bottom of the pouch which hung from his belt. Busy with the selling of his leatherwork at the Sandtun, he had not thought of it again. A sudden wave of guilt shot a chill through his body. It was most likely the cross had come from the monks as they drank water and washed at the hillside spring. Who else would carry such an exquisitely crafted piece of gold?

"Aye, treasures," Arlo repeated. "If it was monks carrying the body then most likely it was a monk they buried and mayhap there were valuables with him."

"But why bury him here, without ceremony?" Todd wondered. "Why hide him away?"

"Because they want him untouched," Fremund suggested. "Perchance this monk is of such high rank, that his body would not be spared by those wanting to take a part of it. His hair, his nails, teeth... Is he so holy that he has to be hidden away or his body would not be left in peace?"

"So holy?" Todd echoed.

"Aye," Fremund replied. "I'd say we have someone of status lying there. But does this man dig for his gold cross or a lock of his hair?"

There was silence as the three of them considered the horror behind Fremund's words. Todd, who lived in Lyminge, where the devout monks and nuns shared a minster, knew how revered the body of a holy person was. Tales travelled along the lanes of Kent and they heard of how pilgrims trailed to places where they could be close to the relics of a saint.

"He could have followed those monks from wherever they came," Todd said, "And perchance he knows the importance of this body, whereas we can only guess. Or, like us, he came across the monks and now he tries his luck at finding something of worth."

They watched in silence, there being no way of learning the answers. The man dug with a steady rhythm. After a while, the onlookers shuffled closer, moving within the ditch, feeling their way until it turned. The reeds grew high and hid them well; the bank was uneven and so their feet found nooks and ledges to support themselves. By the time they were close enough to take a good look, the stranger was inside the hole and clods of earth were spraying up from within it. They were now close enough to smell his sweat as he dug deeper.

"He must be almost there," Fremund murmured. "They buried it well."

"Aye," Todd agreed. "This was important to them."

A sturdy branch was placed across the grave. They watched as a head and shoulders appeared and a pair of hands grasped the branch as the man used it to heave himself out. He brushed down his tunic and wiped his hands on the grass. Picking up a clay flask, he put it to his lips. Tipping his head back, he drank deeply and then eased himself back into the grave.

"He'll find the body soon enough," Arlo said. "I think he's slowed down, taking more care."

"Perchance he doesn't want to damage it," Todd mused. "Although he is content to disturb a grave."

"A grave that shouldn't be there," Fremund reminded them. "There's a story to be told and I doubt we'll learn much here tonight."

A flash of metal and a dull thud heralded the moment when the shovel was abandoned.

"He's nearly done," Fremund said.

The earth continued to rise from the grave, a handful at a time, as if the stranger was feeling his way. He was guided by the gentle light of the moon and stars, but even this was diminishing as the rain clouds gathered over the hills.

"He's coming up," Todd murmured. Again they saw his hands appear, one of them holding something which he was forced to put aside, in order to use both hands to grip on the branch. He pulled himself up and immediately reached for his prize, there seeming to be a desperation as he scrambled about for it.

"What is it?" Todd wondered. "It doesn't shine; it's not metal."

It seemed that the light was not strong enough for the grave digger. He stepped away from the shadows of the trees, and held the object up, moving it from side to side.

"We'll never see," Fremund muttered.

The frustration felt by this man was clear. He turned, tossed the object on the ground, and stepped back towards the grave. It was then, as he stood there looking upwards for a moment, that the most incredible thing happened, stunning the three onlookers. And afterwards, not one of them was able to believe they had witnessed it, nor were they able to express their thoughts.

A golden ray shone down from above. It came from neither the moon nor the stars, but from its own source. It kissed the faces of the cousins and their friend. The light felt warm and full of love; its smell was as sweet as summer flowers in a hedgerow or honey dripping from its comb. Mesmerised, they stared into the light unable and unwilling to shy away from it.

In the centre of the heavenly beam, the stranger stood but it neither caressed his skin nor gave comfort. His body was contorted in agony, yet at first no sound came.

Then it began: a shrill wail, spiralling up through the light beam, losing its strength until it was nothing more than a whisper, like the wind whipping through the marsh reeds. As the very last of it came from his weakened body, the nameless man crumpled and fell into the grave he had desecrated. The heavenly light was gone before the onlookers had pulled themselves from the ditch and, without turning to look at the grave under the willows, they ran. Stumbling and lurching along the track, they searched out the plank bridge and then ran to the shelter of the trees.

At that moment, the clouds almost toppled over the edge of the escarpment, and as they did so, the rain poured from them. A cloak of bulbous droplets hammered down on the marsh, the beach and the collection of tents on the Sandtun.

Eadlyn was sure she woke before the rain started. She had been dreaming it was daytime and the sun was warming her skin; she felt relaxed and drowsy in the healing heat. Lying awake in the darkness, she relived the feeling of comfort brought by the sun's rays. She could hear the children snoring; Clover's leg was outstretched, touching her own. The sides of the tent rippled, as the wind caught hold, and then the rain began.

Huge drops were hitting the hard, sun-dried, soil of the Sandtun. They made a sharp rhythm on the cooking pot left outside and bounced off the walls of the tent. At first the material repelled the rain, but the downpour was relentless and before long the tent was sodden. Eadlyn pulled the children close to her; while they left the sides of the tent untouched, they would stay dry within it.

The leatherwork would be vulnerable to staining if it got wet; Eadlyn recalled Todd speaking about protecting it and she hoped it was keeping dry. She thought of Todd under the cart. The wind would be driving the rain underneath and any moment she expected her husband to be pushing at the doorway of the tent, needing shelter.

With these thoughts wandering about in her mind, Eadlyn began to doze. As the rain eased, she fell back into a deep sleep.

On their second morning on the Sandtun, Todd knelt at the entrance to the tent and pulled back the sodden flaps. "It's been quite a night," he said. "Come and take a look."

Eadlyn crawled out and onto the damp grass; she stood gazing across the land to the beach and harbour. The sky was clear, the sun a soft red ball hanging just above the entrance to the sheltered inlet. Rolling to and fro, with no urgency at all, the sea was low and the sandy beach exposed. All was calm, but the torrential rain, coupled with a high tide, had left its mark on the Sandtun. The usual debris left at high tide had been thrown further than the beach and even beyond the beach track. It seemed as if the waves must have pounded on the edge of the grassy mound between marsh and tidal inlet: fires had been scattered and a fresh layer of sand deposited on the rough ground. Thankfully, the tents and carts had been spared, safe on the highest area of land.

Turning her back to the sea, Eadlyn gasped. Beyond the camp the marshland was flooded. Water had spilled out of the ditches, leaving willows standing within its grey ripples and the tops of reeds dotted about. Sheep clustered on islands of elevated ground and tracks were raised causeways through the wetlands.

A bevy of swans took flight, soaring over the Sandtun, their wings beating through the morning air. "I've never seen..." Eadlyn looked to the sky and then back across the land as she tried to express her wonder. "It's so beautiful. Look how the water sparkles. But the camp... How close we were to being swept away."

Todd put his arm around her shoulder. "Aye, but thank God, we are all safe. The boats are waiting to trade." He glanced towards the harbour with six small boats at anchor. "The men of Francia are here. It will be a good day."

"Aye," Eadlyn agreed. "The tents will be dry before the sun is at its peak and there is plenty of time to collect firewood. It will soon be as if there were no storm, and no harm is done."

She didn't notice her husband tense, or a pulse begin to throb in his throat. Eadlyn's attention was now on her children who had woken and were crawling out of the tent.

Chapter Ten

Standing at the top of the Shipway, gazing out across Romney Marsh and the *Oceanus Britannicus*, Brother Edwen marvelled at the difference in the view. The first time he had stood there, he was weary and the world was in darkness. The sea and creeks had shimmered silver, and the land was a mass of dusky darkness. Yet he recalled a sense of excitement, knowing his journey was almost at an end.

The second time Brother Edwen had stood at the edge of the hillside, he was exhausted. The soil had at first been as hard and unforgiving as rock; later it was damp and his habit heavy with particles of earth clinging to the wool. He had been starving and in need of dipping his body into a cool pool or river. He had glanced at the marsh, the pasture and the sea, but had seen nothing.

Now he was clean, refreshed by sleep and his stomach was full. The four monks had journeyed inland to a settlement called Lyminge and in that holy place the monks and nuns from the minster had fed their ragged brothers. They had allowed them to sleep while their tunics and scapulars were washed, then dried in the summer sun.

There had been no plan in his mind, but as the four monks walked in single file, leaving Lyminge behind and heading for Canterbury, Brother Edwen merely slipped away from them. At first he moved into a field and raced along, level with the road. Then he darted around the edge of Lyminge and walked the road leading to where the Shipway track descended onto Romney Marsh.

And so, Brother Edwen looked down on the flat landscape for the third time. His heart was full of wonder. The tension which had wrapped itself around his body for so long, fell away. The sky was a pure blue and this was reflected in the pools of water and wide channels. There were boats in the sheltered inlet and people on the beach. He recalled Brother Halig's words: "It is as bleak as you could imagine. No one has settled there since the Romans left three hundred years ago," and smiled. If he had not been such a holy man, that smile could have been considered to be a smirk. The tents were out of sight, hidden by the trees, but this place was certainly inhabited, albeit for a short time.

The Shipway track was criss-crossed with trails of water, making it perilous underfoot. The monk took small steps, leaning backwards towards the slope of the hill and the view was now obscured by trees. As he neared the bottom of the hill, he passed women and children with buckets and jugs, no doubt collecting water from the many streams on the hillside. The children stared openly, while the women glanced at him and lowered their faces.

He didn't want to walk across the area covered in tents and carts but retraced the steps he had made under the weak light of the moon. After a short time, Brother Edwen spotted the Roman fort and searched for the track which turned away from the trees. But it was different: where they had walked through a dry ditch, there was now a wide channel of water. However, the track led out from the other side, and so the monk removed his shoes, hitched up his clothes and waded through it. His feet sank into soft mud and the water rose as far as his knees, then he was stepping out and onto the path again.

In the moonlight, Brother Edwen had seen patches of water glistening. But the storm from the previous night had left great pools of water and the ground was very boggy. Flying insects skittered about and the warm air was filled with their soft buzzing. The reeds were sitting deep within the water and so only their tops fretted about in the wind. The track was dry though and safe to walk on until it stopped abruptly by a ditch, the same water-filled channel upon which the golden light had shone, guiding their way on the night they had journeyed with the body of Abbot Botolph.

The monk stood and considered his next move. He had come this far, driven to see the grave in daylight and to assure himself that the abbot rested in peace, with no threat of being disturbed. There was another, less pious, reason for retracing his steps. The golden cross, picked up from the ground just before the body was buried, had slipped from Brother Edwen's leather pouch. "I should never have taken it," the monk said to himself. "It was God's will that I mislay it so quickly, but if I were to come across it, I would not be sorry." He had no wish to trudge all the way back to Middle England, and something as special as this heavy cross may well ease his way into a position in a different monastery. Better to be welcomed as a monk with a gold cross, than accepted as a desperate travelling monk.

"Come on then," Brother Edwen muttered. He slid down the bank, feeling with his feet for the solid plank bridge. This time the water was just above his knees, but it was only a few steps and the monk was soon crawling up the bank. He secured his shoes and gazed at the field. Where it had been well-drained grassland, it now had pools in every dip and the ditches overflowed. Within a few minutes he reached the place where the row of willows now stood deep in water and no sign of the grave remained.

The monk surveyed the landscape, seeing that already the water was retreating and as it did so it would carry any loose earth, smoothing the ground. The grave, still partially underwater, had been concealed by the aftermath of the heavy rains and high tide. "Abbot Botolph is safe," Brother Edwen said, and as he whispered those words his mood was joyful.

The gold cross would not be there, the water would have carried it away, but Brother Edwen's attention was drawn towards something washed up with the debris from the storm. He moved towards the line of broken twigs, shells and leaves, all settled at the furthest point where the tide had flowed. There, sodden and with its pages pressed tight together, was the book of hours. He reached down and picked it up, then prised apart the soaked pages. The writing was faded and illegible. The monk, lost in his confusion as to how the book had surfaced from the depths of the grave, did not hear the footsteps of another man.

Todd had come from the Sandtun, picking his way across the marsh, jumping narrow inlets of water and wading through others. He came alone and hadn't told the others. Having risen early and helped remake the fires, he had checked the tent and his leatherwork was safe. Now Eadlyn was busy with Megan and the children, and the boats would not be pulled up on the beach until the sun had risen further in the sky.

The evening before, Todd, Fremund and Arlo had fled from the double grave, having seen it desecrated. When the stranger fell, his body contorted with agony, the grave had been left exposed. What further damage had been done by the rain and unusually high tide, Todd wondered? On seeing the monk, he faltered, then decided to continue and stood a few feet behind the other man.

While the marsh and pasture had suffered from the high tide and torrential rain, it seemed as if it had smoothed away all signs of misplaced soil around the site of a grave. The piles of earth, removed the night before, had been washed back into the grave and the whole area was now littered with the debris brought with the high-water levels. It was as if a grave had never been dug, and the terrors of the night before had not happened. The water lapped against where Todd believed the grave to be and he found the scene to be soothing. Vivid memories of the previous night began to lose clarity as Todd allowed himself to become absorbed with the cries of the gulls and the movement of the water.

Turning away from the grave, Brother Edwen felt there was nothing more to be done. Abbot Botolph was at peace. He jumped a little but allowed his face to remain passive when he noticed a dark-eyed man standing not far behind him, staring down at the water under the willow trees.

Their eyes met as Todd moved his gaze to the monk's face. "You returned," Todd stated.

Brother Edwen paused, as if considering the words. "Aye, I saw you when I had tools to sell."

"I saw you before that. I saw you with the other monks and whoever is buried here." A silence followed, each man considering his next words. It was Todd who spoke again, "I won't tell anyone. Your secret is safe, and the sea has done a good job of concealing the grave. But I wonder who he, or she, is? Why the body had to be hidden?"

"It is Abbot Botolph. A good man. A saintly man," Brother Edwen told him.

"It wasn't safe to bury him with ceremony and in a Godly place?"

"It wasn't safe; he couldn't lie in peace," Brother Edwen said.

Todd tried to express his thoughts. "There must be a reason and I wouldn't want any harm done. He should be buried in the right place, but perchance he can't be and so this is as good a place as any."

"It's very restful." Brother Edwen smiled slightly.

Todd said nothing about the other man who had been felled by the golden light and shared the Abbot's grave. He allowed the monk to leave the graveside with his mind and heart at ease.

Chapter Eleven

On their fifth day at the Sandtun, the tide was at its highest within two hours of sunrise. The men pulled carts onto the beach while the sky was still a soft pink-blue and the dew heavy on the rough grass of the raised land. The heat of the morning sun was already causing the moisture to lift from the land and a light mist hung over Romney Marsh. The colours of the countryside were muted. Over the past days, high water levels had subsided, and no more storms had come to threaten the peace of the Sandtun.

The only discord came from within the camp. The old woman, Hlappa, continued to prophesy doom. So when she approached Eadlyn and Megan, both women slumped a little but forced smiles.

"I've got our bread to bake," Hlappa moved to the fire, her flat pan held out before her. "I see you're mixing yours."

"Aye," Megan replied. "Our last breakfast here at the Sandtun. I wonder if we'll return next year." If her husband's brother, Arlo, was to find a new wife, then he would have no need for Megan to feed him and look after the camp.

"Last breakfast, you say," Hlappa repeated. "These mists that swirl above the ditches, they send a message."

Eadlyn scowled. "We've no need for your messages. I've heard of no gold coming from the men of Francia."

"I said there was gold on the Sandtun," Hlappa reminded her. "I said nothing of the men of Francia. Someone here has gold and it comes from a place most holy."

Eadlyn thought of the monks but would not humour the old woman. "Our men and children need bread in their bellies, that is our message."

Hlappa turned to the fire, but her voice still carried to the women who mixed their dough. "It will be someone's last breakfast."

Eadlyn and Megan continued to mix, then knead the dough. They worked in silence, not wanting to encourage Hlappa's talk. Having made neat balls of dough, they stretched them outwards to make flat discs. Megan placed the pan over the fire and Eadlyn tossed dough onto the hot metal. Hlappa had moved away, her bread already baked, but she lingered nearby and muttered while looking out to the beach.

Boats were pulled up on the sand, and the men of Francia were looking through the carts. They came on the last day. Perhaps they had missed the best of the goods for sale, but there was a chance of finding something cheap. None of the traders would want to return with leather, or metalwork or clay pots in their carts.

At the start of the day, it was clear Bradwin had been confident of finally selling his clay items. He stood tall and swaggered as he pushed his laden cart onto the sand. The other carts had little to offer the men with silver to spend. This would be the day Bradwin returned to the Sandtun camp with a purse of silver coins when the boats turned away from the sheltered harbour.

With warm bread and a jar of honey, Eadlyn walked to the beach, calling to the children: "Clover, Cym, come and eat with your faeder." The young ones raced across the sands.

Todd turned as he took a coin and handed over a leather bag. "I thank you; my belly was in need of food."

They sat together on the sand, dipping bread in the honey jar. Eadlyn spotted Bradwin at the far end of the beach. His body was slumped where it had been proud. He shook a fist at the departing boat.

"He did not sell his clay," Eadlyn commented.

"Nay, the quality is poor."

"I wish he had sold a little more, just to keep the peace in the Sandtun."

"I understand," Todd nodded. "But they come here for the best. The journey is dangerous and not worth it for a cracked pot."

"I know," Eadlyn sighed.

As they ate the bread, someone came and looked at the last of Todd's belts. He stood to show his work and hopefully make a sale. The man took all three of the belts, waving his hands and jabbering away in a foreign tongue, with a big smile on his face. Then he gestured to a lone leather jerkin draped over the side of the cart. Todd allowed him to try it on and nodding happily, the man parted with his silver.

"Is your cart empty?" Clover asked.

"Aye sweeting, we can pack up our tent and go home."

"I'll be sad to leave," the girl said.

"But we'll come back next year!" her father replied, leaning over to place a kiss on her head of golden curls.

The sun was still not at its highest when the first traders left the Sandtun. They all had to journey up the steep Shipway track and not everyone was lucky enough to have a horse. So the men helped each other pull carts up the hill before waving farewell to old friends. Todd's cart, now empty of leatherwork, had plenty of space for the children, but he insisted they walk up the hill as even an empty cart was a burden for the pony.

"Farewell, friend," Todd said to Arlo, as they reached the Shipway crossroads. "Safe travel."

"Godspeed." Fremund gave Arlo a friendly punch on the arm. "We'll meet again next year."

"Aye," Arlo replied. "The trading was good and I thank you for your friendship."

The two women hugged, with tears in their eyes. "Good health to your husband," Eadlyn said. "I pray we are together again next year."

"I hope so," Megan responded. "I do hope so."

They stepped away from each other and, calling out their farewells, the two families parted. Arlo, with Megan and her children, to journey along the hilltop to Aldington, and the cousins to travel inland to their villages. But as the family going to Aldington moved away from the crossroads, Todd glanced back down the Sandtun and saw Bradwin struggling up the hill with his cumbersome cart.

"I wonder, should we go to help?" Todd asked Fremund.

"Aye," Fremund replied with reluctance. "I'm eager to get home to my wife and son, but we always help each other on the Sandtun, however difficult someone may be."

"We won't be long," Todd said to Eadlyn, as he turned to retrace his steps down the hill.

"Let's look out to the sea," Eadlyn said to the children. "Can you see the boats going back to Francia?" The view never failed to fill her with a sense that all was good in their lives. But when she glanced down the track, she could see the anger on the clay-maker's face as he pulled the cart up the hill. Bradwin had his back to the cousins who pushed the cart, chatting and laughing together, and the twist on his lips, with the red flush over his face, filled Eadlyn with dread. His cart was still full of his clay pots; the last morning at the Sandtun had done nothing to pacify the man. In fact it had only inflamed his anger as one by one the carts of the other traders had emptied, and the boats returned to Francia.

They reached the summit, with Hlappa trailing behind. The old woman coughed and wheezed, as she dragged herself up the final length of the slope.

"Come on woman," Bradwin shouted.

"She's not far behind," Todd tried to calm him. "Come on Hlappa, you're nearly there and you'll be sleeping on your straw mattress tonight!"

"And what of you, in Royal Lyminge?" snarled Bradwin.

"It makes no difference to me," Todd countered, his voice calm. "My home is simple, much like everyone else's."

"But they buy your leather because the King of Kent has favoured Lyminge and his daughter Queen Ethelburga built a church of stone."

"They buy my leather because the work is good," Todd stated.

"Aye, the men of Francia know nothing of Lyminge," Fremund added. "Now we must move on and bid you safe journey home."

"Home to my damp straw mattress, and with my nagging mother." Bradwin gave the cart a push, knocking it into Fremund who still stood beside it.

"I've had enough," Fremund replied, rubbing his bruised arm. "We tried to help you, and now I have a wife to return home to."

The cousins moved from the rear of the cart and walked alongside it. They were no longer laughing and exchanged no words.

"You came back to look at my cart full of clay, to laugh at how laden it is," Bradwin snarled.

Todd shrugged and turned to Bradwin as they moved alongside him. "We came back to help with your cart and still we can do nothing right. We shared our fire and tried to be pleasant, but I've had enough of your anger, and want no part of it."

"You've had enough?" Bradwin's voice was dangerously low; his fists clenched and body tense, like a stag poised to battle.

"Aye, I've had enough," Todd repeated. He began to turn away.

Eadlyn felt her body freeze and the children fell silent, all fearful of the next move, even as their father chose to walk away. It came, with more force and speed than they expected: Bradwin swung his fist in Todd's direction and caught him directly on the bridge of his nose. Todd, fit and strong, was caught unawares and fell instantly. Before the back of his head hit the ground, his face had paled and eyes glazed over. He lay motionless, and for a short time no one did or said anything.

Then came Hlappa's words: "I said death was hanging over the Sandtun."

"Shut up, you stupid woman," Fremund bellowed.

"Stop making such an ungodly fuss," Bradwin's voice was tinged with contempt, and he turned to his mother as he tugged at the cart. "It's nothing but a fall and all he deserves. Come on, you old fool."

If they had taken the time to look at Hlappa, Eadlyn and Fremund would have seen she was even more frail and bent than before. Her skin was clammy, and she trembled, but somehow she put one foot before the other and followed her son up the Shipway.

Kneeling at Todd's side, Eadlyn stroked his ashen face and murmured endearments. She didn't put her fingers to the side of his neck or on his heart, to feel for the rhythmic pounding telling her that he still lived. She knew Todd, who was always so loving and gentle, had been killed by one swing of another man's fist. The children stood nearby, not fully understanding. Fremund was there, crouched beside Eadlyn, his hand on her shoulder. She was hardly aware of his presence; it was just her and Todd alone, with the warmth of the summer sun brushing on their skin.

Fremund only stayed there for a moment before jumping to his feet and running in the direction of Bradwin, who was walking at quite a pace, leaving his mother to lag behind. "Bradwin of Saltwood, you'll not take a man's life and go unpunished," Fremund shouted with all his might.

The shout brought Eadlyn to her feet and she turned to Fremund, "What are we to do? The children..."

"But Faeder is not dead; he is sleeping," Clover wailed, running over to her mother.

"Wake up. Wake up," Cym screamed.

"He won't wake," Fremund said, and then to the children, "We must all be so brave and later we'll go to the church and pray for your faeder's soul."

"He is at peace," Eadlyn said. She heard her words come from her mouth and saw her hands go to the children's heads. Her fingers moved through their golden curls. But she felt nothing; it was as if she looked down on the scene from another place. Perhaps she would wake, and they would all be in their home, with the smell of wood-smoke thick in the air and a lumpy straw mattress beneath them. And Todd would be there breathing deeply beside her, his dark hair falling over his face.

The children began to cry silently, fat tears rolling unchecked down their faces. No tears welled in Eadlyn's eyes. They would come later.

"Others will come up the hill; we cannot leave him here like this." Fremund turned to Todd's cart and took out a blanket. He pushed the tent, their cloaks and the cooking utensils to one side. "Eadlyn, I'm sorry, we must lift him into your cart and the children can sit in mine."

"Of course," she replied, watching as Fremund rolled the body onto the blanket. "Clover, Cym, I must be brave and strong, and help lift Faeder into the cart." Eadlyn moved to Todd's feet. "Shall I stand here, Fremund?"

"Aye."

They both gathered the blanket, and when they were ready their eyes met. Fremund nodded and, using all her strength, Eadlyn lifted her husband's body up to the low wall of the cart. It rested for a moment on the wooden side, they shifted position and lowered him in. Eadlyn placed a kiss on her finger and then touched Todd's forehead. She took the loose folds of blanket and covered his body and face.

Then Eadlyn took the children and gave each one a hug before lifting them into the other cart. She laid her hand on Fremund's arm, "Thank you, cousin." He said nothing in reply. She moved to her pony and took his halter, gave it a gentle tug and he moved forward. With Fremund taking the lead, they walked along the road, moving inland with their backs to the coast and Romney Marsh.

It was a steady climb uphill to Lyminge. Eadlyn's legs ached; she put one foot in front of the other and step by step she neared home. Looking to neither the woodland nor the fields, her eyes were only on the mud and stone of the track. At first, she could hear her children crying for their father but in time their tears were spent and they settled down to sleep on Fremund's blankets.

On reaching the narrow track leading to his home in Postling, Fremund stopped his cart and walked back to join Eadlyn. He put his hand under the blanket covering Todd and extracted the pouch from his belt. "Give me your hand," Fremund said to Eadlyn, as he took her wrist and turned her palm upwards. Then he tipped about a quarter of the coins into her palm; a small package fell with them and he ignored it. "Place these in your purse and when you are home, you must hide them. Todd's brothers will want their share of the money earned, as is their right, but I suspect they will leave you with nothing."

Eadlyn nodded and slid the coins into her own leather purse. "I'll do as you say."

"Now we go on to Lyminge."

"But your wife and child..."

"They will understand I have no choice but to see my cousin and his wife home."

Fremund tied his horse to a tree and lifted the children out of the cart. They both ran to their mother and held on to her dress. Together they walked up the last slope and, as they reached the top, the village of Lyminge was revealed, laid out in a shallow dip, with the stream running through it. The thane's hall took central position and scattered about were villagers' homes of wood and mud, with roofs of reed thatch. There were bread ovens and open fires; communal work areas, such as the hut where Eadlyn did her weaving and the one where she baked bread; areas where families crafted, where clay-makers and metal-workers and, of course, leather-workers laboured. The sounds of village life came from pens of animals and people moving about, calling to each other as they busied themselves with their daily routines. To their left, on the rise of the hillside, the stone church stood taller than the village homes and the minster with its lands was higher still.

Eadlyn's mouth was dry; she felt sick. Somehow she had to walk down the slope and find the words to tell Todd's family that their son and brother had been killed that day. She looked at the cart. It seemed wrong to be taking Todd's body into the village, but she knew she could not leave him. She looked at Fremund, hoping for guidance.

"I'll find my cousins," Fremund said, referring to Todd's brothers.

Eadlyn nodded her agreement and watched him walk into the village. She saw Todd's older brother walk out of their workplace, an animal skin thrown over his shoulder. There was a cry of recognition when he saw Fremund with his distinctive tall frame and red hair. Then a call for the younger brother and when he came, they all stood close to each other. Finally, they turned and looked across the village to Eadlyn and the children. She looked back and watched their progress as they walked towards her and the body of their brother, Todd.

That evening, the children finally slept on their straw mattress, covered by thin woollen blankets. Eadlyn remembered the silver coins Fremund had tipped into her hand and how she had in turn placed them in her own leather purse. The evening sun still gave a little light and Eadlyn went to the doorway of her home; she knelt and let the coins drop on the ground, and with them came a small package, wrapped in a thin piece of cloth. She frowned, not recalling it falling from Todd's pouch earlier and settling in her palm, nor recognising it as her own. With her fingertips, Eadlyn peeled back the layers of cloth and saw a gold cross nestled within the folds of material. She held it up to the last of the evening light and examined the swirls shaped on it, and the dark red stone in its centre, then gathered the coins, wrapped the cross and placed them in a small leather pouch, which in turn she put within her mattress. As she fell asleep that night, Hlappa's words rang in her head: "There's gold on the Sandtun."

Chapter Twelve

Brother Edwen's back was stiff: it seemed as if it were seized in place, never to be thawed. Even though he now lay on a thin straw mattress, he could not relax into it. He had been given a clean shift and it lay soft against his skin; at the first opportunity he would seek out dried thistle heads and place them within the fabric. His penance was not done.

On either side of him, Brother Edwen could hear the gentle snores of the other monks. But he felt as if he still lay on the floor of the oratory, with prayers running through his lips. His back stiff, the stone slabs unyielding.

"You have been on the road for many weeks?" The Abbess had queried when he had returned to Lyminge Minster, the previous afternoon.

"Aye," he had replied.

"You have seen things you shouldn't, perhaps witnessed the sins of man?" she queried. Her features were soft behind her veil. He saw a wisp of pale gold hair, and the snub of her nose pointing upward, but everything else was clouded. It was not fair, she could read every expression in his face, yet hers were hidden.

"I have seen more sins than I would ever wish to," he had confirmed.

"And have you lived in a greater degree of comfort than you have need for?"

Brother Edwen thought of the soft beds of moss and ferns and lowered his head in shame. "Sometimes," he had answered.

"We want no word of your time in the outside world to be uttered within our holy place," the Abbess had stated. "You will spend the day in the oratory, with no comfort. When you join us for Vespers, you will be free to live amongst us."

"Could I… would you permit me to lie in the oratory through the night?" Brother Edwen had asked. "Until Vigils?"

"Through the night?" He couldn't see her frown, but he heard the tone of her voice change as she failed to hide her surprise. "If you feel it will rid you of your sins."

He bowed his head in acknowledgement and respect for her holy state.

Then she had led him from the lobby adjoining her chambers and out into an open area, where the grass was bleached by the sun and neat paths stretched out towards the larger buildings, such as the refectory, dormitories and, of course, the church. There was a sensation of peace, just two nuns and a monk walked these paths, their heads bowed as they almost glided along. Brother Edwen had learnt little of the history of the minster yet. He had observed that only the church and the separate oratory were made of stone, while the other buildings were of wood. On his last visit he had been told that a Roman basilica had stood on this very site and its stones had been used to create these new buildings to worship God.

They had entered the oratory through a narrow, rounded doorway and he stood, allowing his eyes to adjust to the dim light coming from the small windows, set not far from the eaves. The floor was stone, and the walls were plastered without further decoration. A candle burned on the main altar.

"You wish to lie here until Vigils," the Abbess confirmed. "Then you will return to your bed until sunrise and I pray that any faults you have indulged in or any sins you witnessed are cleansed from your troubled soul."

Brother Edwen had placed his body on the stone floor, his arms outstretched so he formed the shape of a cross and, with his gaze fixed on the stone floor, his back to the rafters, he began his penance.

A bell rang to signify the sun was about to rise over the hills to the east. The monks began to stir and swing their legs over the sides of low wooden-framed beds. Brother Edwen did the same, then reached for his tunic, which was hanging on a wooden peg protruding from the plank wall. He exchanged his night-shift for the tunic, taking care to reveal as little of his body as possible and keeping his eyes averted from the other monks. As they dressed, the Prior walked the length of the long room. Then they filed out, with some breaking the line to go to a small outhouse of latticework, situated away from the other buildings. Brother Edwen turned off the main path and waited for his turn to relieve his bladder. The stench was almost unbearable and he turned his face to the nearby woodland. Once inside the narrow building, he stood and watched his urine flow into a shallow channel, before it dropped into a bucket, to be saved for the washing of clothes.

The stone church was a tall building. Like the oratory, it had a narrow doorway and a row of small round-topped openings high in the walls. The roof was made of wooden shingles, while the other monastery buildings had thatched roofs. Walking towards the church, Brother Edwen heard a sudden clatter of pans coming from the kitchens, then all was quiet again, other than the background clucking of chickens in coops and the birds beginning their morning chorus. Even at this early hour, the breeze was light and warm. There was barely a rustle of leaves and the smoke rising from the kitchen fire was moving upwards in a lethargic manner. The sky was filling with newborn light: a mixture of pinks, mauves and grey, yet the sun had not yet risen.

Walking into the church, Brother Edwen was at first struck by a sense of relief. It hit him like a wave, engulfing his body, and afterwards he felt more at ease than he had for some time. "Seven times a day I praise you," he murmured, his lips barely moving. For how many nights had they journeyed across Mercia and into Kent? It began as an opportunity to explore the unknown and only now did Brother Edwen yearn for all that he had missed – the routines of the Benedictine monastery. He stood towards the back of the church and marvelled at the fact that this building had been built of abandoned Roman stones. Perhaps four hundred years beforehand, the Romans had stood in a different building, made of these very stones, and worshipped in their own way.

The sun was rising, although they could not see it, and so the songs from the psalms began. Brother Edwen again felt a gratitude for all which was familiar in the flow and rhythm of the words. Then he listened, more fervently than ever before, as the Prior read a short passage from the scripture. He shuffled a little, his back still stiff and chilled, but as the dawn prayer was said, Brother Edwen felt that some warmth was finally returning to his body.

> "The loving kindness of our God who visits us
> Like the dawn from on high.
> He will give light to those in darkness
> those who dwell in the shadow of death,
> And guide us into the way of peace."

Moving as one gentle wave, the monks and nuns processed in pairs from the church and into the open space between the church, dormitories and chapter house to the north, and the refectory and kitchen to the south. The cubiculum, or Abbess' chamber, stood to the east of the minster buildings, looking towards the settlement of Lyminge. Some of those holy people separated to start their early morning duties, while Brother Edwen followed the others into the chapter house, a low room set below the dormitories. He picked up a book and returned to the courtyard, then sat on a plain wooden bench. He allowed himself a moment to look beyond the minster buildings, towards the gentle swell of the opposite hillside, where neat lines of crops filled one field and sheep grazed in another. Closer to the minster there was a line of wicker beehives and wooden coops for chickens.

Turning to his book, the monk opened it and began to read, his own whispered words joining the others, and so the audible hum of their speech filled the air and the sounds of nature were lost to him. After a while, Brother Edwen stretched a little and looked south, between the kitchen and the refectory, towards a line of trees. A movement caught his attention: a grave was being prepared in the burial area belonging to the people of the village.

Chapter Thirteen

"I thank you," Fremund lowered his head in a show of respect.

"My brother and his son will meet with you when the sun has risen above the hills," the Thane of Lyminge said. "Bring your spear, although we hope for no more bloodshed."

"I'll pray for that," Fremund agreed. He turned to Todd's brothers, one younger and one older than the dead man. "I must return to Brona and the child, but we meet tomorrow."

"Aye, we'll see justice is done," the older brother spoke. "I will come and Alwin must stay with the family."

They were standing in the thane's hall, having just seen Todd buried. A fire burned in a central pit, making the heat within the building unbearable. A hog was roasting above the fire, its skin beginning to brown and crackle, and the rich smell of pork mingled with wood-smoke. A wall of curtains, embellished with stitching to depict flowers and trees, divided the area where the thane worked and ate, with the private area for his family.

"We'll see justice is done," Fremund repeated his cousin's words. "Until tomorrow..."

He moved through the open doorway and immediately felt the heat of the sun on his skin. He had a desire for some mead, or good wine, but walked down the slope to the stream, knelt on a rock and dipped his cupped hands into the fresh waters emerging from the nearby spring. His thirst slaked, Fremund walked up the dry earth track, past homes and animals' pens to the outer edge of the village. Only when he reached the top of the hill, did he look across the dish-shaped valley to the stone church and the burial ground beyond it.

"Sleep peacefully, cousin," he murmured.

The next day came too early for Fremund, after a restless sleep plagued with nightmares about Todd's sudden death. When he rolled out of bed, Brona was sitting at the doorway grinding wheat. The baby was sleeping on a thick blanket. Fremund knelt and took a good look at his son, perhaps for the first time. He was a scrawny child, with a pointed chin and tufts of red hair showing from beneath the linen cloth he was swaddled in. His skin was clear, lips set in a pout, and his eyelashes pale. He was only eight days old and already Fremund had left him to trade at the Sandtun and then to see Todd buried; now he would leave his wife and child again in order to seek out Bradwin of Saltwood. The baby moved a little and a tiny fist emerged; his fingers were so delicate and his nails neatly formed. He opened his eyes, revealing dark blue pools, then closed them again. Reaching out, Fremund ran a fingertip over the baby's soft cheek. Then, letting out a sigh, he stood and turned away.

When Fremund joined the Lyminge road, he looked to the east and saw the other men approaching. Their faces showed no emotion and the four of them merely nodded to each other. Round shields were slung on their left arms and spears were held in their right hands. Bags, carried on broad shoulders, held bread, cheese and a flagon of weak ale. The day promised to be warm, so they only wore their tunics, hose and leather shoes.

Walking on the dusty road, no conversation took place. The men were thoughtful, considering their roles: Harold, brother of the thane, carried a roll of vellum, stating the reason for their visit and expressing the thane's wish that they were granted an audience with the Thane of Saltwood; Fremund would pledge his word that he had seen Bradwin of Saltwood slay cousin Todd with his fist, and state how he had left a man to die without a care. The other two men were there to offer solidarity and to vouch for the placid nature of the dead man, as well as Fremund's honesty. Their minds were full of the scene they might encounter. They pictured hostility from the villagers and Bradwin fleeing as he heard of their approach. Fremund thought of his son and hoped to return to him long before the sun was dipping below the horizon.

Approaching Saltwood from the north, they came to a heavily wooded area. The sounds of men working nearby came in the form of axes slicing through wood and the call of one woodcutter to another. Birds flew high in the canopy of oak, ash and beech trees, and rose as one when disturbed by man. The tang of burning wood mingled with the rich scent of rotting leaves and damp earth.

Although there were no other humans to be seen, the men of Lyminge and their cousin, Fremund, felt the presence of others. They sensed they had been seen and were being watched passing through the woodland; their arrival at Saltwood would be heralded before they walked much further.

On entering a hilltop clearing, it seemed as if Saltwood was a silent village. All faces were turned to the newcomers. Only the chickens, sheep and pigs went about searching for food, or sleeping in the sunshine, unaware of the tension mounting. The men, women and children turned from their duties – whether it was tending the animals, grinding the grain, making repairs to houses or crafting materials in their workplaces. Adults straightened their backs, bringing themselves to full height, while small children slipped behind their mothers.

The elderly thane, flanked by two younger men, stepped forward from the doorway of the great hall. They stood and waited, their faces impassive, showing no sign of welcome. The four who were strangers to Saltwood walked past the villagers, who silently stepped back to clear the path. Then the newcomers stood before the thane and elders of Saltwood, bowing their heads briefly. The building they stood before was taller and longer than the others making up the settlement; its walls were made of vertical planks and its roof was thatch. Smoke curled upwards from a hole in the roof and, as if to emphasise its grandeur, the thane's hall had a set of double doors, each one pushed back to let the summer air flow in.

"We bring grave news," Harold of Lyminge spoke. "I bring this scroll, stating our business. It comes from my brother, the Thane of Lyminge, and tells of the death of Todd, leatherworker from our village. A good man who died at the hands of one of your men, as my friend here bears witness." Harold looked towards Fremund who nodded.

The thane took the roll of vellum and before any word passed his lips he studied it carefully. His mouth tightened and he passed the vellum to the younger men who pored over it together.

"Come inside." The thane gestured to the open doorway. "You will find no hostility here." Then turning to the younger men, he said, "Secure Bradwin the clayworker with haste. Already word of these strangers' arrival will have reached his ears."

Stepping into the thane's hall, the newcomers were greeted by a stunning vista. For although they had entered from a wooded area, the village of Saltwood was set on a spur of high ground, overlooking the Oceanus Britannicus to the south. This view was framed by a wide-open doorway, opposite the one they had walked through, and so the central area of the building was flooded with light and the air was fresh, despite the smoking fire. Gulls swooped and soared, cackling to one another. The sky was open, where it had been crowded by treetops, and the air was a little sharper than before.

Gesturing to benches set around a table, the thane sat and the visitors followed suit. "Allow me to introduce myself," he said. "I am Hugh of Saltwood, thane of this village. And you have come from Lyminge – a place of good honour."

"We thank you for your welcome, Hugh of Saltwood," Harold replied, as he let his spear and shield rest on the dry earth floor. "I am Harold of Lyminge, brother of our thane. I bring with me my son, Aelfraed, also Cedric of Lyminge, brother of the dead man, and Fremund of Postling, cousin to the dead man and witness to his death."

"I would welcome you, but it is not a day for festivities," the thane observed.

"We buried a good man yesterday," Harold told him. "We come in low spirits."

"Some ale perhaps?" Hugh of Saltwood raised his voice, "Alodie, some ale for our guests, if you please."

A woman appeared from the seaward doorway. Her dress was made of a fine woollen thread, dyed in a dark red; it was embroidered at the cuffs of the wide sleeves and at the hemline, which hung just below the knees. An underskirt reached the ground. The scarf, covering her hair, was pinned with a gold brooch; its design was elaborate, and a red stone caught the sunlight. Alodie nodded to the men and they could see her face was pleasant, although lined with age. Moving behind them, she went to the darker recesses of the building and returned with a tray of beakers containing ale.

"I must express my sorrow for the death of your kinsman," Thane Hugh said. "Fremund of Postling, pray tell me what happened."

"We were at the Sandtun," Fremund began. "I was there selling my metalwork and my cousin, Todd, he was with his wife and children, selling his leatherwork. It is something we do every year. Bradwin and his mother were new to trading on the Sandtun. He showed no respect to the old woman, but we said nothing; it wasn't our business. We sold well, everyone did. At least not everyone, not Bradwin. He was angry – angry at us, angry at the men of Francia. But he seemed to take against Todd."

"Did your cousin, Todd, provoke him in any way?" Hugh asked.

"He said nothing much at all," Fremund replied. "My cousin has a... had a calm nature." Todd's brother, Cedric, nodded.

"But you say Bradwin killed your cousin," the thane prompted.

"Aye, we reached the top of the Shipway on our last day. Our carts were empty of goods; we had sold them all. We looked back and there was Bradwin, struggling to pull his cart up the hill. It was still laden with pots. Todd said we should help him; I wanted to get home to my wife and baby. But we went and then he started, saying we were laughing at him, because our carts were empty. Todd would not laugh at an other's bad fortune. He, my cousin that is, said he had had enough of Bradwin's anger. That's when it happened: Bradwin swung his fist at Todd and felled him. He came down so hard, and that was it; Todd was dead."

"Did Bradwin show any remorse?"

"Remorse?" Fremund repeated. "Nay, he walked off at such a speed. I'd say that he didn't realise he had killed a man, but he knew it was time to leave."

The thane turned to Harold, "Your brother, Thane of Lyminge, sent you in his place today. Tell me, Harold of Lyminge, do you trust the word of this man?"

"Aye, I do," Harold answered. "Fremund is an honest man, whose mother came from our village and settled not far away. He is a good man and a fine metalworker."

"I place high value on your word." Hugh of Saltwood turned to Cedric and spoke, "Your brother – was he a placid man?"

"Aye, he never had a temper."

There came the sound of feet on hard earth; the pace was urgent, and the men turned, expecting news of Bradwin. The thane's men entered the hall and paused, looking at the group around the table.

"You can speak before these men," the thane said.

"We have him in his home. He was packing a bag in haste, with his old mother looking on. We left men surrounding the building, all of them trustworthy."

"Bradwin's actions speak of a guilty man and we know of his temper." Thane Hugh rose to his feet.

"Aye, we do."

"But he must have a fair hearing, so bring him to me to face the charge of killing a good man." The thane walked towards the far doorway and turned to his guests, "I want no more of this in my home. Come my friends."

He led them to an area, open to the cliff edge and clearly used as a meeting place. Logs were placed on the ground, and roughly shaped into long seats. Three heavy chairs faced the seats; the thane sat in one of them and gestured for them to sit facing him. Even before Bradwin was brought before the thane, the villagers began to emerge and silently fill the seating area, until there was only space to stand. Their faces were serious, and the occasional murmur came from their lips. Fremund and the men from Lyminge sat looking ahead, but all around every eye was fixed on them. The sun beat down on their backs and the toes of their boots pressed on dusty earth. The air was both sweet, from where it swept across sun-warmed thatch roofs, and salty from where it rose from the sea below. Tangy woodsmoke mixed with both.

Then came a shuffle of feet and the soft movement of tunics, accompanied by a wave of whispers throughout the on-lookers. Those on the front seat still looked forward, but they knew Bradwin was now with them. The thane stood and commanded, "Bring him to stand before us."

Two men, with rough tunics, broad shoulders and great hams of hands clamped around the upper arms of the prisoner, brought him forward. Dragged between these burly men, Bradwin looked to be scrawnier than ever, his brown hair more ragged and his eyes more hooded. Yet his defiance still showed in the twist of this thin lips. When the men stood Bradwin to the side of the thane, his eyes roamed across the front row of men seated, and for a moment they rested on Fremund, who turned his gaze to the ground.

The thane's men sat beside him, and then he resumed his own seat. "People of Saltwood, we are here today as grave news has been delivered by these men who sit before me," Hugh of Saltwood began. "It is said that four days ago a man from Lyminge was killed at the hands of one of our own. Now we bring the accused before us to hear his account."

A guttural wail came from the back of the villagers, it continued long after any person would have expected it to cease, rising and falling as if the agony were more than one person could bear. Turning around, Fremund saw the shrunken body of Hlappa kneeling on the ground with her face turned to the cloudless sky.

"Be quiet you fool," one of the women spat, then reaching down she picked up a stone and threw it in the direction of the old woman. It hit her on the shoulder, and she fell silent, lowering her head so it was cradled by her claw-like hands.

Fremund looked back towards Bradwin, his face showed no sign that he too had just witnessed this scene.

"Fremund of Postling, step forward and tell us how you know this man," the thane ordered.

"We met at the Sandtun," Fremund replied, having stood up and moved before Hugo of Saltwood. "I was there selling my metalwork; my cousin was a leather-worker and he too was selling on the Sandtun."

"Your cousin was Todd of Lyminge," Thane Hugo clarified.

"Aye, he *was*."

"Tell me the nature of your cousin."

"He was a gentle man, a hard-worker and good to his family," Fremund stated. "He caused no trouble ever."

"Did he cause trouble to Bradwin of Saltwood?"

"Nay." Fremund could not help but scowl in the direction of the accused man. "Nay, Todd was kind to the old woman, Hlappa, and we shared our fire with them, despite not liking the way Bradwin spoke to his mother. He, Bradwin, was angry all the time. Angry at us because we sold more than him and scornful to his mother."

"What happened on the day your cousin died?" the thane asked.

Fremund told him again about the incident when they had reached the top of the Shipway track. The villagers, who had been mostly silent until this point, began to whisper and mutter. Fremund, looking out at perhaps fifty faces, became nervous of them turning against himself and the other strangers who accused one of their own. But the thane appeared supportive and introduced Harold of Lyminge, asking him to read the words written by the Thane of Lyminge.

"I declare the word of Fremund of Postling to be honourable. His mother's family is from Lyminge and he is known to be a good man. His cousin, Todd of Lyminge, was a steady man with no anger nor ill-feeling to other men. We mourn his loss." Harold read the words clearly and all were silent.

The thane nodded his thanks and turned to Bradwin. "You are accused of killing a man for no good reason. Not in defence of yourself or your property, not

111

by accident either. What do you have to say about this?"

"Dead," Bradwin snarled. "He wasn't dead; it was just a friendly nudge." But even as he said those defiant words, his voice faded away and the last was just a whisper.

"He wasn't dead?" the thane thundered.

"How could he be?" Bradwin protested, pulling away from the men who held him, but he stood no chance against their strength.

"At your own fist, as declared by his kin." Hugo of Saltwood stood and addressed the men and women before him: "Can anyone vouch for the good name of this man? He has stood here before and his temper is well known."

"He's a good man." A frantic screech came from the back. This was then accompanied by raucous laughter and several stones were thrown in the direction of the desperate woman, Hlappa.

"A mother's word has no bearing on this matter," the thane roared. "Now leave her be. She will suffer enough. Bring the man to stand before me." Head lowered, Bradwin was almost dragged to stand before the thane, who then continued, "Bradwin of Saltwood, it shames me to state that your temper has finally caused death. Of this there is no question. At sunrise you will hang at the gallows. You now return to your home, which will be guarded at all times. Your mother may stay to see you hang and will leave our village tomorrow. Where she goes is no concern of mine. Your family are no longer of Saltwood."

Chapter Fourteen

"Todd did well to sell everything at the Sandtun."

Eadlyn started; she had been bent over the loose stitching on Cym's tunic and had not heard Cedric's footsteps as he approached. "Aye, he did." she said. She turned and looked up at Todd's older brother; he was dark, as were the whole family, but whereas Todd's eyes had sparkled and his expression was always friendly, Cedric was more reserved.

"And you have the money he earned." It was not a question.

"Of course. It is to be shared with you and Alvin." Eadlyn stood and turned from her place at the bench outside their home. She walked inside. It was dark and her eyes smarted from the smoke drifting from the open fire. Reaching inside a trunk, Eadlyn pulled out Todd's leather pouch which had hung from his belt. It was heavy with silver coins.

"We'll be taking care of you now," Cedric announced, with no hint of love or compassion in his tone. "We'll give you food – we get plenty in exchange for the leather – and whatever else you need."

"I thank you," Eadlyn bowed her head.

Cedric opened the pouch of coins and poured the silver into his hand; he seemed to assess the amount lying there. He looked at Eadlyn, and then at the coins, before tipping them into his own pouch and pulling the drawstring tight. "You are part of our family, and your son will one day work alongside us," Cedric stated. "It is our duty to look after you. I will see you have all you need."

Fremund was right, Eadlyn's thoughts screamed in her head: *Todd's family say they will care for us, but they leave me with nothing of my own. I thank the Lord that cousin Fremund knew to leave us with something.* She watched Cedric walk away to his own home and for the first time Eadlyn felt rigid with fear for the future of herself and that of her young children.

It was six days since Todd's death. Six days of being an on-looker as first his body was buried near the stone church on the opposite hillside, and then the news was shared that Bradwin of Saltwood was hanging from the gallows. Eadlyn's feelings were numbed, while she had no choice but to continue to work and care for herself and the children. As the sun continued to shine upon Lyminge, the bread still needed baking and the fire still needed tending. Eadlyn did it all, with the children trailing at her skirts and her sister, Janna, nearby to offer support.

Eadlyn had uttered few words; she didn't know how to express her thoughts, and no one pressed her to do so. She had no choice but to carry on with her tasks as mother and provider, but now she also gathered wood, collected water and hauled the three goats from the pen within their home to their grassy enclosure every day. Her voice before the children was as cheery as she could force it to be, but inside she was lost and knew Clover and Cym felt the same.

Watching Cedric walk away, questions formed in Eadlyn's mind: What did he mean when he said he would feed them? And what of the other things they needed, such as the material for clothes and repairs to the home?

No sooner had Cedric gone than his younger brother, Alwin, approached. Eadlyn had not returned to her stitching and watched him from her position by her doorway. Alwin too had both dark skin and hair; his face was narrow and his eyes never met Eadlyn's – not now as he stood before her or when he saw her about her daily chores, as they passed each other during the day. Eadlyn thought her emotions had died with Todd, but when she looked at Alwin, she had a sensation of fear run through her body. "Good afternoon," she said.

"I've come for the goats," Alwin stated, with no words of greeting preceding these.

"My goats?"

"You have no need for them, and I have a fair-sized plot."

"They are my goats," Eadlyn scowled at him.

"We are all as one family. Cedric and I will care for you now." He turned away and Eadlyn noticed lengths of rope hanging from his hands. Alwin had come prepared to take the animals. No more words were said and Eadlyn did not follow to watch him take the goats. Instead she recalled the bread she had left cooling on the open racks near the bakehouse. Looking back at Cym's tunic, still in need of stitching, Eadlyn vowed to do it later and walked down the hillside to the village centre.

The next time Eadlyn spoke to Alwin, she was kneeling at the Nailbourne stream in the centre of Lyminge. The shawl she moved about in the stream was heavy with water and would be awkward to wring out. When she sensed someone stood behind her, Eadlyn had to haul the sodden wool with her as she turned. Somehow she knew that presence brought trouble to her, despite nothing being said yet. Alwin had not merely paused to ask how she was, it was not his way. He had sought her out for a reason, she was sure of it.

The sun was hot on Eadlyn's body and the back of her neck was sticky. Although fresh from its path through the rock and earth, the water from the stream did not cool her as she had thought it would. Eadlyn's headscarf was slipping back and tendrils of her hair fell forward, sticking to the beads of sweat on her forehead and irritating her. *What does he want from me?* she wondered. *He already has my goats, what more can he take? They say they want to help me, but all I feel is threatened by these brothers whom I should be able to turn to at this time.* Determined to say nothing and wait for Alwin to speak, Eadlyn started to squeeze the water from the shawl. It dripped at her feet. *I should have waited for Janna,* she thought. It was easier to work alongside someone when washing larger items, but since Todd's death Eadlyn had chosen to spend time alone or with her children.

"How do you fare?" Alwin asked, his tone pleasant.

"I keep busy and we have food in our bellies," Eadlyn responded. "I can hope for no more."

"You're lonely no doubt."

"The children bring comfort." Eadlyn continued to twist the cloth. Some of the water dripped down her dress, and she looked at the trails. They would dry within minutes in this heat.

"Cedric and I have been talking," Alwin said, his words were tentative, and Eadlyn raised her eyes to investigate his face. He was gazing beyond her, to the church on the spur of land overlooking the village. "We have decided that you and the children should live with me and our modor. She is an old woman now and would welcome your company."

"Live with you?" Eadlyn repeated. *What does he mean by this? Surely I am not to share his bed?* Nausea rose in her throat.

"You're a year or so older than me, but still able to bear children." Alwin made his thoughts clear.

"I thank you, but I shall manage on my own," Eadlyn replied, trying to keep her voice free from any emotion.

"It has been arranged," he stated. "Modor is pleased; she is fond of you."

"And I am fond of her, but I will stay where I am." Eadlyn turned away, gathered the wet scarf in her arms, and started walking up the grassy slope to her home – one of a row belonging to Todd's extended family.

"I will wait a week," Alwin told her departing back.

It was no distance to her home, not for a healthy young woman. She stepped over grassy hillocks and stony patches with long strides. In some ways, Eadlyn felt more alive than she had done since Todd's death. Her mind was filled with disgust for Todd's brothers and their bid to control her. How could her dear husband be of the same blood as these beasts?

Over the next seven days, Eadlyn passed Alwin several times when she walked to the nearby woods to gather firewood, or to and from the village centre. Her days were busy as she collected water, baked bread and worked in the weaving shed. She often had the children with her and was glad of it, feeling Alwin dare not speak of his proposal in front of them. On the seventh day, eighteen days after Todd's death, Alwin came to the home and asked to speak to Eadlyn alone. They stood on the land to the side of the plank and thatch home, looking out towards the village.

"You have not been to see me," he said.

"I had no need to."

"I thought you would," he replied.

Eadlyn said nothing.

"It was a good offer," Alwin continued. He turned away, and she watched him return to the shed where he worked on the leather with his older brother.

The next day, when Eadlyn and the children returned home after working in the weaving shed, she jumped to see a figure sitting at the table within their home. Her first thought was that Alwin had returned, determined to claim her as his wife. But the tension soon passed as this was no tall young man, but the bent figure of an old woman. It was Todd's mother, known as Elder-Modor by the children. Eadlyn was fond of her and greeted Elder-Modor with a hug.

"We've been at the weaving shed," Eadlyn said. "But let me bring the fire to life and we'll drink chamomile together." She gathered logs and pushed at the glowing embers in the hearth with a poker. "And then I must warm the pottage. I see Cedric has left us some more food." A basket of vegetables and grain, with peas or beans, was left in the doorway of their home every few days. The milk, perhaps from their own goats, was delivered daily in a jug.

"You're a hard worker," Elder-Modor said. "I knew Todd was lucky to have you as his wife."

"I was lucky too," Eadlyn said.

"And now Alwin is to take a wife..."

"A wife?" Eadlyn repeated, her voice high.

"Aye, he told me today. He is to marry Bertana, whose father farms the land towards Ottinge. She is plain of face but healthy enough."

118

Eadlyn, speechless, nodded her understanding.

"My son said I was to pack up my belongings and come to you," Elder-Modor continued, "He said it was all arranged."

"Oh? I've not spoken to Alwin... at least not about this," Eadlyn replied. She reached out to the older woman, placing her hand on her forearm. "But I am pleased, very pleased. It is a wonderful idea."

"I hope so." Elder-Modor's smile faded. "I get so sleepy and a little forgetful, but I'll try to be a help and not to burden you."

"You will be a great comfort," Eadlyn reassured her and she called to the children, who had gone to gather the eggs. "Clover... Cym... I have good news: Elder-Modor is coming to live with us!"

The children came running in. *It looks as if they have something to tell me,* Eadlyn thought. But the worry on their faces changed for smiles of joy, and Eadlyn was pleased Alwin had sent his mother to be with them.

"Where will she sleep?" Clover asked.

"Now Faeder is gone, you have been sharing my bed, so Elder-Modor can sleep in yours," Eadlyn suggested.

The children considered this and nodded happily, but they had other concerns in their young minds. Clover held up her empty basket and said, "The chickens have gone."

"Escaped, surely not?" Eadlyn went to the doorway. "I was certain they were secure."

Elder-Modor broke the news: "Alwin took them; he says his new wife will provide you with eggs."

The pleasure of having the old woman to live with them was replaced with a grey cloud wrapping itself

119

around Eadlyn. "Why can we not collect our own eggs?" she asked.

"Cedric and Alwin want to care for us," Elder-Modor replied. "They want to help in any way they can."

In the distance a tiny voice screamed in Eadlyn's head: *But this is not helping. There is no reason for them to take our goats and chickens.* Those unsaid words were muffled by the cloud which stifled her, pressing on her limbs and slowing her thoughts. "I see," was all she said, as she turned to take vegetables from a basket and prepare them for the cooking pot.

Three weeks later, when the crops in the fields were golden brown, the grass was dry and the ground dusty, Bertana of Ottinge walked through the lanes from her father's home to the church at Lyminge. Her oldest brother carried a new sword, to be gifted to Alwin of Lyminge after the ceremony. A harness of the best quality had been crafted for the horse kept on the Ottinge farm and three leather jerkins had been made for Bertana's father and her brothers. She came from a family of men, with her mother long gone and no sisters surviving.

Eadlyn and the children watched the procession from their place by Todd's grave in the churchyard. She had already seen Alwin arrive with Cedric; his own sword hung from his belt and it seemed as if he wore a new tunic for his wedding. Elder-Modor had reported Alwin had taken the customary bath the day before and even the old woman had hauled a bucket of water up the hill from the Nailbourne.

As Bertana neared, Eadlyn saw she was almost as tall as her brothers. Her brown hair fell straight down her back and was entwined with ribbons. Her dress ⌐ red wool was trimmed with embroidered cloth at the cuffs and hem. "She looks very fine," Clover said, her eyes wide.

"Aye, she does," Eadlyn agreed. "She is strong and healthy. I'm sure Alwin will be pleased with his wife." She held out both her hands for the children and together they walked from Todd's grave to the narrow doorway of the church. Already the people of Lyminge were gathering outside, hoping to hear a little of the wedding ceremony, for there was little room inside the church.

From the warmth of the sun, the comforting scents of the hedgerows and ripening crops, to the stale darkness of the church, the difference was marked. Spots of light beaming down from the small round-topped windows played about with Eadlyn's eyes, causing her to narrow them so she could allow the features of the building to become clear, along with the people in it. The space was bare of furniture with only the altar cross and candles on the narrow table beneath the east window, and the red sanctuary lamp burning in front of the tabernacle.

Eadlyn and the children sidled towards Elder-Modor and stood next to her, their faces turned towards the doorway. More people came in and the view to the doorway was obscured; the children, standing close against Eadlyn's legs, were agitated as they pressed closer still to their mother. She scooped Cym up and he was soothed, but Clover clung to Eadlyn's free arm. "It won't be long now," Eadlyn whispered.

A hush fell over those in the church. Eadlyn moved a little, knowing the ceremony was about to begin. Now Alwin and Bertana were revealed to her, standing at the open doorway. She was flanked by her brothers and father, while he had Cedric at his side. A baby started crying... people shuffled about... soothing noises and whispers moved amongst the people. And so when the priest began to prepare Alwin and Bertana to take their vows, none of his words could be heard. In the entrance to the church, pledges were exchanged, and plain gold bands placed on their fingers. Eadlyn knew it to be happening but could follow none of it.

When Alwin and Bertana entered the church for mass the new sword was hanging from Alwin's belt. Bertana's hair was now covered with a scarf and she had taken possession of his sword. Times were peaceful in the Kingdom of Kent and his sword had seen no battles; now it was in safe-keeping and would pass to her son.

The priest took the lead, walking down the centre of the church, waiting at times for the people to move aside, and as they did so once again others jostled for position. The stone church, in which the air had felt so cool not long beforehand, was now warm from body heat and rich with the scents of sweat mingling with the perfume wafting from pomanders. The candles on the altar table let out an acrid smoke. Eadlyn glanced at the open doorway and wondered if it would be acceptable to stand outside with the rest of the villagers. She pushed forward, with Cym still on her hip, and Clover holding onto her skirt.

"Let's sit here," Eadlyn suggested to the children, and they flopped on the dry grass. Memories of her own wedding played in Eadlyn's mind, while life in Lyminge carried on, almost as if Todd were forgotten.

That evening Eadlyn lay awake on her straw mattress; the children were sleeping beside her and she could hear Elder-Modor snoring in her bed. Voices could be heard as members of Todd's family left the wedding party and returned to their homes. She heard a raucous laugh and believed it to be Bertana. There were footsteps outside; they passed by and again the laugh rang out. If it were the newly-wed couple then no doubt they had enjoyed their fill of mead. It was tradition to drink the honeyed wine for a whole cycle of the moon after the wedding; it made the bride's womb more receptive to carrying a child. Eadlyn wondered if there would soon be the signs of a baby being born into the family. She shifted a little on her mattress, closed her eyes and fell asleep.

Chapter Fifteen
Early Spring
681 AD

Eadlyn tried to allow her thoughts to wander back to the long summer days, when her children ran free within the village, the days were warm and the food both fresh and plentiful. She tried to include Todd in her thoughts, but increasingly his image was fading. His voice still came to her as she served the meals, tended the children or walked through the village, and she was grateful for that. She did not hear him as she laboured in the tannery. Todd and Eadlyn had spent no time together there. He had rarely worked on the early stages of preparing the animal skins, as his skill at crafting leather into quality items had soon been noticed by his family, meaning that he progressed in the trade quickly.

Hard as she tried, it was impossible to feel the warmth of the sun. Although the darkest days of winter had passed, there was still a frost in the mornings and little sign of the leaf buds opening. Eadlyn's hands were chapped, despite her rubbing fat into them morning and evening. She looked at her knuckles now; the skin was tight and red, and she felt the sores opening every time she flexed her hand a little. Grasping a flint, she scraped down the animal pelt, removing the coarse hair with every stroke. Eadlyn transferred the flint to her left hand and allowed the right hand to relax. She raised the flint and continued to scrape downwards; the hair drifted down, falling at her feet.

After a while, when she had long given up trying to imagine the summer sun still shone down on Lyminge, Eadlyn moved to the corner of the wooden building. She picked up a broom and brushed the hair into a pile, where it joined the debris from many weeks of work in the tanning shed. Looking down at the rotting fat and hair, Eadlyn had one reason to be grateful it was still cool – the stench in the summer was nauseating, and the flies intolerable.

The skin was stretched tight across an upright wooden frame and Eadlyn stood surveying it, feeling the chill breeze on her back, but knowing she needed the light from the wide-open doorway. Leaning forward she rubbed the flint against an area she had missed, and a few more hairs fell, landing on her apron before she brushed them off.

"Modor..." Clover stood at the doorway, her face gaunt and hair dark. The gloss of her wheat-coloured waves were gone until Eadlyn washed them when the chilly weather of winter and early spring had passed. "The bread is ready."

"I thank you, my dearling," Eadlyn said, smiling at her daughter, her heart warm with love. She wiped her hands on her apron and took it off, hanging it over the frame which held the leather.

Mother and daughter walked together, past the shed where Todd's brothers cut, shaped and stitched the leather. Then past the homes where Todd's brothers lived with their wives and children, and on to their own home.

The first thing Eadlyn noticed when they walked through the doorway of the wooden home was the fire was barely smouldering and yesterday's pottage had not been put to warm over it. Todd's mother dozed on her mattress. Eadlyn sighed and turned to Clover, "Elder-Modor is sleeping again; we must heat the pottage before we can eat."

"She sleeps a lot," Clover commented. "They said she would help us, but they sent her here so we could look after her."

"Aye," Eadlyn replied. "But she has worked hard in her life, raising her three sons and two daughters. No wonder she is tired now." *That girl is wise*, she thought, *she sees how her uncles found a reason for her to live with us and not burden their own wives.*

"Perhaps she'll tell us some stories later," Clover suggested.

"That would be nice," Eadlyn smiled. She may forget to keep the fire burning or heat the pottage, but Elder-Modor was a wonderful story-teller, bringing to life the times she remembered as a younger woman and stories passed on by her own grandmother.

Eadlyn placed some wood on the fire, then prodded and blew on it to encourage the flames. She took the iron pot containing the remainder of yesterday's supper and hung it over the fire.

"I've brought some more wood in," Clover said, as she added logs to the pile they kept inside the home.

"You're a great help to me." Eadlyn dropped a kiss on her head. "Where's Cym? Is he with Janna?"

"Aye, but I told him to come back to eat," Clover said, and for a moment it seemed as if the burden of her chores was too much for the girl who was only seven years old.

"He'll come soon enough," Eadlyn reasoned. "And the pottage is still cold."

After Todd was buried, his brothers said Eadlyn must work for them. Not as a skilled crafter of leather, but working in a lowly job as a tanner, preparing the leather for them. It was the way they all started, and in a few more years Cym would be learning beside her. But he would progress and learn other skills, whereas she was destined to remain scraping the skins and preserving them, unless she were to marry again. Eadlyn looked down at her dirty dress and smelt her hands; the perfumed balms could not hide the odour ingrained in her skin after months of working on the animal hides. No worthy man would want to marry her now and besides, Todd had been a good husband whom she was not inclined to replace. Eadlyn's life was set out before her – she would work at the leather and her skin would smell no better than a pig's; it would be a lonely life only made tolerable by her family. Eadlyn prayed she would not be a burden to her own children when she reached the age when she could no longer work.

There came the sound of a child's footsteps on the hard earth and Cym came into the home, his cheeks glowing and eyes bright. He still had the soft rounded limbs of a young child and was untouched by the worries of having to care for the home and family, as well as go to work. Under the watchful eye of their Aunt Janna, the children spent several hours a day in the weaving shed, sweeping the floor, and running about doing chores for whoever called out for them. Clover would often spend the time rolling fibres from wool, hemp and nettles together, working with another child who would turn the length of loose rope onto a stick. With other children, the brother and sister would roam the woodland and hedgerows looking for the berries and mushrooms which would be used to dye the textiles.

"I been getting lichen from trees and rocks," Cym informed his mother as he ran in.

"With flint," Clover informed. "Scraping it off."

"I didn't have flint," Cym scowled at his sister.

"You're too small," she replied. "You'd hurt your hands."

"What did you do then?" Eadlyn asked, kneeling to look into her son's face. "How did you help?"

"I collected it from the ground and put it in a bowl," Cym said.

"And was it fun?"

"Aye, better than sweeping the floor." Cym beamed at his mother, but his eyes began to roam towards the pot hanging over the fire and he sidled towards it.

"Better than collecting nettles," Clover said, her forehead creasing into a frown.

"Aye, I had to do that when I was no older than you," Eadlyn told her, as she leaned forward to stir the pottage. It would not be long now; as soon as the weather warmed up the fresh young nettles would be thriving in any disturbed soil and before they flowered and turned too woody, they would need harvesting.

"Did you get stung?" Clover asked.

"Aye," Eadlyn replied. "Lots. But where nettles grow..."

"...We'll find dock leaves!" Clover continued.

"Now, let's have something to eat." Eadlyn picked up a wooden bowl and began to ladle the thick pottage of beans and root vegetables. "Cym, my sweeting, can you wake Elder-Modor please."

The old woman moved on the bed, which had once been the children's. She sat herself up, pulling

128

off the blankets and adjusting her shawl so it was snug against her shoulders. "How could I sleep with the three of you chattering away?" she asked. Her eyes were watery, her cheeks rosy and her smile was toothless.

"Oh Elder-Modor, you needed to wake as the meal is ready," Clover told her.

"Aye, it must be time." Elder-Modor shuffled across the room, and sat at the bench alongside Cym. "I forgot to keep the fire going, didn't I?" she said to Eadlyn. "I'm sorry, my sweeting."

"It was no trouble." Eadlyn laid her hand on Elder-Modor's shoulder. "Look, the food is warm now, and Clover has made some bread."

Clover had taken over Eadlyn's daily task of making bread for the family. Guided by her mother's sister, Janna, the girl mixed hot water, yeast and oil, then added the frothy liquid to wheat flour. She mixed it with her hands before kneading it into a smooth dough. Eadlyn missed the friendship of the other women as they worked side by side preparing the dough and took it in turns to keep a close eye on the bread oven. She missed the warm sticky mixture that clung to her fingers and the satisfaction of seeing it form a smooth dough. It would soothe her chapped hands now, if only she could mix the dough in the morning, rather than take a cold flint and scrape the leather.

"This is lovely," Elder-Modor said, soaking her bread in the gravy from the pottage. "When we have honey, you could put that in the bread, Clover. It will sweeten it. There will be honey when the thane gives his spring feast."

"Aye, there will be," Eadlyn agreed.

"And a roasting pig," Clover added.

"Something to look forward to," Elder-Modor smiled, dipping more bread in the liquid and chewing it with her gums. "But now we need to think of our next meal; I'll cut the leeks and soften them in the pot, Eadlyn. And put the beans in to soak."

"That will be a help," Eadlyn said. "The leeks burn my hands, while they are so sore. But they say there's a chicken coming for our supper, and we'll appreciate that!" She referred to Todd's brothers who supplied their food in part-payment for the hours Eadlyn laboured in the tanning shed.

"Aye, we'll thank God for keeping our bellies full if there is chicken in the pot today!" Elder-Modor smiled.

"And afterwards, will you tell us about Queen Ethelburga?" Clover asked. "Please Elder-Modor."

"Of course, child. We'll speak of her story."

The short time with her family lifted Eadlyn's spirits. She walked back to the tanning shed, looking across the village to the thane's hall and the feasting hall; the latter being a reminder to them all of the time when the King of Kent presided over Lyminge. The stories of these times had been passed from Elder-Modor's own grandparents and she knew, in turn, Clover would relish telling the tales to her own children.

Several simple plank bridges crossed a narrow stream which emerged from a spring, giving the village a supply of good fresh water. Eadlyn smiled to see a child skipping across a bridge; she carried a basket, probably containing food. Women gathered around the bread oven, at the door of the weaving shed, or paused to exchange the news as they passed by each other. Eadlyn felt a pang of loneliness: their home and the tanning shed were on the edge of the village, limiting her contact with other women. Her feet walked the muddy track between home and work, often not straying from these two places for days at a time.

She thought of Clover who, in many ways, had taken over her role within the home and Eadlyn's heart swelled with pride for the girl who was proving so capable. She thought of Todd's mother who came to live with them not long after her son died, and brushed away the tears beginning to form. The old woman was very dear to her and her company valuable in the winter evenings when it was too dark to sew, and they huddled under blankets, the smoke from the fire meandering upwards but leaving its sour soot on everything it brushed past. During these times when darkness fell so early over their village, Elder-Modor brought the past to life: they saw beyond their own fireside, to times of great banquets and the days when a widowed Queen presided over the minster she founded on the hill overlooking the village.

Eadlyn glanced across at the minster: the tall stone walls and roofs of wooden shingles belonging to the church and oratory, and the domestic buildings of wood and thatch. She wondered about life inside it and, on entering the tanning shed, her head was still filled with the stories of a young woman, Ethelburga, who had led such an adventurous life.

The stench of rawhide and chicken droppings assaulted Eadlyn even before she had stepped through the doorway. Todd's older brother was there, looking over the stretched skin; he had moved the frame nearer the light.

"I thought it would be time for the dung," Cedric said, nodding towards the wooden bucket.

"Aye," Eadlyn responded. There was nothing else to say about it.

He moved to the doorway. "You're happy with the flint? It did a good job."

Eadlyn nodded, "It was much better."

"I'll bring a chicken before the sun reaches the hills."

"Elder-Modor is looking forward to it," Eadlyn told him. "I thank you. We'll eat well tonight."

That was her payment. The brothers provided Eadlyn, the children and their mother with all the grain, beans, meat, fruit and vegetables they needed. The children were given material for the work they did in the weaving shed. No silver sceattas passed through their hands. Eadlyn was bound to them, unable to manage without the food they gave in exchange for preparing the leather for them to craft.

After tying the huge apron around her slim body, Eadlyn surveyed the hide and then the bucket of chicken droppings. Turning to face to the doorway, she breathed in the fresh air and held her breath before plunging her hand into the bucket and scooping out a small amount with her fingers. She had to breathe though, and took in a little air before wiping the fresh droppings onto the skin. Spreading it out the best she could, Eadlyn returned to the bucket and repeated the task several times before standing before the skin and working the droppings into it with the tips of her fingers.

As the sun moved through the sky, Eadlyn worked over the whole of the skin. She had emptied the bucket and was picking any loose droppings from the ground when Todd's brother returned, holding a plucked chicken by its legs. She took a rag and wiped her hands, trying to scrape the dirt out from under her nails. He stood watching for a moment, then placed the chicken on a bench.

"The skin fares well," he said.

"Aye, it does." Eadlyn dunked her hands in a dish of water. They stung and it did nothing to remove the staining nor the stink from her fingers. She thought of her lavender-scented balm and longed to rub it into her skin. She removed her apron and hung it up. "I thank you for the chicken."

Todd's brother nodded. "In another year, Cym can come and learn these tasks."

"I rely on him to work with Clover, to gather firewood, collect water and so many jobs."

"Women's work."

"Aye, but I'm doing the man's work, so the children must do these things to help me." Eadlyn scowled; he wouldn't notice, the light was too poor where she stood with her back to the doorway.

"You have Elder-Modor."

"We welcome Elder-Modor's company and wisdom, but she sleeps all day," Eadlyn pointed out. "When I returned for our midday meal, the fire was almost burned out, the pottage still cold and she was sleeping."

"I'll speak to her," he replied. "We don't ask much of her."

"Nay, we don't but she is old. I thank God for Clover and the help she gives me."

"Aye, she is a fair child and will make a good wife one day."

"She will," Eadlyn said. "But she is only seven years old."

Eadlyn wandered home before the sun settled behind the treetops and the minster. Walking away from the tannery, she passed the sheds where the leather was crafted and the homes where Todd's brothers lived.

The chicken was swinging from her hand. When she reached her home, the fire was burning and the leeks had been cut, just as Elder-Modor had promised.

"They gave you a chicken then?" Elder-Modor stated.

"Aye, it will be in the pan soon," Eadlyn replied. "Fetch the vegetables, Clover, and the beans."

Removing the knife from her belt, Eadlyn looked at the chicken and prepared to remove its flesh. The bird was not large, but with root vegetables and beans, there should be plenty for tomorrow's midday meal as well as their supper that evening. She put the bird on a bench and pressed the knife into its skin. Her sore hands would have to wait; the children would soon be complaining their stomachs ached for food and there were still the vegetables to cut.

Before long, the meal was simmering, and the smell of meat juices mingled with the woodsmoke. Eadlyn sat pressing the balm into her sore hands, enjoying the sensation of softening the mixture and allowing it to seep into her skin.

"Elder-Modor, will you tell us about Princess Ethelburga?" Clover asked.

Eadlyn looked towards the old woman, also hoping for stories to keep them entertained after supper.

"Aye, when our bellies are full, I'll tell you about that young princess who travelled far before fleeing the north and making Lyminge her home," Elder-Modor announced. "And we'll remember her life as a song; it's easier to pass on that way. Then in years to come, your own children and their children will know the tale of our princess-queen as well as we do today."

Chapter Sixteen

"Tell us about Ethelburga, Elder-Modor," Clover pleaded, when the supper was eaten and the bowls wiped clean. The fire still burned bright, leaving the corners of the home in darkness.

"Do you remember how our song goes?" And so Elder-Modor began the tale:

"Her hair had the sheen of copper,
Tumbling in curls from her head.
Fair of skin, and rosy of cheek,
The sparkle of life in her eyes,
Clear as the spring of Lyminge.

"She was the daughter of a King," Clover reflected.

"Aye, King Aethelburt of Kent, and his wife, Queen Bertha. The King's wife was a Christian and so he was baptised, becoming the first Christian King of Kent. It was my own elder-modor who told me about the King; the stories were passed on from her own modor."

"Did she know the King, your elder-modor?" Cym asked.

"My own modor served him in the royal feasting hall," the old woman explained. "She would help prepare the food and place it on the tables. She never spoke to him, of course, but he would give a nod or a smile, to say his thanks for the food served. He was grateful for his food, more thankful to God than to those who raised the animals or grew the crops."

There was silence as they thought of the ruins of the great building, now part-used as a barn for animal feed, and partly as a meeting hall for the villagers, with much of its long plank walls being taken down and re-used on the thane's own home, and the homes of his brothers. The children had never known its long wooden walls, perhaps four times longer than their own home, or the massive doors that opened to let the light in. Eadlyn remembered it, not at its finest, but still as the most prominent building amongst those scattered close to the stream which meandered through the village. She recalled the roof collapsing under heavy snowfall one winter and the men gathering to decide what was best to be done with it. The King of Kent had not favoured Lyminge for some time, and so the thane decided to reduce the size of the royal feasting hall and make better use of the building materials.

"Ethelburga, pure in heart and soul,
A child of our King of Kent.

Jewel of our Christian kingdom." Clover recalled the song, as taught by Elder-Modor. "Did she live here as a child, or before she married a king?"

"Nay, sweeting," Elder-Modor replied. "Mayhap she was in Canterbury, or some other royal place. But she visited with her brothers and sisters and Queen Bertha."

Clover frowned, trying to imagine the princess as a girl of her own age running about in the village, jumping across the stream and feasting in the great hall. "She went to Northumbria – *Northumbria, benighted kingdom, still held in Pagan times.* What was it like in Northumbria Elder-Modor? How long would it take her to travel there?"

"Travel there?" Elder-Modor considered the question. "How would you travel there, do you think?"

"I'd ride on the thane's horse," Cym announced.

"I wonder how long it would take?" Elder-Modor said. "The Princess would ride a horse, I expect. But she would have to wait for good weather, perchance it would take a few weeks? But if you were to go, Cym, and there was no horse to ride, it would take months."

"He has little legs," Clover pointed out.

"Aye, but I was thinking of him being bigger."

"Did she talk about Northumbria, when she came here?" Eadlyn wondered.

"Aye, and it's not like any place we have ever seen," Elder-Modor began, her voice became low and as the fire flickered, it seemed as if she had wondrous things to tell:

"Away to the north she rode,
Her nature fearless and bold,
Northumbria, benighted Kingdom,
Still held in pagan times.

She told tales of a bleak and savage land, with areas of high land, free of trees and covered in a wiry plant that would survive the harshest of winters and still have rich purple flowers. A place where the snow would settle for months at a time and the mists would smother the land, chilling her to the bone. A godless land, with few settlements."

"A godless land?" Clover repeated.

"Aye, remember the song:
To pagan King Edwin she ventured,
Pledged as his Christian bride.
Paulinus, the bishop, her guide
To save Ethelburga
From heathen wiles."

Elder-Modor told the brave tale, pausing to ensure the children were listening, and continued:

"King Edwin lay open to truth and beauty
Yet the faith of Rome he denied,
Even when saved in battle
And his tiny new-born survived."

"He didn't want to be a Christian?" Clover queried.

"Not at first child, but listen:

To Bishop Paulinus he spake:
'I wait for a sign.
Give me victory in battle,
Save me from my wounds
And then I shall honour your Christ'."

"But did he become Christian?" Clover asked.

"Aye, but it was two years after his wedding," Elder-Modor confirmed. "He was baptised in another northern town called York, and soon thousands of people were following his example:

Survived and convert he did.
The waters of Baptism gushed forth
And thousands of pagans saw the light
Of the one true Christian faith."

"It all went wrong though," Clover continued the story. "Listen, I remember the words:

But a heathen slew our good King
And fair Ethelburga took flight.
Bearing treasure from Edwin:
A golden chalice and cross.

Have I got it right, Elder-Modor?" the girl asked.

"Aye, child, you have."

"Back she sailed to her brother,
Now ruling the Kingdom of Kent.
Her children and trusty Paulinus,
ever at her side." Clover paused, frowning.

"There in our Christian Lyminge," Elder-Modor sang softly.

"Stood the sleeping Roman villa.
'Take this as your own,' said the King,
From Roman stones her monastery rose."

*"*Let me finish it..." Clover's voice was excitable as she sang:

"Queen Ethelburga took the veil
And Abbess of Lyminge became,
Fair and brave and full
Of saintly loving-kindness."

"And that is how the princess became a Queen and then an Abbess," Eadlyn said, as she scooped Cym up and settled him in the bed they had shared since Elder-Modor had come to live with them. "My own elder-modor used to speak of her building the minster from the stones left by the Romans."

"Aye, and not only the minster but the church that looks over us," Elder-Modor reminded them.

"She is buried there, by the church," Clover added. "She has a big tomb because she was so good. Faeder has no stone; he has a mound of earth."

"Your faeder was good too," Eadlyn reminded her. "He was kind and fair, even to the man who killed him. Your faeder had been trying to help him. But Queen Ethelburga had built the church and she was a Queen, as well as the daughter of the King of Kent. She was royal and good; that is why she has a tomb."

"I like it where Faeder is, near the trees," Clover said. "It's peaceful. I wouldn't want to be in that tomb, listening to them pray all day."

"I don't think they pray all day!" Eadlyn smiled to herself as she placed a large log on the fire; it should smoulder all night. "They work hard on the fields and look after the bees so we can have their sweet honey.

139

And they brew the mead our cousin Fremund enjoys so much!"

"Aye, they work hard," Elder-Modor agreed. "I went there to buy the lavender oil, to make the balm for your poor hands."

Eadlyn reached for the pot of balm and opened it; she brought it to her nose and breathed in the floral scent. "It gives me such relief from the pain." She scooped out a little and began to massage it into her fingers. "Time to go to bed now, Clover. Let's speak more of past times tomorrow."

Over the following weeks the breeze coming through the open doorway of the tanning shed became less sharp. Eadlyn moved the frame so while her hands scraped with the flint or massaged the chicken droppings on the skin, she looked out over the shallow bowl of the valley where the village was built. Almost overnight, the buds on the trees sprang open to reveal fresh green life. It seemed as if the chickens were more vocal in their pens and the pigeons in the woods behind the tanning shed cooed in their search for a mate. The grass became lush and grew long against the sides of the buildings. Well-worn tracks remained muddy and new paths were formed from the work sheds to the homes of the villagers.

It was as if Lyminge came out of hibernation. For so long the people had stayed within its confines. For months their diet had been restricted to dried, smoked and salted food. They had watched their piles of logs diminishing and crept out in search of dry wood, hunting it down amongst decaying leaves and under woody bramble stems. Bedding became damp and straw mattresses mouldered. The time between sunset and sunrise had been a lonely one.

Now fields were being prepared for crops, animals taken to fresh pasture and people began to journey between the villages. Sometimes these travellers were in the business of trading goods, but more often they were visiting family members. Through these men and women, news of the wider world was shared. The people of Lyminge learned of important places, such as Canterbury and Dover, and the people who lived there.

The skin Eadlyn worked on was becoming pale as she scraped against the flesh, prising it away with the sharp edge of the flint. It had already been soaked for days before Todd's brothers had taken it, sopping wet with the urine in which it had lain, and stretched it out on the wooden frame. For the next day it dripped on the dry earth floor, while Eadlyn began to work on it. Tiny pieces of flesh rained down, coating the skirt of her apron. Beyond the foul flesh and the monotony of working the flint over it, there was much activity within the village. She could see men repairing a roof, the women at the bread oven, and children herding pigs.

From the south, a tall red-headed man came over the brow of the hill and into the settlement. Rather than walking to the centre, he moved around the edge, heading towards the area where the skins were turned into leather and then crafted into bags, belts and bridles. Eadlyn saw him coming and spoke to Todd, who she sometimes liked to imagine was standing there beside her, "Here's your cousin." In the past those words would have been said with a hint of disapproval, but now she saw a friend. This was the person who had been there with Todd when he was killed and had supported her on the journey home, then passed on the shocking news to Todd's family.

As Fremund came closer, picking his way around the worst of the muddy patches, Eadlyn left the leather and, still with the flint in her hand, she walked out of the tanning shed towards him. There was a flicker of recognition in his eyes, and then a frown of disbelief as he surveyed the filthy apron, her stained fingers and gaunt face. Then he smiled, trying to hide his thoughts and, as he took the last few steps towards her, he put his arms out, clasping her upper arms in an awkward show of affection.

Eadlyn, at first more conscious of her own appearance than Fremund's, looked at him more closely and now it was her turn to show dismay. "Fremund, Cousin... has it been a harsh winter for you?"

"Brona died of a fever just one cycle of the moon ago."

"And your son?" Eadlyn asked, somehow knowing his response.

"Aye, the boy as well." He looked to the ground. She studied his face: Fremund's skin looked paler and more weathered than before, his hair and beard more ragged, and his cheekbones were prominent under his freckles.

"I'm sorry," were the only words Eadlyn could say. "The Lord has his reasons we cannot begin to fathom."

"He does." Fremund looked to the opposite hillside and the rounded end of the small church. Turning back to Eadlyn he continued, "But you have your own sorrows and now I come to find you here. Who bakes the bread, tends to the fire, prepares the supper and weaves the cloth?"

"Clover does most of it, under the guidance of my sister, Janna. And as for the fire, if Clover is not there, then Todd's mother tends it. And if she falls asleep then it may burn out. I'll be home to make the pottage; will you eat with us?"

"I know your sister; she is a good woman. But Todd's mother, why does she tend your fire?"

"She lives with us," Eadlyn told him. "I have to work here on the skins, and they give me the food we need."

"It's not the way I would treat the wife of my cousin," Fremund said. "Aye, I'll eat with you and be happy to do so. Mayhap, I'll bed down in a barn tonight and return home in the morning."

Eadlyn looked back towards the skin. "I must..."

"I'll go to see these cousins who treat you so poorly," Fremund said. "And then my own sisters."

"You'll find your sisters in the weaving shed," Eadlyn told him.

He turned and walked, taking long strides towards the shed where Todd's brothers worked. Just as Eadlyn was about to return to the skin, she saw he had turned and was coming back to her. Leaning down a little, Fremund kept his voice low: "Did you keep the silver coins?"

"Aye, they are in the mattress." She did not mention the gold cross nestling with them in a small cloth bag.

"I'm glad of that."

Eadlyn didn't speak to Fremund again that afternoon, but she saw him walking amongst the houses and workplaces in the village. When she returned home, the fire was burning steadily and Elder-Modor was sitting at the doorway making a tunic for Cym. "I saw Fremund today," Eadlyn told the old woman.

"Aye, he came here and said he would be back to share our pottage."

Reaching for a small brush with firm bristles, Eadlyn placed it in a bowl along with carrots and turnips. "He came with sad news."

"I know," replied Elder-Modor. "I pray he'll find a new wife..."

"But his wife, Brona... it was only last month, and the child too." Eadlyn frowned, understanding Fremund was a man who would want a wife and children.

"Perchance he comes to Lyminge to find that wife."

"He said nothing of it," Eadlyn told her. "I wouldn't expect him to." She took the bucket outside and began to brush the dirt off the vegetables. Then she placed them on a wooden bench which leaned against the plank walls of her home. Removing the knife from her belt, Eadlyn cut the vegetables into chunks, then pushed them back into the bucket. When she added them to the iron pot, she saw they needed more liquid, and asked, "Do we have water?"

"Nay, I was going to ask Clover..."

"I'd like the walk," Eadlyn said. "I seem to go only from the home to the shed."

Setting off down the hillside, Eadlyn was soon walking amongst the remains of the great feasting hall and crossing the stream, known as the Nailbourne, by one of several plank bridges. She passed the bread oven, now empty of loaves, and the weaving shed. Pausing to say, 'good afternoon', Eadlyn exchanged news with women in the village and waved to others. It felt good to be back in the heart of it and now the days were becoming longer she would have the freedom to do some of those chores which took her out of the home and down to where the women met, as they washed clothes or baked bread, and the children played.

The hill began to rise steeply towards the church overlooking the village from its place on the hillside, and here a spring bubbled out from a crevice in the rocks. The ground around the base of the spring was very muddy and the thane had ordered that good flat stones be placed there in order to make the spring easier to access and safer to use. Stepping carefully on the wet stones, Eadlyn leaned forward and placed the jug against the flow of clean water. The jug filled and she emptied the water into a bucket. After repeating the action several times, she stepped back and turned towards home. Clover and Cym were running up the opposite side of the shallow valley; it looked as if Clover was holding a bundle of something and Cym clutched a small basket. Eadlyn smiled to herself and, struggling with the heavy bucket, she walked back.

When Fremund arrived, the pottage was simmering over the fire and the children were threading clay beads onto leather laces. Eadlyn was rubbing balm into her hands and Elder-Modor was placing wooden bowls on the table. He stood looking in through the open doorway, a smile fixed on his face, his tall frame blocking the last of the sunlight.

"We're pleased to have you visit us," Eadlyn said. Her words sounded stilted; they were unused to visitors in the home.

"I'm happy to be here, to see you all again," he replied. "I hear good things about Clover and Cym. They work hard for the good of the family."

"Aye, they do," Eadlyn said, "But Cym is so young." She reached for a leather mitten and removed the cooking pot from the frame, then placed it on the table.

"You need a new frame for the fire," Fremund commented.

"Nay," Eadlyn brushed his concern aside, "This will last another year, it is just a little twisted, but is strong enough."

Fremund said no more; he understood there was no money other than the silver sceattas Todd had earned at the Sandtun. He thought of the empty chicken pen behind Eadlyn's home. Perhaps if they were to replace the birds taken by Alwin, then the eggs could be exchanged for things needed in the home? Fremund decided to speak to Eadlyn and Elder-Modor about this after they had eaten. He could put some of his own chickens in a basket and they would be welcome to have them. They provided more eggs than he needed now that his wife and child were gone.

Eadlyn was grateful to the children that evening. They kept the words flowing, allowing everyone to speak about Todd and share the good memories. But their presence meant that some things were left unsaid. Eadlyn knew nothing of Bradwin being hanged; she didn't know that Fremund had witnessed it and the memories of that day haunted him more than Todd's death, which had come so quickly there had been no time to think of it beforehand. They could not discuss the old woman, Hlappa, who had foretold death. Perhaps she was lucky enough not to know beforehand that it came at the hands of her own son. Eadlyn wondered about Hlappa and where she had gone after seeing her son hang, having been banished from Saltwood, as determined by their thane.

When Fremund left – he had decided to journey home by the light of a full moon – it was with the intention to return within a few days. He would bring a basket of chickens and a newly-made frame to stand over the fire. Eadlyn may deny it, but within weeks their pottage would fall into the fire as the cooking frame gave up the fight to stay whole. Fremund felt a duty to care for his cousin's widow and this new occupation would keep his thoughts from his dead wife, and his lips from the noggin of mead.

Chapter Seventeen

The sun had reached its peak in the pale blue sky and was sending a little warmth through the wisps of cloud when the family sat down to eat their reheated pottage.

"Fremund is back!" Clover exclaimed, her voice high and eyes shining. The others looked up in surprise to see him once again at their doorway. "We have plenty to share, don't we Modor?" the girl looked towards her mother for approval, then continued, "I made enough bread."

"Aye, you're welcome, Cousin." Eadlyn stood, her smile uneasy. For so long now it had been just the four of them in the home.

Fremund stepped forward and they saw the basket he had placed by the doorway. "Nay, I'll not eat your food," he replied. "But I have little need for all these chickens. How can I eat a dozen eggs all in one day, when there is no one to share them with?"

"You could exchange the eggs?" Eadlyn suggested.

"I could, but I have my metalwork to make and trade," he told her. "And I feel a duty to care for the wife of my dead cousin. Todd and I grew up as close friends."

"Eight chickens!" Clover announced, having risen from the table and counted the birds in the woven basket.

"How many eggs will we have?" Cym asked.

"If you are lucky then eight a day," Fremund answered, placing a hand on the boy's shoulder.

"Eight eggs!" Cym echoed.

"And if you were to eat only four, then you could trade those eggs," Fremund told them.

"What would we trade them for?" Clover asked.

"Mayhap something you need, such as a new pot or some fresh straw for your bedding, or the grain you need to feed the chickens."

"Todd's brothers give us food, but little else," Eadlyn said.

"Aye, they do," Fremund agreed. "And now if you need something else, you could use your eggs in exchange."

"I thank you," Eadlyn said, her tone thoughtful. "You are a good man and now you must eat with us as we are grateful. Please sit and share our meal. We must give something in return."

"There is no need to thank me," Fremund said. "I'll be looking for more ways to be fed! It's lonely sitting at the table with no company." He smiled, the thin lines around his eyes crinkling. "I have something else for you. I made this, hoping it may be of use to you, if your pot stand were to break." He returned to the doorway, reached down, and produced a metal frame.

"We needed a pot stand," Elder-Modor said. "Eadlyn told you we didn't but every day I feared ours would break."

"I thought it would last," Eadlyn replied.

Since Todd died, she had become increasingly unwilling to accept help. Anything given from his family was offered with reluctance, there seeming to be little acknowledgement for the hours she spent scraping at the leather or pressing chickens' droppings into the hide. Elder-Modor and the children gave such comfort, but the dark days of winter had been long, and it was as if a heavy cloud had settled over her. Now the days were brighter, and the sun was bringing some warmth to her skin, Eadlyn felt the heaviness in her body begin to lift. Her sister, Janna, was a great support but she felt a distance between herself and Todd's family. Cousin Fremund was the first to show a sign of friendship towards her, other than dear Elder-Modor. While Eadlyn found it hard to accept both the chickens and the pot stand, she could not deny both were welcome.

Elder-Modor fetched a bowl and was spooning pottage into it for Fremund. He reached forward and pulled a piece of bread from the loaf. "I thank you," he said. "This is fine bread, Clover."

Before long, the bread was being used to wipe the last of the pottage from the pan, and Elder-Modor said, "Let's place the new stand over the fire."

Fremund stood and, taking the leather glove, he lifted first the pot and then the stand from where they straddled the fire. He put his own stand in place and hung the pot on it. "I'll exchange this stand for your old one," he said, lifting the old one. "I can make it strong again and mayhap it will be of some use."

"Of course." Eadlyn gave a rare smile, as she placed the bread in a clay pot to keep it fresh. "It seems like a fair trade."

A few days passed and one afternoon, when the rain fell as a soft mist, and everything felt damp, Todd's elder brother walked into the shed where Eadlyn worked alone. He carried a basket of beans, root vegetables and flour.

"You have more chickens," he stated, placing the basket on the earth floor.

"Aye." Eadlyn was sweeping the scrapings of animal flesh into a pile. It would need to be taken away soon; she would speak to the boy who trundled around with a cart of waste.

"Do we not feed you enough?" Cedric asked.

"Of course." Eadlyn kept her face lowered and her voice steady.

"Then why do you need more chickens?"

"There are things we need other than eggs," Eadlyn replied. "The thatch is thinning and how will I pay Orson Thatcher, if I have no money?"

"How will a few extra eggs pay for a thatcher?" Cedric walked over to the skin and examined it as best he could in the poor light. He ran his fingertips over the smooth surface.

"They won't pay for a thatcher," Eadlyn admitted. She felt foolish to have suggested something that was so far out of her reach. "But I must repair the roof before long, and perhaps they can be exchanged for a bundle of wheat straw, and I'll patch the roof myself!"

Feeling defiant, Eadlyn looked up at Cedric, to see the amusement in his face. "Perhaps you could?" he conceded. "You and the girl could bind the wheat tightly, and the children could seek out some pliable hazel, while it grows fresh in the springtime. You'll need it to make the spars to hold it all in place." He looked at her filthy apron and the stained hem of her dress. "I'm sure it is just the thing you could do."

"It seems as if I have no choice, if we are to stay dry," Eadlyn persevered. "And your own modor too; she will suffer if the roof fails us."

"There will be no need for that; you are to fix it yourself." There was a note of triumph in his voice. Cedric turned towards the doorway.

Eadlyn scowled and felt her body tense. How could she climb on the roof and fix the thatch with only a seven-year-old girl to help her? How cruel they were, these brothers of Todd. How could they leave her to struggle so, when their own brother had been such a good man?

"Where did you get the chickens from?" he asked, as he walked through the doorway.

"I was given them," she replied.

"If they were a love token, then you must consider your place living here with us," he said, turning back to see her reaction.

"A love token?" Eadlyn's eyes flashed her fury at him. "Who would be thinking of loving me, while my hands stink of chicken droppings and my skirt is littered with animal hair and worse?"

"True," Cedric nodded his agreement.

"And..." Eadlyn was not done with him. "The home is mine, built by Todd, with help from my father and uncle who supplied much of the wood. It is not yours to take from me."

Cedric shrugged and walked away. Eadlyn swept the floor with long vicious swipes, sending the animal hair flying about. *How dare Cedric speak in that way. Does he think I like to have my clothes so ragged and my hands so sore from working at the leather? The home is mine, mine to do as I wish with.* These thoughts and more rattled about in her mind; Eadlyn's stomach felt tight and her throat restricted. There was so much she must say, but dare not. But the seeds of discontent were growing and from that day Eadlyn began to question if there was more she could do in order to improve her life.

The next day brought strong winds, sweeping aside the misty rain, but fresh problems came for the villagers. When Eadlyn returned for her midday meal, the chickens' coop was listing, although for the moment it remained secure. "Look what the wind has done," she said to Clover, as she wound twine around the pieces of wood, while trying to pull them upright. "Sweeting, after we have eaten would you please ask Egfrid if he could make some repairs. We mustn't lose our chickens."

"He'll be busy today," Clover said. During the day she went about her chores, wandering from her home to the bakehouse, the spring and the weaving shed, and seeing much of what happened in the village.

"Aye, but he'll come to help us," Eadlyn said, as she tied a knot and straightened her back. Egfrid was the husband of Janna, her sister. "How many eggs did you collect this morning, Clover?"

"Seven," announced the girl.

"Do we have any left from yesterday?"

"Three."

"Give six to Egfrid, please. I know they lost three chickens to a fox last week and will appreciate the eggs." Eadlyn felt satisfaction run through her body, as they walked away from the coop. "Look how cousin Fremund has helped us already. We are able to give eggs in exchange for the repairs to our coop and the chickens will stay safe."

That night the wind gathered more strength, moving across the valley, pressing on buildings in its path. In the small home on the rise at the edge of the village, the wind found a path through the gaps between planks and streamed in. The fire flickered and struggled to keep its hold on the logs. The slender flames which rose from the rush-lights were whipped about and there was no possibility of keeping them alight. Sitting around the fire, the family huddled under blankets, and Elder-Modor spoke of past storms. When they went to bed, the children soon fell asleep but Eadlyn lay there, listening to bundles of thatch lifting and falling back with a gentle slap.

Morning came, and with it a lull in the wind. For the family waking on their straw mattresses, there was an unusual light in the home. One side of the roof had patches of thatch missing, and when they threw open the door to view the damage from outside, dark rainclouds could be seen gathered to the north.

"What will we do, Modor?" Clover looked at Eadlyn; her face showing concern.

I wish she did not need to worry about these things, Eadlyn thought. *It seems as if she is unable to be a child.* She studied the clouds for a moment and then turned back to Clover and spoke: "The rain will come through our roof and onto our beds if we don't move them."

"But where will we put them?"

"We can sleep in the animal pen!" About a quarter of their home was separated by wattle fencing and beyond that was the area where their goats had once been kept at night. Shortly before Todd's death one of the goats had died. Afterwards, Alwin, Todd's younger brother, had suggested that he care for the goats with his own. At the time, Eadlyn had thought this was an offer of help, but recently she began to regret giving away her source of fresh milk. Now she was glad of the space, enabling them to at least keep the bedding dry.

"I miss the goats," Clover announced.

"I was just thinking the same." Eadlyn said.

"We could ask for them back?"

"I think they see them as their own now," Eadlyn replied. She placed a hand on Clover's shoulder. "Come on, we must rouse Elder-Modor before the rains come."

By the time the rain was dripping through the thatch, a section of wattle had been removed and two beds made where the goats had once slept.

"We'll need fresh straw in the mattresses soon," Elder-Modor commented.

Eadlyn thought of the silver sceattas and the gold pendant cross hidden within the dusty greying stems of straw. Perhaps it was time to move them to a safer place of hiding? "Aye, we'll change the straw when they cut it later in the year. We usually do it after going to the Sandtun..."

They would not be going to the Sandtun this year. Where Eadlyn had been invigorated by the challenge of moving the bedding, her body now felt heavy with regret. She wondered if Cedric or Alwin would want to go. It was something she had done for many years, at first journeying from Lyminge with her parents, brother and sisters. Her father had been a woodcarver and sold his boxes, bowls, and spoons there. Todd had been at the Sandtun with his brothers and parents. Although they came from the same village, it was at the Sandtun where the affection had grown between them. Eadlyn wondered if she could bear to be there without Todd? *I would love to be at the Sandtun;* the answer came to her immediately. *I always looked forward to it so much. And even if he cannot be with us, then to be at that place would bring me closer to him.*

The rain was gathering in three pools on the earth floor of their home. Eadlyn and Elder-Modor stood surveying the damaged roof while Clover sat on the floor grinding wheat into flour. Eadlyn thought of Cedric's amusement when she had suggested the extra eggs would pay for the thatcher and her own assertion that she could do the job herself. As Eadlyn stood there, frustrated by her inability to pay for or repair her roof, Cym walked in with a basket of eggs.

"I have eight today," he said.

"That's wonderful," Eadlyn replied and a grain of an idea began to form in her mind. They needed six eggs a week to trade for the grain the chickens ate. The rest were for their own use. "Cym, could you give me the basket please?" She took two eggs out and left the rest in the basket. "Elder-Modor, I have an idea. I'm going to see the thatcher."

"God's luck," Elder-Modor responded, seeming to know what was on Eadlyn's mind.

It was still raining but Eadlyn was fuelled with hope and, after placing an additional shawl over her headscarf, she left the home with Cym skipping alongside her. They walked down the slope towards the village centre, away from the row of homes belonging to Todd's family and away from the sheds where leather was made and crafted. They walked past the remains of the royal feasting hall but did not cross the stream. Instead they walked up the slope towards the church and then to a home, not unlike their own, which had a large barn beside it.

"Good morning," Eadlyn called at the part-open doorway, standing back from the thatch as a steady flow of water dripped from it.

156

"Come in, come in," Merewyn, wife of Orson Thatcher, appeared at the doorway with a baby on her hip and a young boy peeping around the skirt of her dress. "What brings you here in the rain? Have you suffered damage from the winds?"

"Aye, and now the rain is here, we've had to move our beds." Eadlyn shrugged her shoulders, and continued, "I was hoping to see Orson. Is he nearby?"

"He just went to fetch water, and won't be dawdling," Merewyn replied. And as she spoke, her husband came through the doorway with a bucket of water from the spring.

"Good morning, Eadlyn," Orson said, placing the bucket on the ground. "How do you fare?"

"I am well," Eadlyn said, "but my roof has been thrown about by the wind and now the rain is coming through."

"And there's just yourself to do the repairs..."

"We can't send Elder-Modor up on the roof!" Eadlyn grinned. "Orson, I have nothing much to trade. Todd's family give me food and nothing else." She thought of the silver sceattas but knew they must remain her secret. News that she had money must not spread about the village. "But we have chickens and they lay well. I could bring you eggs, perhaps twice a week, for as long as you like..." Eadlyn lifted the basket to show him. "Would you thatch our roof in exchange for eggs?"

"With six children to feed, I'd gladly thatch your roof for eggs," Orson grinned.

"I have six eggs here, and Clover will bring the same in three days," Eadlyn said. "Would you be happy with that?"

"Aye, I would." Orson agreed. "Now tell me, you've not lost the whole of your roof, have you?"

"Nay, but we've had to move our beds into where the goats used to sleep," Eadlyn told him.

"You're sleeping with the goats?" he asked, and even in the dim light of his home, the furrows on Orson's brow could be seen.

"The goats are gone," Eadlyn replied. "We only have the chickens."

"That's a shame," Merewyn commented. "There is always a need for milk."

"Alwin has the goats and he gives us milk," Eadlyn told them. "I must be grateful for that. And glad we can move our beds into their area!"

"Not for long," Orson said. "I'll come on Monday to take a look at the roof and hope to patch it the same day."

"I thank you," Eadlyn said, turning to the doorway. "We'll appreciate that. I fear if we wait for the next storm then we'll have no roof left."

"You've plenty of friends in Lyminge," Merewyn said. "There's no need to worry."

Eadlyn stepped forward and gave her friend a quick hug. "I thank you, Merewyn." She had lost touch with so many people over the last few months. Working until dusk on the animal hides was a lonely existence.

When Eadlyn walked back outside, the sun shone bravely, although still flanked by dark clouds. "Look at that," she said to Cym, pointing towards a bright rainbow. It stretched from the hills beyond their home to the church and minster on the opposite hillside. "Isn't it beautiful?" The storms and rain may continue in Lyminge, but it seemed as if the clouds surrounding Eadlyn were finally going to pass.

Chapter Eighteen

For months it had been barely light as Eadlyn walked the short distance between her home and the shed where she worked on the hides. She followed a track through the long grass, passing by the homes of Todd's family, past the shed where they worked on the leather, then the stores and finally to her own workplace. These were all on the very edge of the village, set apart from the other homes. Behind them the woods grew thick and dark, and from these woods came the grunts of wild boar, and the scream of the foxes. If she were to venture to the centre of the village, it would often be by moonlight, with frost forming on the ground and the air sharp on her skin.

Now Eadlyn walked to work and back in daylight, albeit the soft light of early morning and late afternoon. If she wanted to visit her family, or fetch water from the spring, then she no longer scurried, half-hidden by the darkness.

The leather apron she wore while working on the hides, took the worst of the flesh and hair Eadlyn scraped off the skin. Much of the debris fell to the ground, often sliding down the apron first. But some of it clung to the skirt of her dress, and even her headscarf became soiled as she lifted her hands to push it back into place or to sweep a stray lock of hair from her face. Every day she brushed her dress before leaving to go home, but over the past months it had become nothing more than a shabby rag, stained with mud at the hem and with the evidence of her work doggedly clinging to the woollen fibres.

A few weeks beforehand, Cedric had eyed her with distaste, agreeing that no good man would consider her for his wife. *I don't want to be anyone's wife,* Eadlyn scowled as she recalled the scene, *but I'll not have a man looking at me and thinking I am no good, just because the hem of my dress is dirty and my nails are stained from working droppings into leather.*

Moving her hands closer to her face, Eadlyn inspected her fingers, and her stomach felt heavy. However bold she tried to feel, there was nothing to be done for her hands. *I'll soak them in water and lye soap*, she vowed to herself. But she knew there was not enough time in the day to allow herself this luxury; besides, making the soap was time-consuming and the jar of soft mixture had to be used sparingly.

However, Janna had given Clover some natural coloured woollen cloth. Enough to make tunics or dresses for the whole family. Clover had earned it for her work in the weaving shed, just as Eadlyn did before Todd died. Now Eadlyn spread the cloth over their table and stood with a knife in her hand, ready to cut the length of material needed for her own dress.

"Can you hold the wool steady..." Eadlyn gestured to Clover. "Here and here, like this. Now I will cut it carefully. We mustn't waste any."

It was a beautiful day; the light was good and clear. They had been to church that morning and after the midday meal Eadlyn planned to sit on the bench outside their home and stitch her new dress into shape. It was not just Cedric who eyed her with distaste, or perhaps it wasn't as much distaste as pity. Whatever it was, Eadlyn was no longer going to walk across the village and up the slope to church in a soiled dress and headscarf.

"This will be the dress I wear when I am not at work," Eadlyn told Clover. "This one," she waved her hand across the ragged cloth falling from her shoulders to her calves, "will be to wear to the shed and nowhere else."

"You'll look beautiful, Modor," Clover said, her grey eyes wide and serious.

"Or at least clean!" Eadlyn grinned.

"She will look beautiful," Elder-Modor spoke from the bed.

"I thought you were sleeping," Clover replied.

"Nay, child, I just rest my eyes and enjoy listening to you talking with your modor. Cym will be back soon; it doesn't take the boy long to deliver eggs."

"Aye, he'll soon be back," Eadlyn confirmed.

"I was thinking." Elder-Modor slowly swung her legs out of the bed. "I was thinking that the day is so warm and there is no chill in the breeze; let me heat some water and help you wash your hair after we have eaten. I added some rosemary and lavender to the soap. It will be a wonderful feeling to wash the grease from it."

"I thank you, Elder-Modor." Eadlyn walked over to the old woman and gave her a quick hug. "I feel lucky to have you."

"Even though I fall asleep and forget to heat the supper?"

"Aye, even if the pottage is still cold when hunger gnaws at my stomach!" Eadlyn picked up the pot and hung it from the frame made by Fremund. "That reminds me, it's nearly time to eat."

True to her word, as soon as their bowls had been emptied of beans and root vegetables, Elder-Modor was filling an iron pot with water. Eadlyn walked through the village, across the wooden bridge and filled the bucket from the pool which gathered by the spring. Feeling conscious of her forlorn appearance, she rushed along, not wanting to stop and talk to the villagers. On her return, the pot of warm water had been placed on the ground by the hedgerow and the jar of lye soap was in Elder-Modor's hand.

'We must do the children first," Eadlyn said. "Then we'll warm more."

First Cym and then Clover knelt on the grass, leaning forward, and Elder-Modor dunked a jug in the iron pot then poured warm water through their hair. Eadlyn sank her fingers into the soft soap and massaged it into the children's scalps, loving the sensation on her hands. Their hair was rinsed, and the process repeated.

Then Eadlyn helped Elder-Modor wash her thin iron-grey hair. Finally, she was rubbing the lye soap into the roots of her own hair, then pulling her fingers through the wet waves, smelling the rosemary and lavender on her hands before continuing the process. The scent of the soap lifted her spirits and rubbing her hair vigorously with a cloth was invigorating. Eadlyn left her hair uncovered, tumbling over her shoulders and down her back. She moved to sit on the bench in the sunshine at the front of the home, her sewing on her lap.

It was whenever she had the chance to sit on that bench Eadlyn appreciated living on the edge of the village. With her back resting on the plank wall, she was sheltered from any chill winds from the east and

162

could look across the shallow valley in which the village nestled. She moved the needle in and out of the woollen material, concentrating on making small, neat stitches, and occasionally looking up to take in the scene.

It was a Sunday, so no one was working in the bakehouse or the weaving shed, at the blacksmith's fire or thatching a roof. But the water must still be collected, and the animals needed tending, and so there was plenty of activity within the village. In the home, Elder-Modor was making lye soap with the children. They had been given animal fat in exchange for a jar of the finished soap and been saving the wood ash from their fire. Eadlyn smiled to hear them chatting and singing as they worked.

On the opposite side of the village, the rounded end of the church was clear to see. Eadlyn's attention was attracted to a figure walking around the church grounds. There was no sign of either the monks or nuns who lived in the minster; Eadlyn wondered what they were doing. Her concentration moved back to her stitching, but her thoughts stayed with those who lived at the minster and she reflected on their lives, so structured through their prayers and routines.

When Eadlyn looked up again, there was a figure striding around the eastern edge of the village. She turned back to the fabric on her lap and pushed the needle in and out. She raised her head again as the children came outside with a bowl of soft soap to show her.

"It's cousin Fremund again!" Clover's voice was high. "Has he come to visit us again?"

"I don't know, my sweeting," Eadlyn frowned. The figure was much closer now, and Clover was right, it did appear to be Fremund. He had jumped across the stream with ease and was walking up the slope towards them. She put her sewing aside, ready to stand and greet their cousin.

"It is him," Cym squealed. "Look, look, he's waving." He raised his arm and waved back before he went running down the hillside and was scooped up into Fremund's arms.

"I wonder what he wants, coming here again," Elder-Modor said from the doorway. She turned back into the home and soon reappeared with a bundle of tightly knitted cloth. Handing the cloth to Eadlyn, she said, "Cover your hair."

Eadlyn looked at the material in her hands. This was not her ragged, stained headscarf. This was something new, something clean and soft. She turned towards Elder-Modor and asked, "Where...?"

"It's something I was given, but an old woman like me has no need for a new headscarf. Take it and put it over your lovely clean hair. We can wash the old one, and you can wear it when you work."

Allowing the cloth to unfold, Eadlyn then held it out and placed it over her hair. "It's very kind of you," she said, once more grateful for the love and company the old woman had brought to their home.

"I came to see how the chickens are!" Fremund produced a small sack of grain from behind his back. "A gift for them!"

"Come and see them." Clover took his hand in order to lead Fremund to the coop.

"They've settled in well," Eadlyn told him.

"Producing eggs every day?" he asked.

"Aye, they lay well," Eadlyn replied, as she trailed behind Fremund and the children, still fastening her headscarf.

164

"We give eggs to the thatcher every week," Cym informed.

"To the thatcher?" Fremund queried.

"The roof was damaged a few weeks ago," Eadlyn explained. "In the storm."

"We had to sleep in the goat pen," Cym continued with relish.

"The goat pen?" Fremund repeated. They were by the coop now; he knelt to look at the birds, his red hair shining bright in the sunshine.

"Not with the goats," Cym told him. "We have no goats. But we moved our beds because they were getting wet."

"We paid the thatcher with eggs," Eadlyn took up the story. "If we hadn't been able to give eggs, we could not have repaired the roof."

Fremund stood up and turned to look up at the roof. "I'm so glad I could help. I thought only of feeding you and now you're able to use them to trade."

Eadlyn reached out, placing her hand on his forearm, "You gave us more than chickens. You gave us the chance to be able to survive without begging from Todd's brothers. We won't forget your kindness."

The chickens were inspected, and it was agreed they were content in their new home. Then Fremund sat with the family in front of the home; they drank ale together, and dipped bread in honey. Elder-Modor spoke of the past, retelling the family stories. Eadlyn picked up her sewing; she continued to stitch the sides of the dress, pulling the needle through the two-tone colours of grey and pale grey wool. It made a pleasant scene, she thought, as she became accustomed to Fremund joining the family group.

As Eadlyn completed the stitching on the body of the dress, Fremund suggested it was time to leave. "Eadlyn, would you walk with me to the village boundary?" he asked.

"Aye, that would be nice." She stood up, thinking it would be good to stretch her legs and to look across the village from a different viewpoint.

The children got up to follow. "Nay, he asked your modor," Elder-Modor held them back.

Eadlyn turned to look at Elder-Modor, a slight frown on her brow, her eyes questioning. But the old woman merely smiled and placed her hands on the children's shoulders. Fremund set off, his pace slower than usual. They walked in silence for a few minutes, skirting the eastern edge of Lyminge. As they approached the track leading to the south, Fremund stopped and turned to face Eadlyn. "I respect the way you are looking after your family, but it's not right that Cedric and Alvin took your goats, they work you hard and expect you to care for their modor."

"They could have shown more kindness," Eadlyn admitted. "I would not let them take the goats if they were to come now, but I was numb... grieving."

"And Elder-Modor gives you company?"

"Aye, I am very fond of her," she replied.

"Eadlyn?"

She did not reply but looked up at him and for the first time she saw Fremund not as Todd's bothersome cousin, or the only male family member to show her support since Todd's death. Eadlyn looked at Fremund and wondered if... if perhaps he was thinking of a future with her. She recalled Elder-Modor pulling the children back, and the old woman suggesting that Cousin Fremund might come to the village for a wife. Her mouth dried. She hadn't thought this before... and

166

hoped she misunderstood. A chill prickled her skin, and she pulled her shawl tighter.

"Eadlyn," he repeated. "Clover and Cym are fond of me, and they are fine children to be proud of. I don't think they would mind, so I wondered what you would think of us becoming husband and wife?"

"Elder-Modor..." Her excuse was weak, and she knew it. "I couldn't leave her..."

"Of course, not unless she wanted to live with one of her other sons. But what about you, Eadlyn. Do you think we could live happily together?"

"I've never thought of it," she replied. Now a mild panic ran through her body. He was right, of course he was. The children liked him and being with him reminded them of happier times. He had shown a caring nature which had gone unnoticed before. They had saved their home this time by exchanging eggs for the thatcher's labour. But what would happen next time they needed something? Could she really be both mother and father to the children, and care for an old woman who would become increasingly frail over the next few years? The voice in her head screamed: *no, I don't want to marry him; I don't want to marry anyone; I want to manage on my own; I have the chickens and soon I will find a way to buy some goats. Every month I will grow stronger and braver and I will look after my family.* But there was another voice, a steadier voice, one which spoke to her slowly and reasoned with the frantic scream: *he seems to be a good man; I know him to be a hard worker and he has shown he cares for us. Think of your children. Think of keeping them safe.*

"Perchance you could consider it now," he said, and reaching forward he trailed his fingertip over the skin of her face, now soft from the lye soap with which she had washed her hair and cleansed her face.

Her heart, so attached to Todd for many years, gave a treacherous lurch and Eadlyn wondered what it would be like to lie with Fremund. She looked into his eyes and found herself liking their clear blue, whereas before she had loved the mystery of Todd's dark brown colouring. Did his hair give him a temper or was it just an ancient tale, as old as the flint hills, that a red-headed person was liable to have fiery outbursts? She looked at his lips, full and pale pink, with his beard neatly cut around them. How would he kiss her? She had only ever kissed one man. Would this man's tongue taste of the mead he enjoyed so much? All these thoughts came at once, pressing against one another in those few short moments when his finger touched her cheek and moved down to her neck before he pulled away.

"I don't know," was her only reply.

"You can think about it while we stroll a little way up the hill," Fremund suggested. "You've not left Lyminge all winter and barely walked further than the shed where they make you work." He flashed a grin at her, "Would it harm you to go beyond the village homes?"

"I would love to walk beyond Lyminge," Eadlyn declared. "I'd love to run with the children, to climb these hills," she waved her hand to the east and the steep hills beyond the pastureland. "Or to explore past the minster and to go along the lanes until we stand on the edge of the hills and look across Kent. My spirits have been so low and I long to leave the village boundaries, if only for a short time."

"You always loved the Sandtun," he reminded her.

"Aye, to stand at the Shipway and look across Romney Marsh, and wonder about the people who live in that bleak place makes me feel alive."

"Would you go there with me?" Fremund asked.

"I don't know," she said again.

They walked on, leaving the last of the simple wood and thatch homes behind them. The lane was narrow, the hedge of trees and bushes high. Neither of them spoke. On reaching an opening in the hedge, Fremund took her arm and guided Eadlyn to the edge of the field. They stood looking up at the steep hillside.

"Cym would feel like King of Kent if he could climb that hill!" Fremund commented.

"Aye, he would." Eadlyn agreed.

They were standing close to each other, their sleeves almost touching. He turned so they faced each other and said, "I think we would live well together. I wouldn't have wished either Todd or Brona dead, but we are alive and must think of our own happiness and the comfort we could bring one another."

Eadlyn's headscarf, hurriedly placed over her hair when he had approached earlier, was coming loose; she reached up to adjust it. "You're a good man, Fremund," she said. "But I am becoming used to being on my own and had not thought of this."

"I know." He placed his hand over hers and pushed her scarf back, then ran his fingers through her tumbling curls, the colour of ripe wheat. "I've always loved your hair... and the freckles on your nose."

Mesmerised, she let him pull gently at her hair. It was so soothing, so relaxing, and she felt the tension flow from her body. Her own arms were at her side; she dare not reach out to touch him. She studied his face: the freckles, the fine lines, the shades of fire in his beard and the brilliant blue of his eyes. He moved his hand from her hair, and she felt regret, but now he traced the shape of her jaw and neck, down to her collarbone. She felt almost as if she had turned to stone, her lips slightly open.

When he leaned down to kiss her, she didn't object, although still the voice in her head screamed that she must stop. He tasted of the honey they had just shared, and his beard was scented with sweet woodruff. Fremund had also been cleansing himself from the soils of winter. His hand was on her hip, and he pulled her closer so now their bodies touched and Eadlyn pressed against him, dormant senses awakened. She allowed her hand to move to the small of his back. They parted a little and looked into each other's eyes, both uncertain.

"Lie with me now?" Fremund looked at the fresh grass at the side of the field. Taking her hand, he moved it and placed it over his bulge, showing her that he was ready.

Her own desire was no less than his own, but the voice in her head still beat a steady rhythm: *no, not him, move away.* "Nay, Fremund," she said. "I must go... go back to the family; they'll be wondering..."

And without saying another word or even waiting for him, Eadlyn turned and ran back to the lane. With her headscarf still in her hand, she fled towards Lyminge, only slowing when she reached the village boundary.

Chapter Nineteen

"The walk did you good; there's a bit of colour to your cheeks," Elder-Modor commented. She was sitting on the bench, helping Clover stitch the hem of her new dress.

"Aye, the views are beautiful, the hills... the..." Eadlyn fiddled with her headscarf.

"Will Fremund be back soon?"

"I hope so, he makes me laugh," Clover said, her gaze still on the stitching.

"I expect he is busy," Eadlyn said, feeling the warmth spreading through her cheeks. She moved into the home, away from Elder-Modor and her prying eyes. "I must add to the pottage or there won't be enough to fill our bellies at supper-time."

It was dim inside the house. Eadlyn could hide away in there and allow the pulse throbbing through her body to calm down. It was cool, and she felt a respite from the sun which suddenly seemed to shine too bright. Eadlyn snatched at the bag of beans and, dipping her fingers in, she threw several handfuls into the pot. Then she took the basket of vegetables and placed them on the table. As she did this, Elder-Modor came through the doorway, and Eadlyn gave a silent sigh of despair.

"I wondered if Fremund has thoughts of you and he..." Elder-Modor began. "You and he being together and if he did, then you must think of yourself and the children and not grieve too much for Todd who has gone from our lives."

Eadlyn pressed the knife through the turnips, chopping the white flesh into uneven chunks. "Nay, it's not what I want. Look at us, we are doing very well." She tipped the turnip into the pot and turned to the old woman. "We need more water. I'll have to go and fetch it before the pottage dries up."

*

"This reminds me of when we go to the Sandtun," Clover said, smiling up at Eadlyn.

Mother and daughter were walking the same road which led to the south. The hedgerows were now rich with spring growth and the track was dry but not yet dusty. Lyminge was behind them and if they were to stay on this track they would, after some time, reach the sea. The traders had not yet returned to the Sandtun this year; they awaited another two cycles of the moon before word came that it was time to journey to the coast.

But Eadlyn's thoughts were not on the Sandtun; it was six days since she had seen Fremund and she was nervous that he may return to Lyminge. She had been restless in those six days, taking any excuse to stride out across the village to fetch water or wander through the woods in search of fallen branches for the fire. As the sun set behind her, she had sat beside Todd's grave and wondered what was best for her future and that of her children.

Eadlyn and Clover approached the gap in the hedge where Fremund had led her off the road and they had kissed. It was the place she had betrayed her

172

memories of Todd and, stepping through into the field, Eadlyn felt the colour rise in her face.

"If we walk across this field, we can follow the stream all the way to Etchinghill," Eadlyn said to Clover. "Won't it make a pretty walk, with the steep hills to our left?"

"Aye, but Modor, do you think Cousin Fremund might help us buy some goats? He liked helping with the chickens."

"I'm sure he would." Eadlyn's fingers went to the leather pouch hanging from her belt. "But I heard about these goats needing a home and I have two sceattas to buy them with."

"Two?" Clover repeated, her eyes wide. "Can I see them?"

"If you would like to." Eadlyn paused and loosened the lace on the pouch. She carefully withdrew a coin and held it on the palm of her hand. It was small, no bigger than her thumbnail; the surface had raised marks in the form of lines and dots, with two lines forming a cross. Clover leaned forward and turned the sceat in her mother's hand. The other side of the coin had crude lines and a circle.

"And with this tiny coin we can buy a goat?" Clover asked, a frown on her face.

"Aye, because it's made of silver."

"And silver is very precious," Clover said. "Did uncle Cedric give you the sceat because he took our goats?"

"Nay." Eadlyn smiled down at her and put the coin back in the purse. "Nay, your faeder earned these at the Sandtun and I have kept them very safe until we needed them."

"I like knowing that he can help us," Clover said, as she started walking again. "Can we run to the stream, Modor?"

It was pleasant walking along by the water with the steep hillside to their left and open pasture to their right. Sheep grazed on the hills, their pitiful bleats carrying on the light breeze. The path was a little rough, but Eadlyn felt the tension easing as she strode out, trying to keep up with Clover's youthful scamper. A bird of prey hung in the air above them, and Eadlyn marvelled at how still it could be and how sharp its eyesight was to spot a field mouse or vole in the grass below. The bird swooped and she wondered if it caught its victim. As it vanished, something caused a flock of starlings to rise from a small copse; they soared high and then swooped in one fluid movement, before turning back on themselves and sailing off to the north. Closer to hand, the grasshoppers chirped, while black-bodied beetles and small spiders moved about in the long grass bordering the stream.

Before long, a small collection of homes came into view, all made of either wood or mud, with thatched roofs. They nestled around the stream, with the line of hills sheltering them from the north-easterly winds, and thin columns of smoke drifting upwards from where the fires burned, no doubt each one with a pan of pottage hanging above it. Not one of the buildings was as substantial as the thane's hall in Lyminge, and Etchinghill had no church in which to worship their Christian God, but merely a wooden cross where the people would gather.

There were pens with long-legged hairy pigs, and coops for chickens. Goats, known for their determination to escape, were in secure enclosures. Beyond the cluster of homes, lines of crops spread out in the fields, and Eadlyn saw men with rounded backs walking the hillside, a small barrow being pushed before each one of them, as they gathered loose flint.

One by one, the women who washed clothes at the stream, the men who repaired homes and fences within the village, and the children who ran about, turned and stared at the newcomers. Eadlyn walked up to one of the nearest, and spoke, "I am Eadlyn from Lyminge, my husband was Todd the leather-maker. I am looking for a man who had goats for sale and was told to come here."

The woman looked back through her dark eyes, with their heavy lids. She pondered Eadlyn's words before giving her reply: "Aye, there is a man with goats for sale. He lives near the old oak tree, over there."

"I thank you." Eadlyn gave a nod and, with Clover at her side, she walked past the men, women and children of Etchinghill, and on to the small home near the oak tree.

An old man sat on the bench outside his home. It was a building made almost entirely of thatch, with two sides coming down from the ridge to the ground and only the triangular ends being made of vertical planks. He sat at the end, with the open doorway behind him. In his hand was a piece of wood which he appeared to be shaping. His hat was large on his head, concealing his face until he looked up and spoke, "Strangers, do you come to see me?"

"Aye, we come from Lyminge," Eadlyn said, waving her hand in the general direction of their village. "I'm Eadlyn and my daughter, Clover, is here with me."

"You came to see me?" he repeated. His eyes were so watery, he could barely see. And, as he stood, he reached to support his gaunt frame on a sturdy stick.

"We heard you have goats for sale," Eadlyn began. "Could we see them, please?"

"That's right," he said, leading the way to the side of his home, where four goats were kept in a small enclosure.

"They're too strong for me," the old man said, pointing his stick at the animals. "Always pulling and getting into mischief... they need a strong hand."

The goats, two of them tawny in colour, and two of them grey and white, seemed to be in good condition. Their rough coats were clean, their eyes were bright, and they were well-fed. Two had swollen udders, and one looked as if she was expecting kids.

Eadlyn opened the gate and walked amongst the goats; she inspected their hooves, their eyes, ears and udders. "They look to be in good health," she said. "We are looking for milkers."

"You'll get plenty from these two," he said. "My daughter came and milked them just an hour ago, I'll give you a beaker to try. The little one, she will be ready for a billy goat before long. You can see the other one is expecting. This will be her second lot; we had no trouble from her last year. I'll want more for her, I reckon she has two kids in there and they're worth money."

"Aye, they are," Eadlyn replied, "but that is more work than I'm ready for and I don't know I can afford the grain for them. "I'll give you two sceattas for the milkers and the young one. I'll put her to a billy, but she's not proven to be a good mother. And that will give me time to get used to them before the kids come."

"I was wanting three sceattas for them," the old man said.

Eadlyn pondered this while continuing to handle the goats. They were strong, but not tall. *Would Clover be able to handle them on her own if needed? It is a lot to ask of the girl, but if they produced milk, then it could be used to make cheese and butter.* She thought of the eggs she had traded for the thatch repairs on her roof. *Is there a trade to be done here?*

"I have three sceattas," Eadlyn said. "That's all I have. I will give you three for all four goats. And three times a week until harvest time my daughter or myself will bring you cheese or milk from these goats."

"I'll miss them..." the old man began. "Perhaps I'll keep the one expecting and sell her kids for more."

"And perhaps they'll die, or she will," Eadlyn said. "I'll take the two nannies and be happy with that. Two sceattas, you said?" She began to open her pouch and withdrew two coins.

At the sight of the silver, the old man became keen for more. "Three, you say," his voice animated. "Three for all the goats and you'll bring me milk?"

"Aye I did," Eadlyn said. "But my daughter is young to manage four goats while I'm out to work all day. We'll be pleased to have two." She offered the coins to him. "Clover, we'll need to fasten this rope around their necks."

"Nay, a strong girl like yours and a hard-working woman like yourself can manage the four of them, and the kids," the man said. "Do you need more rope? I have some inside..."

"Well..."

"And to know your girl was coming with a jug of milk or a bit of cheese... I'd be happy to know that," he continued. "It's no distance at all from Lyminge."

177

With Eadlyn keeping three of the goats, and Clover holding the more sedate pregnant nanny, they left Etchinghill behind them. The goats, eager for freedom, pulled at the rope, but mother and daughter were also in high spirits, and at times they ran with the animals. Their path followed the course of the stream and soon the stone church on the hill, and then the thatched roofs of Lyminge, could be seen.

"Modor, how will we manage when the kids come and there is so much work to do?" Clover asked, but she could not contain the joy in her face and the little frown she gave was short-lived.

"I'm going to tell your Uncle Cedric that I will no longer work all those hours on the animal skins," Eadlyn announced and, as she said those words, she felt her back straighten a little and she held her head higher. "I will work in the morning and for just a short time after our midday meal. Then in the afternoon I will milk the goats and make cheese."

"But Cedric gives us our food," Clover said.

"That's not all I will do," Eadlyn proclaimed, as she gave the youngest goat a sharp tug on her lead. "I will work on our strip of land to grow beans and carrots and turnips."

"But Modor, we have no land."

"I am going to ask the thane for some," Eadlyn said. "Cedric will still give us some food, but we'll grow our own as well!"

When they arrived home, Elder-Modor was dozing on the bench outside, her back resting against the plank wall. She roused herself on hearing the chatter between Eadlyn and Clover, and the bleating of the goats. They paused in front of the old woman, eager to show off their purchases.

"I expect you're thinking I've done nothing but sleep all morning," Elder-Modor said. "But you'd be wrong, I've been very busy."

"You deserve a rest now then," Eadlyn said, hoping to find the pottage heated through over a healthy fire. But when she glanced through the doorway, she saw no warm glow from the logs.

"Aye, I do deserve a short sleep," Elder-Modor said. "I've been moving the straw around, as if I were twenty years younger!"

"The straw?" Eadlyn queried. "Didn't Orson-the-thatcher spread it out for you?"

"He would have done; he's a good worker," Elder-Modor told her. "But I decided to refill our mattresses and use the old straw for the goat's pen. Orson left them some fresh hay to eat, so they won't mind about the straw."

"You emptied the mattresses?" Eadlyn repeated and, as she looked through to see the old straw strewn over the floor of the goats' pen, she felt the colour drain from her face.

Chapter Twenty

Fumbling at the gate, with three goats at her legs and her daughter looking on, Eadlyn could feel the agitation rising. Why did they have to fight so hard to reach the grass? If only they could show some patience the goats would soon be rewarded by an enclosure with this season's lush grass, untouched for so long. She lifted the gate again, but not quite high enough; it came down awkwardly, catching the side of her hand. She cursed under her breath; it would be showing a fine blood blister in no time. Eadlyn tried again, and this time the gate opened, swinging open far enough to allow one goat to pass. But the foolish beasts would not wait and before she could lean forward to push it further, they were shoving their way through, pulling her with them and, as she let go of the rope, they surged forward and somehow Eadlyn found herself falling in the gateway. The fourth goat, still held by Clover, stood firmly on the back of Eadlyn's hand, before her daughter let it go.

"Now we'll have to chase after them before they do some damage to themselves and get all tangled up," Eadlyn said. "Why did we buy four? Please God, we'll be able to manage them."

Clover, visibly surprised by her mother's change of humour, tried to pacify her. "Look at how they like our paddock. They had no grass at all in the pen where the old man kept them. Don't worry, Modor. They'll soon calm down."

"Aye, they will," Eadlyn attempted a smile. She held up her hand and said, "I'm sure we have some cream for the bruising."

They set about trying to herd one goat at a time into a corner and soon removed all the twine from their rope collars.

"I'll find Cym; he'll want to see them," Clover said.

"He will, and I thank you for your help," Eadlyn said. "Now I'll go to see if Elder-Modor needs any help with our beds. Won't it be good to have a freshly filled mattress? I have some lavender to place in them, so they'll smell sweet."

But on entering the home, Eadlyn barely looked towards their plump mattresses; instead she moved a section of the wattle fencing and stepped into the goats' pen. Her body and spirits slumped. The area wasn't big and the straw was only a thin layer over the mud floor, but none of the light from the doorway fell into the pen: a dusty darkness fell on the whole area. She had no choice but to kneel and search with her fingertips for the pouch containing her last sceat and the golden cross. Sliding her feet across the floor, rather than risk standing on the pouch, Eadlyn decided to start against the far wall. Kneeling, with her back to the main living area, she started moving her hands in a circular pattern, feeling for the soft leather. The straw was musty and immediately she felt the stale particles rising upwards, she breathed them in and they caught on the back of her throat.

She had not been searching for long when Eadlyn became aware of Elder-Modor standing at the wattle partition. The old woman had made no sound but merely looked on. Eadlyn shuffled to the side and continued her search. The knot in her stomach was tight. Elder-Modor would be confused, and Eadlyn hated to think of her being upset, knowing she had done wrong but not understanding why.

"I have to look for something," Eadlyn gave a weak excuse.

"Should I have left the mattresses?" the old woman said. "Should I have let you do it yourself?"

"Nay, you were trying to help and now we'll have such comfort at night," Eadlyn replied, forcing her voice to be light, while her throat constricted and the stale dust built up as a layer on her tongue.

"Can I help you find what you've lost?"

"It's best no one knows about it, not even you," Eadlyn tried to explain. "I'll find it soon enough."

She moved back a little and continued the search. It seemed to take an age, and then Eadlyn's fingertips touched on the soft leather. She stood, with the pouch nestling in her palm, and backed out of the pen. Elder-Modor had taken to her bed for a rest, so Eadlyn stood outside and slipped her fingers into the pouch. It was wide open at the neck; she had not secured the lace when she had hurriedly removed three sceattas that morning. The single silver coin remained in the pouch, but the golden pendant cross was gone, no doubt still amongst the straw in the pen.

At least the sceat is of some use, Eadlyn thought. *To sell a gold cross would raise questions as to where it came from. It brings questions to my own mind: why did Todd carry it in his pouch? What secrets does it hold?*

Time after time, Eadlyn returned to the goats' pen that day, searching amongst the stale straw for the elusive pendant. By early evening, the goats were brought into the pen, and it seemed likely the gold would be trampled underfoot during the night. When the family settled on their fresh mattresses that evening, the home was once again alive with the sound of goats, as it had been in the time when Todd was with them. For Eadlyn, the joy of bringing the goats into their lives had been short-lived. Now, frustrated, all she could think of was the golden cross.

A couple of days later, and Elder-Modor looked on as Eadlyn trudged away from the home to labour on the animal skins. She was fond of the young woman her son had chosen to marry. As fond as she would allow herself to be when life was so fragile and at any moment someone close could be taken away. The old woman looked towards the stone church on the opposite slope of the hill. It gave her comfort to know that Todd now lived in a better place. She had prayed for him regularly and was sure his sins were few. His soul would have reached its heavenly home.

Elder-Modor was bothered by Eadlyn though; her spirits were changeable, and Todd's mother believed she knew the reason. Cousin Fremund had shown kindness to the family, and then asked to walk with Eadlyn as he journeyed home. When she had returned, the young woman was flushed and excitable. Elder-Modor believed Fremund would make a good husband: he was a skilled worker and well respected; he was lively and enjoyed the company of the children. If he liked to drink too much mead, then she was sure this could be calmed with a firm hand. Eadlyn was clearly confused: experiencing an attraction for this man she knew well, her mind was turbulent with new emotions, yet still missing her own dear husband. It might not be clear to Eadlyn, but with the wisdom of age, the older woman knew exactly what ailed Todd's wife.

Over the years it had become easy to lose count, and Elder-Modor no longer knew how many seasons she had lived, although it was longer than most. Her brother and sisters, and the friends of younger days, were no longer in this world. Her breathing was weak and vigour fading fast, but her mind was as sharp as always. Remembering faraway days was easy though, and the stories passed on from her own elder-modor. She also recalled being left with three boys when her husband went to fight with the thane and was fatally wounded in battle.

Like Eadlyn, she was young and spirited and it was not long before she took a man in her bed, or in the copse – whatever suited her best. Before long she was carrying the daughter of one who was not her husband and neither was he inclined to take her as his wife. The girl was weak and died before she was two years old. Elder-Modor had learned a lesson in life, and she was grateful that if Eadlyn were to be tempted, then Fremund would not leave her alone with child. He would marry her and be glad of it. In fact, there was no reason why the happy event had not been announced already. Life was short and full of peril; they should take comfort from each other while they could.

The old woman could think of nothing else that could be bothering Eadlyn, whom she loved as a daughter. The cloud of grief was lifting; Eadlyn was showing herself to be resourceful. She needed a husband in her life, and all would be well.

With her mind still on that rogue who pleasured her in the copse and in his barn, Elder-Modor reached for her shawl. As she dragged it from the trunk containing her few belongings, the pendant cross, caught up in its threads, travelled within the soft folds and nestled against the small of Elder-Modor's back.

At the doorway of the home, Elder-Modor looked across the village, beyond the church to the minster. At the thought of walking up the hill, her chest tightened. But she thought of Eadlyn's troubled soul, and her hands, so red and chapped. Muttering to herself, "It will be worth my trouble, to see the girl's smile," the old woman set off, her back bent and step unsteady. As she moved, the golden cross hung on by just one tenacious thread and rocked gently to and fro.

Walking amongst the buildings of the minster was very soothing for Elder-Modor. She had already paused at a bench by the church and recovered her energy for the final steps to where the nuns and monks lived in one communal area. There was a calm about the place you did not experience in the village. Amongst those who lived in their homes around the Nailbourne stream, people called out to one another, their voices competing and jarring. Here, only the necessary words were used; the tone was always low and calming. Sometimes there was the hum of scriptures being read or prayers being uttered, but the sounds never vied, they merely flowed side by side.

The old woman, a visitor to the holy place, lingered outside the stone-built church and oratory. She was almost cocooned by the buildings, with the refectory and kitchens to her left, the church, chapter house and dormitories to her right, and the Abbess' and Prior's quarters behind her. Before her, she saw movement amongst the smaller outbuildings used as store and work rooms. She wondered about the Romans who had built the first house of God here. The stones they used had been lifted, cleaned and re-laid to form new buildings: the church and oratory. Elder-Modor mused on the style of the Roman basilica, probably quite different from the tall plain Saxon church, with Roman tiles surrounding the small, rounded windows. Closing her eyes, she listened: there was the hum of insects, the murmur of the monks and nuns and, jarring the peace, the sound of a meal being prepared in the kitchen – a knife coming down on a wooden board and the moving of iron pans.

The slim wooden door to the church began to open and Elder-Modor walked on, not wanting to impose herself upon these peaceful souls. As the view to the fields opened, she saw robed figures moving amongst lines of crops, and working on maintaining wooden fences. Nuns with additional veils, moved amongst the beehives and she could see a honeycomb glistening as it was lifted free from the wicker hive. Closer to hand, there were herb gardens, and it was here a low building stood, its thatch almost reaching the ground.

Elder-Modor walked into the stillroom and bowed her head to the nun. "Good day to you," she said.

The nun offered a shadow of a smile. At least it seemed as if she did; the veil hid her facial features, but it twitched a little as she spoke and moved her lips or eyes. "Good day," she murmured from her position behind a solid wooden table. She held a cleaver in one hand, and the fingers of the other hand moved herbs on the chopping board. To her left, a pestle and mortar already contained dried flower heads.

There was no discomfort in the near silence. Elder-Modor walked through the minster to the still room about once a week. She felt she knew this nun, although few words passed between them.

"Does she suffer with her hands?" The nun asked, referring to Eadlyn.

"Aye. I'm in need of balm for her."

"I have fresh calendula and marigold," the nun offered, turning towards the shelves and picking up a jar.

"I thank you." Elder-Modor began to turn away, the jar of balm in her hand. Then something drove her to turn back and appeal to this nun who knew nothing about the turmoil of falling in love when your husband had not long departed this earth. "My Eadlyn, her spirits are all mixed. What can I do? How can I help her?"

The nun stood still, perhaps contemplating this revelation. She said nothing in reply. Elder-Modor offered no more; she merely waited. After a moment, the nun busied herself gathering a small cloth bag and selected a few of the plants hanging from hooks on the ceiling. She gave no indication to show she was aware of the old woman standing there, until she pushed the filled bag across the table. "Melissa balm, columbine and borage," she said. "To hang from her wrist or belt."

"I thank you," Elder-Modor replied. She bowed her head and turned away.

On stepping out into the sunlight, with the balm and filled bag in her wicker basket, Elder-Modor proceeded to walk towards a smaller building. Two nuns were in it, pulling large veils from their heads. The room smelt sweet, and the old woman's mouth watered in appreciation. "A honeycomb, please," she said, offering her own pot to place it in. A piece of golden sweetness was placed in the pot.

This time when she left the nuns, Elder-Modor heard their whispers: "May God be with you."

Next Elder-Modor ventured amongst the monks, to a place she rarely visited – the brew-house. Her desire to see Eadlyn settled, led her amongst the aromas of yeast, honey and barley. On leaving the brew-house, her basket contained a small flagon of mead to offer their guest, Fremund, when he next found a reason to walk along the deep lanes to Lyminge.

Finally, Elder-Modor emptied her basket of some bread, a pot of lye soap and some woollen thread. She placed these offerings on a shelf in a sheltered area near the kitchen. This was the way of the minster; the nuns would never ask for payment but gratefully received any offerings.

All this time the pendant cross had been hanging from a loose thread on Elder-Modor's shawl. Its tenacity was such that it had endured the journey across Lyminge and through the minster. But now the shawl swung about as it became caught up with the basket. The cross let go of its fragile grip and tumbled down the shawl, then her dress, before it fell to the ground. It slid, without grace, to the base of a bench.

There was no sign of the old woman when Eadlyn returned from her work in the tanning shed. She scanned the living area, expecting to see a sleeping body in a bed, or at least someone tending the pottage. With a sigh, she lifted the pan onto the stand and prodded the fire into life.

Then Eadlyn continued her search for the golden cross, this time moving her fingers amongst soiled straw; the goats had spent several nights in the pen by now. "This is the last time," she muttered to herself. "My mind is so tormented." In many ways the cross had no worth for her, but it was her very last link with Todd. Found in his money pouch, not long after his death, the pendant cross held mysteries. Somehow it related to the Sandtun, Eadlyn was sure of it.

While her fingers moved automatically over the straw-strewn floor, Eadlyn's thoughts returned to the Sandtun. She recalled those mornings when the mist hung low over both the marshland and the lagoon, and the sound of the sea lapping on the sandy beach. At those times the area was both soothing and magical. She remembered the coming together of families and the communal meals, the gathering of shellfish and the pleasure of receiving fresh fish from the men on the beach. *Perchance I will go there next year,* she thought. *I'll find a way, and not marry Fremund to do it.*

The pottage began to bubble and Eadlyn knew it was time to give up the search. She wiped her hands, picked up a wooden spoon and stirred the thick broth of beans and vegetables. Looking out of the doorway, she spotted the children walking from the bakehouse with the bread, and not far behind Elder-Modor was coming with a basket slung over her arm.

Elder-Modor could see Eadlyn's spirits were low. It showed in the slump of her shoulders and the small smile which gave no spark to her eyes. She offered the balm, with the bag of dried flowers and herbs. "To lighten your heart," Elder-Modor said.

"I thank you. My hands are sore today," Eadlyn raised the scented bag to her nose. "And my heart... I'm just a little weary."

"The bag can hang from your belt or above the bed," Elder-Modor told her.

"It will cheer me, just to know you were thinking of me!" Eadlyn replied. "I'll wear it when I'm not at work and place it by the bed at night."

Elder-Modor, still believing she understood Eadlyn's heart, continued: "I bought a small flagon of mead for Fremund; I feel sure he'll visit again soon. He'll appreciate us thinking of him, I know he will."

"Fremund?" Eadlyn repeated, as she ladled pottage into bowls. "I expect he is busy with his work and… and whatever keeps him occupied."

"Aye Fremund." *I can see she thinks of him every hour, why else would she be acting as if her head is full of the salt air she breathes on Romney Marsh? What is it that she searches for? I know – he has given her a love token and she hid it under the mattress, and now it is lost amongst the old straw. Is that the cause of her distress?* Elder-Modor smiled, at last believing to understand the whole story of Eadlyn's agitation.

Chapter Twenty-One

Brother Edwen was seated on one of the benches running along the length of the outside wall of the refectory. Leaning against the wooden wall of the building, the monk held an open book on his lap. His eyes followed the ink, and he appreciated the beauty of the loops and upright lines, forming letters and words on the vellum pages. Words flowed from his lips, barely audible but, when melded with the whispers from others sitting alongside him, a pleasant hum drifted up the plank wall, and outwards through the open spaces linking the buildings of the minster.

An insect landed on Brother Edwen's calf. He tried to endure the irritation. It remained there, preparing to suck his blood. The monk read with more vigour. The insect clamped its jaws onto his bare skin. Brother Edwen lowered his hand and swiped the insect away. He watched it fall to the ground and crawl to the shelter provided by the underside of the bench. As he was about to turn back to his book, the monk's gaze fell upon an alluring golden glint of light. Frowning, he leaned forward and picked an object up, immediately pulling it into his palm.

While curiosity burned into his hand, Brother Edwen continued to read, the words running through his mind then drifting away as seeds float on a summer breeze. Time passed slowly before the monk was able to move with the others into the refectory.

Once seated, he secured the golden cross within the folds of his tunic. The meal – bread, cheese and pickled vegetables – was tasteless. The monk thought only of his precious find and nothing of the food. From a raised platform to the side, one of the Brothers took his turn at reading about the life of a saint; Brother Edwen heard none of the words.

Finally, the holy people of the minster left the refectory in pairs, then moved in different directions. Brother Edwen walked the path trodden by Elder-Modor just that morning. Not far from where the old woman had bought her balm, the monk fetched a hoe from the tool shed. He walked to the back of the shed and opened his hand. A chill ran through his body and he felt his head go light. How could this be? St Botolph's pendant cross, lost on the wilds of Romney Marsh, was there sitting in the palm of his hand. He looked briefly to the heavens, to the white clouds and pale blue sky, and marvelled at their clarity, then across the well-managed fields. No answer came to him.

Brother Edwen's gaze returned to the cross and he drank in all the details: in the centre a dark red stone glowed, and from that point all four spokes splayed outwards as sturdy arms; the circular domes of gold on them were evenly spaced and smooth to the touch. The scrolls encircling the domes flowed across the surface of the pendant. The decoration was simple, but every part of it was crafted to make this cross an object of beauty and to show that a craftsman of high-standing had created it for someone of great worth. This was indeed made to adorn the neck of a most godly monk. He turned it over: the back was plain, showing the slight indents where it had been hammered into shape.

Hanging from the monk's belt there was a pouch. He was allowed no money or personal possessions, but sometimes he had the need to carry a square of cloth, a jar of balm or a small tool. He tucked the cross into his pouch and walked to the fields. The next hour was spent with a hoe in his hand, removing weeds between the beans and peas. As he did so, Brother Edwen's troubled mind was soothed, and the rhythm of the task restored a sense of calm to his body. *I will pray to Saint Aidan and in time the answer will become clear to me,* the bemused monk thought. And from his lips the prayer flowed:

"Give me peace,
Empty my mind
Of the trivial.
Leave me alone
With the holy saints,
Let God's message come clear
And the truth be mine
So I am prepared,
For the next step
As shown by God, Amen."

Three days and nights passed and, in that time, the soft white clouds and blue skies were replaced by a sky of stony grey. Strong winds came from the east, whipping at tender young leaves on vulnerable crops. The sun, at best, was weak and doing nothing to encourage new growth or warm the limbs of those who worked and prayed in the minster. Brother Edwen welcomed the biting wind and grey skies; it suited him to suffer. He prayed constantly, letting nothing other than the pendant cross enter his mind, as he dwelt on what to do next. Several times, he stood at the door of the Abbess' chamber. But how could he confide in someone whose face he could not see, since it was so well hidden by her veil?

On the evening of the fourth day, it all became clear. It was as if the low-lying clouds had lifted, although in truth Lyminge still suffered from the dull sky and chill winds. But the cloud of indecision had been raised from Brother Edwen. Without seeking permission from the Abbess, he separated himself from the others after Vigils and, rather than return to his bed, the monk moved through the darkest shadows of the minster's buildings. He picked up a bag, containing food and a flagon of ale, from where he had stowed it under rough sacks in the tool shed. Reaching towards the tools, he took a short-handled trowel and left the shed. Then Brother Edwen walked across the fields of crops, knowing the tracks and the gaps in the hedgerows, although he had never travelled them by night. In time he left the minster's land and journeyed along a narrow lane, which rose upwards until he stepped out onto the open land through which the Roman road, named Stone Street, passed. He was now on the edge of an escarpment and could see nothing of the valley below; in the darkness it was nothing but a black pit. He turned left, knowing that by dawn he would stand on the edge of another steep hillside and this time he would be looking down on Romney Marsh.

The road became a deep cutting in the land and Brother Edwen took each step with care, slowly descending the hill. As the countryside opened again on either side, he saw nothing of the woods or fields; although the sky was gradually lightening to the east, they remained swathed in darkness. He passed no other travellers on the road and no villages. The monk thought of those many days when they had journeyed through Mercia and into Kent. Now alone, and without the leadership of Brother Halig, or the company of the other monks, this short walk to Romney Marsh seemed to lack the adventure he had sensed on his last journey there.

By the time his companions at Lyminge Minster were gathering for the office of Lauds, Brother Edwen was slumped on a grassy mound beside the edge of the Shipway track. Bleary-eyed and his body heavy, he found the view of Romney Marsh at dawn uninspiring. The land, in its various shades of dull green, continued without end. The sky was a blanket of grey and, when he looked behind him, the first rays of the sun's light were weak. The plaintive bleating of sheep and their lambs was muffled by the dampness in the air. There came another sound: the surge of an incoming wave, the sound of its froth playing at the edge of the beach, and finally the deep pull of the tide retreating. He recalled the boats he had previously seen in the sheltered harbour and the traders on the beach, but he knew it was not yet the time for them.

The monk snatched a few mouthfuls of his bread, broke off a chunk of cheese, and drank deeply from his flagon of weak ale. Then he descended the Shipway, taking each step carefully; the track was steep, with rivulets of water running down it, and loose stones scattered on the surface. Before he reached the bridge leading to the Sandtun, Brother Edwen followed the track along the base of the hills, then turned and stepped out across Romney Marsh, along causeways and plank bridges, until he neared the three bent willows and the grave of Abbot Botolph.

Chapter Twenty-Two

Eadlyn's sleep had been restless, her mind occupied with the golden cross. She felt certain it had some special significance and, in her dreams, its red stone radiated light, luring her towards it. Yet when she reached out, there was nothing. While she slept, Hlappa's words 'There is gold on the Sandtun' were repeated over and over. What did the old hag know of the gold? *If I could seek her out and ask her, then I would,* Eadlyn thought to herself in those first dream-like moments of waking. *But even if I knew where she was, then she would only talk in riddles. Besides, she is the mother of the man who killed my husband, so I cannot speak with her.* Most likely the old woman, cast out of Saltwood on the day her son was hanged, would be dead by now. Nearly a year had passed.

While the children still slept, Eadlyn moved out of her bed and wrapped a thick shawl around her shoulders. Barefoot, she pushed the door open and went outside. The sky was growing brighter to the east and she could make out the shapes of buildings gathered around the Nailbourne stream. Across the shallow valley, the small stone church stood dark and featureless. The air was damp and the wind brisk, as it had been for the last few days. She returned to the home and placed some wood on the fire, then blew and prodded it until the flames came to life. A pan of water already hung over the fire and Eadlyn added some sprigs of rosemary to brew.

In no time at all the children were out of bed and pulling on their clothes. "Can we help with the goats, Modor?" Clover asked.

"Of course," Eadlyn replied. The goats could not be moved from the indoor pen to their enclosure by the children alone. "We'll keep the two milkers here and take the others out. Then, Clover, you can sit with me and learn how to milk them."

Eadlyn was now starting work a little later and finishing earlier in the afternoon. She had been to see the thane and he had given her a strip of land to the north of the village. While she milked the goats morning and evening, as well as beginning to labour on the land, Eadlyn's day was filled with more work than ever. And although breaking up the soil in preparation for growing vegetables was equally hard on her hands, she was happy to be free of the animal skins and could look forward to growing some of their own food.

With the goats settled in their enclosure and a bowlful of porridge in her stomach, Eadlyn walked on the damp grass to the shed where she would strip the hair and fat off a cow's hide until she left for her midday meal. The door to the shed was closed, and she pulled on a metal bolt. It was covered in dew and left the sweet smell of iron on her skin; Eadlyn wiped her hands on the long grass at the side of the building. She had barely fixed the open door in place when a boy from the village appeared. Ragged, with no shoes on his feet and holes in his tunic, he said nothing but stood about as if waiting.

"Are you looking for someone?" Eadlyn asked.

"Aye, Cedric the leather-maker told me there was work for me."

"Work?" Eadlyn repeated. Perhaps he could sweep the floor and remove the pile of waste. It was not much but enough to earn his family a filling meal. "If you want Cedric, then he's in there." She pointed to the shed in which the leather was crafted.

At that moment Cedric appeared. Watching him approach, Eadlyn felt a ripple of fear dart through her body. There was something about the way he held his head and the intensity of his gaze, which made Eadlyn sense his defiance. There was trouble coming, and it seemed this boy had something to do with it.

"Ah, here you are," Cedric said, giving a nod of his head in the direction of the boy. Then he turned to Eadlyn, "You can show this boy how to scrape the fat off the skin. Mind he takes care and learns how to do it properly. And after your midday meal, you can both start on the hair."

"As you wish," Eadlyn replied.

"He'll pick it up in no time and you'll be free to tend to your crops and your goats," Cedric said.

"He is to help me every day?" Eadlyn queried.

"Nay, he'll be working alone by the end of the week. You can fend for yourself now or marry again if you please. This is a boy's job, as you've said yourself."

"But how are we to manage?" Eadlyn asked, her limbs stiffening and chest constricting.

"You'll do very well, I'm sure." Cedric dismissed her fears. "You'll have a sack of grain and a bag of beans every week for the care you give to our modor, and here..." He opened the pouch hanging from his belt and extracting a sceat, he said, "Take this as a token of my goodwill; you'll be needing tools or seeds if you are to have crops ready by the summer."

Eadlyn snatched at the coin and held it tight in her palm. "Very well," she said, trying to keep her voice steady. "But you can show him yourself if you want the hide cleaned." She walked away, her back straight and head held high.

Eadlyn had no wish to go home and tell her family that they must now manage without the support of Todd's brothers. Her bold decisions had led to her being cast from her work and, however lowly it was, it provided much of the food on their table. *I have proved myself unable to be both modor and faeder to the children,* Eadlyn told herself. *No man would leave his job with only four goats, some chickens and a strip of land which has not yet been prepared for seed. I have shown myself to be foolish. I must go to Fremund while my hair still shines, and my body is able to bear his children. He is not a bad man, and I found myself attracted to him, despite my misgivings. I will go now.* She looked down at the stained dress, now only worn while she worked on the leather, and put her hand to the tatty headscarf. *It hardly matters that I wear these clothes; the next time he sees me I will wear my good dress. Our passions will linger in his mind, and he will think of them when I tell him I will be his wife.* But before she had walked more than a dozen paces, Eadlyn's thoughts had changed: *It would be foolish to go in these rags, when I am about to go right past my home. I wouldn't walk to the bakehouse or the spring in this soiled dress, so I will not walk to Postling in it.*

With an abrupt turn, Eadlyn walked into her home. The children were still at the table finishing their porridge. Elder-Modor was chopping vegetables for the pottage, she turned with surprise and spoke, "Is everything well? Have you forgotten anything?"

"All is well, but Cedric has no need of me today."

"No need?" the old woman could not disguise the concern in her voice.

"Do not worry; he says we'll still have grain and beans." Eadlyn did her best to soothe the old woman. She slowed down and rather than snatch at her clothes in her desperation to be on the road from the village, Eadlyn took her time in getting dressed in her new tunic and she brushed her hair before placing the scarf over it. She secured the scarf with a pretty brooch, given to her by Todd after one of their visits to the Sandtun.

"Are you going somewhere?" Elder-Modor asked.

"Aye, I must go to Postling."

"Can I come?" Clover asked.

"But then who would bake the bread?" Eadlyn asked, placing a kiss on her daughter's head. "I'll take you next time, sweeting."

"Postling?" Elder-Modor repeated.

"Aye, Postling," Eadlyn confirmed, and she left without sharing her plan.

Once she had left her family, Eadlyn allowed herself to dwell on the conversation with Cedric. The words ran through her mind and she responded to him under her breath, letting the scene grow. Angry with herself and allowing no time to think any further before going to Fremund, her pace was brisk as she told herself over and over that she was unfit to care for the family alone. Soon Lyminge was behind her and she was heading south. The day was miserable, as had been promised by the grey dawn; it suited her mood very well.

The road to Postling came, for there was no great distance between the two villages, and Eadlyn's temper had not eased. It was narrow with open pasture running up to the hills. Where she had previously been hemmed in by the sunken lane and hedgerows, Eadlyn could now look across the fields to the steep hill on her right. There were lambs with their mothers and a farmer with his dog; watching the activity in the field finally relieved some of the tension in her body. Eadlyn slowed her pace and even paused to look at the small lambs gambolling about. A donkey with a cart passed her on the lane; she found a smile and friendly greeting came easily to her, and the smile flowed through the whole of her body.

Eadlyn began to think more of the small successes she had managed over the past weeks: the new dress, the repairs to the thatch, and the goats. She recalled how washing her hair had lifted her spirits and wondered how the sceat given by Cedric and her one remaining coin could best be used to help the family. She thought of her strip of land and the satisfaction she would feel when it was clear, and the seeds were sown.

To her left there was a small copse, and Eadlyn knew a wise woman lived in the heart of it. She looked towards the wooded area and the track running across the field in the direction of the trees. It seemed to beckon her, and she paused. Should she continue on the road to Postling and seal her future with Fremund, or perhaps she should seek the advice of this unknown woman? *I will go just a little way... and if she is there... and if she welcomes me, then it will do me no harm to speak with her,* Eadlyn told herself. She turned and walked along the track, which was no more than a slight hollow in the grassy field. Hazel, ash and oak trees, their leaves still young and green, stood in a cluster before her. As she approached, Eadlyn could see the outline of a small dwelling amongst them.

The cottage in the copse was no larger than a pen where goats or a pig might live. It was low, with the thatch roof almost touching the ground. Eadlyn felt if she were to stretch her arm out, she would be able to touch the ridge of the mossy roof. The fire was smouldering in a pit outside the home, and here the old sage sat on a bench beside the fire. She had a basket next to her and her small brown hands were working at some wool, pulling it into a usable yarn.

Although her hands were busy, the woman watched Eadlyn walk towards her and perhaps she sensed the young woman's heart beat in trepidation. She was swathed in a headscarf and shawl, but Eadlyn could see her features were small and neat, and her eyes a bright blue in the brown face. She also saw the wise woman was not as elderly as she had at first believed and there was kindness in her eyes.

"What brings you here to see me?" she asked. "I sense you are not lost and that you choose to be here."

"I hear you have wise words," Eadlyn said.

"Who says that?" the woman asked.

"The women of my village." Eadlyn waved her hand in the direction of Lyminge.

"I seem to know things," the woman agreed. Her voice was soft, tempting Eadlyn to draw closer. "You might not like what I know, but I'll tell you nonetheless."

"I've nothing to give you in return." Eadlyn paused, looked about the clearing in the copse, and continued, "I came without thinking... without a proper plan."

"You had a plan," the woman said. "But now you doubt it."

"Aye, that's true."

"And you'll pass by again and remember me, Mildrithe, and bring me a little something."

"I will," Eadlyn agreed.

Mildrithe gestured to a log serving as a second seat. She sat and studied Eadlyn for a moment and the young woman returned her stare, feeling at ease. After a moment, Eadlyn's gaze moved to the black beetle ambling along the dry earth, the spider climbing up the log and the delicate patterns the lichens made. She looked upwards at the grey sky and watched the blackbird settling on the slender branch of an ash tree. The air was still and rich with the scents of decaying leaves, rotting wood and smoke from the fire. The only sounds were those from the copse: the rustle of leaves, the crows on the highest branches and the shifting of a log on the fire.

"You've lost something, and you despair of finding it," Mildrithe said. "It was something precious. I sense it was gold. It was precious, yet you had no use for it."

"Aye, it was gold," Eadlyn agreed. "It was something special. I was keeping it safe. At least I thought it was safe..."

"I see you searching for it. On an earth floor, with reeds or straw?"

Eadlyn nodded, "Aye. But no more. I have lost hope."

"You are right to stop. The cross will come back into your hands. Do not search; it will travel far, and your time would be wasted. But there is something else," Mildrithe paused and frowned, as if trying to read Eadlyn's thoughts. "You have your own journey but yours is a journey of the heart. There is something

203

troubling you; I sense uncertainty. And I sense that you feel as if you have done wrong by your loved ones."

"I do feel that," Eadlyn agreed.

"You've done nothing wrong, but now there are two paths ahead of you." Mildrithe looked into the distance as if she saw those paths, and then continued, "You are lucky, for either path will bring happiness, but one will lead to a deeper contentment than the other. If you choose the way you believe to be more difficult then perchance you will struggle at times, but your hard work will bring success."

"Should I make my choice now?" Eadlyn asked. "I had made it and thought it was the right one."

"But you faltered."

"Aye, I was beginning to."

"Then wait. There is no need to rush." Mildrithe looked back to her wool and it seemed as if she was finished. Eadlyn stood up, a little uncertain. She took a few steps, and was about to give her thanks, when the wise woman spoke: "Wait. I see gold and in the centre something glows red. Not the red of a fire; this is a darker red with deep energies. When you see this red... I believe it to be a stone. When you see it the answer will come. The red stone will show your future."

"I thank you," Eadlyn said. "I know the red stone you speak of and I will wait as you say." She gave a nod and a small smile, but Mildrithe was now absorbed with the wool, teasing it into a thread. Eadlyn left the copse and retraced her steps back to the road.

Chapter Twenty-Three

Now he stood at the grave of Abbot Botolph, the most holy of men, so honoured by the monks from the monastery in Boston, Brother Edwen felt humbled. He was weak without the direction of Brother Halig. But God had led him to remain in Lyminge, and in time He had brought Brother Edwen to find the pendant cross. Saint Aiden had soothed his troubled mind and then encouraged this pilgrimage to the grave. Where the lone monk had felt comforted by the saints, he now felt unsure. *This is no good,* he scolded himself. *You have been led back to Romney Marsh and the cross has been returned so you may ease your conscience and allow it to rest with the Abbot.* With these words firmly in his mind, Brother Edwen, closed his eyes and envisaged a golden light casting a warm glow over his body, empowering him, and bringing comfort.

Then he knelt on the damp grass and began to dig with his trowel. He had no intention of uncovering the body. He would merely make a deep hole and place the golden cross in it. It would lie forever close to the body of Abbot Botolph, where it was intended to be. The rhythm of the digging was therapeutic. The ground, not yet hardened by the summer sun, yielded as he eased the trowel through it. He felt sheltered by the willows, and the sheep grazing nearby were of no concern to him.

Once the hole was as deep as Brother Edwen's forearm, the soil began to fall back on itself, and it was necessary to widen it to dig deeper. A little further and the monk was satisfied. "It will lie close enough," he said to himself. He opened his leather pouch and took out the cross, moving it to and fro, so the weak light of the sun was caught in the red stone, revealing its true colour. Then he placed it on the ground, safe on a piece of embroidered cloth.

For no good reason, Brother Edwen decided to take a moment to tidy the hole he had made. He removed loose soil on the tip of his trowel and smoothed the sides. The trowel caught on a piece of rag and he pulled at it, causing it to rip. Frowning, Brother Edwen, looked down and saw a human limb. He had not meant… not meant to disturb the Abbot. His throat tightened. He had done wrong. Very wrong. What to do now? All confidence in his task was gone.

Then other thoughts came flooding through his mind: this was not the shroud the holy man had been buried in; that was of high quality – a thick pale wool. The rag he pulled upon was coarse and dark. And the arm, or perhaps leg, was still covered in dark hair, where Abbott Botolph had been old and his hair white. Brother Edwen had been misguided and he knew this now. Hurriedly he leaned down, grabbed at the pendant cross, and flung it in the direction of the hole. He pushed at the loose soil and half-filled the hole then stood, grabbed his cloth bag and ran from the grave under the willows.

The desperate monk knew that by returning to Lyminge his absence would be questioned, but he could think of nothing except the peace within the stone walls of the church and soft murmur of the whispered words when the monks and nuns read in the courtyard. The lines of seedlings in the fields beckoned him, and the warmth of an egg fresh out of a nest. Sweat poured off him as he took the steep Shipway at a fast pace and kept walking without pausing for mile after mile. When he did stop, it was to drink the last of his ale and to wipe his brow before continuing.

As he entered the minster's grounds, those holy men and women were gathering for their midday meal. *Can I slip amongst them?* the desperate man thought. Will they notice my soiled tunic? *Have they noticed my absence?* How he longed to be one of them, without the terrible secret of Abbot Botolph held in his heart. He slowed his pace, threw his bag into a low hedgerow, and joined the queue forming to enter the refectory. But minutes later, just as his taste buds were watering at the smell of strong cheese and his hand was reaching for the bread, a young monk walked up behind him and said: "The Abbess wishes to see you in her chambers."

"We cannot allow a man as holy as this to lie in a land which is almost heathen," the Abbess declared and, although her features were clouded by her veil, Brother Edwen knew she could no longer calm the emotions previously held deep within her. "Romney Marsh – they say it is a godless place – where mists rise from the land to form spirits that prey on the innocent." Her voice now had a touch of hysteria about it; Brother Edwen took a step back.

"It is where he lies safe."

"He is not safe," she almost snapped, although it hardly seemed possible for this gentle Abbess to speak in such a way.

207

"Not safe? There are only four of us who know of his grave and so it is safe from desecration."

"No soul is safe, buried alone without proper ceremony," the Abbess continued, her voice still high, although now seeming a little calmer. "He, who should be secure of a place in heaven, will be lost forever until buried as is his right."

"It was his wish to have his body left intact. Not to be moved about from place to place – a limb here, his heart there. It was Abbot Botolph's wish to be buried in peace," Brother Edwen stated.

"He knew nothing of what he was saying," the Abbess declared. "His wish would be to do good to others. He would want the pilgrims to visit his shrine and to give silver to the holy places they visited. We have no such male of great worth here at Lyminge and will welcome him to lie near Queen Ethelburga."

"Welcome him?" Brother Edwen repeated, hardly daring to understand her words.

"Indeed, and when he is buried to the north of our altar... to the right of God, you, Brother Edwen, will rise to a more revered position. It will not be forgotten who brought good fortune to Lyminge."

"Of course," he said, while a chill ran up from the stone slabs beneath his feet and throughout his body.

"Now go and tell those good men in the kitchen to feed you, then seek solace in the peace of the oratory," the Abbess ordered. "And after Vespers you will return here and tell me exactly where the body of Abbot Botolph lies. No one should venture on Romney Marsh without guidance from someone who knows the land."

Brother Edwen merely nodded his agreement and left the Abbess' chambers.

Chapter Twenty-Four

With his hunger satisfied, Brother Edwen stood in the courtyard of Lyminge Minster. He had been happy with his life there. The presence of God and the saints nurtured him both within the walls of the church, the chapter house and all the other buildings in which life was orderly and peaceful. He enjoyed the gentle rhythm of tilling the earth, planting the seeds and watching new life emerge, and all this sheltered by the folds of the Kentish hills. If he were to end his years here in silent contemplation, able to watch life in the village from the vantage point of the minster set on a spur of high ground, then he would be content. But that was not to be. Now the Abbess was demanding more than he could give to her or to the minster. The resting place of Abbot Botolph would never be disclosed by him and so he must leave or face whatever punishment she would decree. *Perchance I will spend the rest of my life in her cell,* Brother Edwen thought, as he gazed towards a small building set not far from the outhouses which covered stinking pits of bodily excrement.

Having reached for his bag, previously abandoned in the hedgerow, Brother Edwen walked in the direction of the storerooms and work-sheds. Here he refilled his flagon with weak ale and had to be satisfied with that. There was no means of taking food during the day, although he had hidden some bread and cheese in the folds of his tunic while eating his meal. *I will have to eat whatever God provides in the hedgerows,* the monk thought, recalling the long walk to Kent with the body of Abbot Botolph.

In the tool store, Brother Edwen took a hoe. *The Abbess will not recognise me in the fields*, he reasoned. *One monk looks very like another and if I work my way along the beans, then as I reach the end of the row, I will slip away.* And with his plan in place, the monk walked to the field where he often laboured and went through the motions of his afternoon's work, all the time moving further from the minster's buildings.

For some reason he could not fathom, the flat landscape of Romney Marsh still beckoned Brother Edwen. He had no other place in mind where he should go. Word would pass between Lyminge and the hallowed walls of Canterbury, Minster-in-Thanet, Folkestone and Dover; no doubt the godly Abbess would seek him out if he were to find a home in one of those places. He had no desire to travel north and explain himself in his home monastery. And so his legs took him back along Stone Street, and by the time the prayers of None were being offered in Lyminge, and throughout the land, Brother Edwen was once again viewing Romney Marsh from the elevated position of the Shipway Crossroads.

When he had last looked across the marsh, just earlier that morning, it had all been grey: the sky, the sea and even the land. Now the blanket of cloud had begun to break up and the sun was shining through as it lowered itself in the sky. The land was changed to all shades of green, from the dark swathes of reeds to the soft green of the willow trees and the bright fresh spring grass. The water in the dykes glistened and in places they took the blue from the sky. It was as if the land were being hurried along, for the clouds raced and cast their shadows, making the colours on the land ever-changing. Caught up with the thrill of it, gulls soared and dived; Brother Edwen envied their freedom but gathered his cloak close around him, feeling ill at ease with their mocking cackles.

"I am free to venture across this land!" he said aloud, doing his utmost to feel defiant, as if saying those words would make it be. But even as he spoke, he was unsure he wanted to be free of the Benedictine ways. "I can travel a little, see this part of the world and settle in another place where news of Abbot Botolph has not yet reached," Brother Edwen reasoned. "If there is a path across this land then in time it will lead me to a place where I can once again serve the Lord."

And so, Brother Edwen, a man from a noble family, who had been pledged to God at an early age, set off down the steep Shipway track. He reached the wide sea inlet at the bottom of the track, but rather than walk through the band of trees fringing the marsh, Brother Edwen stepped on the wide plank bridge leading to the Sandtun. Pausing for a moment, he marvelled at the force of the tide surging inwards, watching it press against trees growing out of the bank, and push at reeds and rushes. Then he moved off the bridge, and took the sandy path running along the top of the beach.

There were two men on the beach, both standing to survey a series of poles which were standing proud while the sea plunged forwards. At their sides were small handcarts, awaiting the catch of fish the men hoped to have snared within the unseen net. They were the only humans in sight; the monk had seen no farmers or labourers as he descended the Shipway. The area of exposed land between the sea and the marsh was empty of any signs that people ever lived and worked there for a few days a year. It was littered with debris from the sea, a sign that during the winter months it was sometimes overcome by the tide, and a thin layer of sand raced along the top of it, riding on the wind. There was a definite track between Sandtun and beach, and Brother Edwen knew that it would turn to eventually meet up with the three willows and the grave of Abbot Botolph. But that was not his destination and he wondered if a junction in the path would offer another route, taking him to a previously unknown place. Would it supply the monk with the chance to explore Romney Marsh and assuage his curiosity about the place?

It would do no harm to approach the fishermen; they were already watching his progress. "Good afternoon, friends," Brother Edwen began, aware of his inexperience when it came to speaking with people who came from a world outside a minster or monastery. "I am hoping to cross Romney Marsh, does this path lead to..." He paused to consider where he may want it to go, as his true desire was to explore the area. "...Does this path lead across the marsh and into Sussex."

"To Sussex?" one of the men repeated, his face showing confusion.

Brother Edwen saw then that these were simple folk who travelled no further than from their village on top of the hill, to the Sandtun and beach. He had been too ambitious to put thoughts of Sussex in their minds. For one who had travelled across Middle England, to think of walking to Sussex was nothing, if only the

Romney Marsh would allow such a thing. "Or to any other place? A village perchance?"

"Oh aye," the men chorused.

"It goes this way and that, but it will take you to Romney and if you were to take a boat, then on to Lydd."

"Or you can follow the line of hills away from the coast," the second man suggested. "It would make an easier path."

"If you go by the marsh, it's no easy walk. You'll see no folk for hours or days, and if the mists come down, you'll have no way of knowing which direction you're going in."

"I'll take my chances," Brother Edwen said, with a bravado he did not feel.

"Aye, you do that," the first man agreed. "But wait awhile and get some fish in your belly. We'll light a fire, and you can cook them on hot rocks."

"I thank you," Brother Edwen replied. "But I have nothing to give you in return."

"You do," the fisherman told him, "My friend here, his daughter is sickly and his son too. You're a man of God, will you pray for them?"

"I will," Brother Edwen said, feeling grateful that he had something to offer. "Morning, noon and night, I will pray for your children, and you too."

Chapter Twenty-Five

Sitting at the bench in front of her house, with a bowl of turnips and carrots beside her, Eadlyn could see the people begin to gather on the patches of open land around the Nailbourne stream. She pushed the bowl aside and called out to Elder-Modor: "I'm going into the village; there's time to finish the vegetables later." And, having gathered the folds of her good dress, so it was free from her ankles, Eadlyn walked briskly down the earth track, her eyes darting about, taking in everything. In her hand she carried a small wicker basket with just five small brown eggs in it.

Twice a week, the centre of Lyminge became a market. Farmers brought carts of their produce along the lanes from all directions, and the village became the colourful heart of the valley. Neighbours from Etchinghill, Postling and Ottinge would come, and news flew about from one person to another. Not only the stories of people in the local villages, but there was always a report of life in some place further afield. It was true that the thane and his family were able to travel to Canterbury and Dover several times a year, but not the churls or the slaves. These people, who worked for themselves or slaved for the thane, stayed in this village, rarely travelling further than they could walk in a morning.

Amongst the high spirits, which came with the bartering for goods and the exchange of news, there was a more subdued presence in the form of the monks and nuns from the minster. Living side-by-side with the villagers from Lyminge, these holy people were less well known than those who came from across the fields or along the lanes. The nuns were isolated by the veil they wore to hide their features. These holy women came in pairs, bringing eggs, honey and soothing balms to the market, but if a villager were to pass the same nun in the grounds of the minster, they would not know if it were the one who had whispered a few words as a pot of honeycomb was passed from one hand to another.

The monks had no veils, and although their hoods fell low over their foreheads, they could be recognised by their features. A villager might pass by a monk in the churchyard or minster and think: "I saw him selling ale at the market last week." There would be no flicker of recognition, and no greeting exchanged, but the monk was known.

Eadlyn, who had been kept from the market for eleven long months as she laboured on the animal skins, felt her spirits soar to be a part of it again. Only five days after losing her job to the boy from the village, she had nothing but a few eggs to barter, but to be able to walk amongst those in the market was pleasure enough.

The thane's wife mingled with the people. Eadlyn admired the beauty of her dress which hung in soft folds of dark green, showing it to be made of a good quality wool. She longed to reach out and touch the intricate pattern of swirls on the embroidered band at the hem and cuffs. Her scarf was pinned in place by a circular gold brooch, inlaid with coloured stones, and at her waist a pomander swung from her belt. Eadlyn felt compelled to linger by this woman who was said to be a distant cousin to the King of Kent, and so related in some way to Queen Ethelburga, whose story deeply fascinated the whole family. If she were to get close enough, perhaps Eadlyn would breathe in the scent from the pomander, or be able to describe the pattern and colour of the brooch to Elder-Modor, who was resting at home and would love to hear of these details.

As Eadlyn moved amongst the people, she became aware of a hush falling upon the marketplace; both the villagers and visitors looked towards the church on the hillside. Two nuns were walking down the track, each with a basket in their arms. Eadlyn frowned, not understanding why this caused so much interest to those who were used to living beside the minster. Then she saw the light catch the pectoral cross hanging at the neck of the nun and noticed the gold band she wore on her finger. This was the Abbess herself, leaving the minster to mix with the people at the market. She was a tall woman, with a straight back and slender figure. No one could be sure of her colouring; her hair and face were partially concealed by her veil, but as she stepped amongst the people, they saw her hands on the basket were pale. And so, they knew the Abbess to be fair of skin, and it was rumoured that a wisp of hair hanging loose between her scarf and veil was pale gold in colour.

Curious to know what was in the Abbess' basket, Eadlyn moved away from the thane's wife in her fine dress, to the holy woman in her habit of natural wool. The Abbess was speaking to the women around her, seeming to want to engage with them. *How strange it is that not only has she left the minster, but she has something to ask or to share with us; I have never known her do this.* As these thoughts ran through

Eadlyn's mind, she sidled closer until she could see the delicate hands wrapped around the handle of a basket and within that basket there were small pots of herbs or balm, each one covered with a scrap of cloth and secured with twine.

"One of our monks is missing," the Abbess was saying; her voice was soft, yet it reached the ears of those who were keen to understand the reason for her being there. "He left the minster not long after noon yesterday, and we are worried for him."

"A monk is lost."

"She is here asking about one of the brothers."

"Have you seen a monk on the road? The Abbess is looking for him."

Her concerns were repeated, yet no one came forward to say they had seen a monk on any of the roads leading out of Lyminge.

"Do you know in which direction he was travelling?"

"Was he a young monk?"

"Is he dark or fair?"

The people in the marketplace were curious. They could not ask – they dared not ask – why he would leave the minster. But they could question and form their own opinions as to the reason for his absence.

"I do not know in which direction he left," the Abbess replied. "I come here to ask if he was seen in the village, or in the distance as you worked on the fields or tended your animals. He is a young man, tall and strong, with thick brown hair and pale skin."

She moved, or some said drifted, so elegant was her manner, throughout the marketplace, offering her small jars of soothing balms and herbal teas. The women flocked to her, curious and perhaps hoping that to be near to this good woman would bring them

217

closer to the Lord in Heaven and the saints. But no one had seen the monk, who in time they learned was called Brother Edwen.

"Pass the word," the Abbess whispered. "If anyone recalls seeing him, then please come to me at the minster. I pray he is safe and welcome any news of him."

The people agreed they would: in fact, they were eager to be a part of helping her. After a while, it seemed as if she were satisfied that her word had been spread and the Abbess left the marketplace to return to her minster on the hill.

Eadlyn stood and straightened her back. She leaned on her fork and looked along the strip of land she had been working on for the past few days. The blanket of grey cloud had finally been blown away and at last the sun was warming both her skin and the soil. Eadlyn's spirits were rising by the day and, if her hands were stained brown from working on the soil, at least the scent of chicken droppings had faded. She still massaged the soft balm into her skin and for short times during the day her hands smelt of the herbs scenting it. The children had been enjoying working alongside her, pulling their own small barrow and picking up loose flints which would hinder the growth of new seeds. And so, another means of making a trade was born – the barrows of flint could be exchanged for labour with a local builder.

It was mid-afternoon, and the children had gone to collect water at the spring, when Eadlyn saw Fremund walking towards her. Her cheeks became hot at the memory of their last encounter, now more than two weeks before. But she raised her hand in greeting and looked down at her soiled dress and apron in dismay.

She didn't realise the beauty that came from the pleasure she felt in working on the land. Her eyes now shone, her cheeks were no longer gaunt, and where her scarf had come loose, her golden hair shone with the sun's rays upon it. Her dress clung to her moist skin on her back and between her breasts. Even with smudges of earth on her cheekbones. Fremund had never seen her looking so pleasing.

"I thought I should leave you alone for a while," he said.

She looked at the ground, remembering their last meeting. "Aye, I needed time to think."

"You've been working hard, but why are you not with the animal skins?" Fremund asked. "I went there first and saw a young lad. He would say nothing about where I could find you. But then I found young Cym and he told me you'd be here."

"Cedric had no need for me anymore," Eadlyn told him. "He saw I'd bought some goats, and we had the chickens too. He decided I was able to manage for myself." She looked along the strip of land and grinned, "And perchance I will feed the family myself."

"Don't try so hard that you have no need for me," he pleaded.

"Oh Fremund, I still think of Todd as you must of Brona, I'm sure you do," she replied. "But you need a wife in your bed and a child in your home, I know that."

"And you...you need a husband in your life."

"I'm not sure of that," she said. "In time I will, but not yet."

"I'll come and see you every now and then, and if you need anything then you know I'll help the best I can." Fremund smiled down at her, his expression gentle. "And if I'm lonely then mayhap I can join you all for a share of your pottage sometimes."

219

"Of course, you may, Cousin," Eadlyn reminded him of the family connection: he needn't come as a lover to her home. "But for now, I have my own path to follow." She thought of Mildrithe and the two routes open to her.

"Perchance our paths will meet one day?"

"Perchance there is another young woman who will charm you?" Eadlyn retorted.

He ignored her comment and countered, "You called me cousin and if I can't be your husband, then cousin I will be. It's no distance to Postling if you need anything."

Eadlyn knew how close she had been to going to him in Postling and blushed to think of what might have happened had she gone. To think of his caresses still made her restless. Desires had been awakened and she wondered how long it would be before she could satisfy them. She turned away, knowing he had seen her blush and that it gave him hope.

Now looking towards the village, Eadlyn let out a cry, "Oh no, not the goats!"

"The goats?" Fremund echoed.

"Aye, do you see Clover? She's chasing one and it's heading for the village." Holding up her tunic so it was free of her shoes, Eadlyn ran ahead of Fremund, away from her strip of land and across the field.

Fremund was soon beside her and they left the field together, he matching his strides to hers. "You'll need rope to hold it with," he said. "Let me go to Clover while you fetch some."

"Aye, I will," Eadlyn replied, her words coming out in a short burst. "And I'll check the fence."

They separated, Eadlyn running to the left, skirting the edge of the settlement, and Fremund going straight down the slope towards the Nailbourne, thane's hall and the village centre. For Eadlyn, the grass was long and ground uneven, causing her to stumble on loose flints and tufts. She was forced to slow down, and passed the leather-making sheds, then the homes of Todd's brothers, at a brisk walk. Turning to the back of her own home, Eadlyn was relieved to see the three remaining goats were still in their enclosure. Elder-Modor was battling to close the gate while the young goat pressed up against the gap, eager to be placing her lips on new grass and to seek out other delights. As the old woman turned, the goat took her chance and pushed through. Eadlyn lunged at it, grabbing the goat by her collar but falling heavily on the ground.

"It's all my fault," Elder-Modor cried out. "I said to Clover we could take them in for milking."

"You were trying to help," Eadlyn replied, still sitting awkwardly on the ground, with a hand on the goat's collar and another firmly holding a horn. She eased herself up, feeling where the bruises would begin to show very soon. Leaning over the sturdy little goat, Eadlyn ushered her through the small doorway leading into the pen within the home. "She can wait here until I have time to milk her."

"Poor Clover, how's she going to catch the goat?"

"Fremund will help her." Even as she said the words, Eadlyn knew she was giving Elder-Modor fresh hope.

"Fremund?" the old woman enquired. "I knew he'd be here sooner or later. I thought it would be sooner."

"He has his own home and his metal-work to keep him busy," Eadlyn responded.

"What will he be thinking when he sees these goats and you labouring on the land?"

"He'll be glad I'm not working on the animal skins," Eadlyn retorted. "And Fremund has seen the land, as Cym told him where to find me. Now I must fetch the rope so we can lead the goat back."

Within minutes Eadlyn was running towards the village; she grinned with satisfaction to see Fremund wrestling with the wayward goat. As she watched, he scooped it up in both arms and, with Clover running alongside him, he began to walk towards her.

When she reached them, Eadlyn tied the rope onto the goat's collar and it walked, now subdued, back to the home.

"Elder-Modor let her out," Clover said. Her face was flushed and brow glistening.

"I know." Eadlyn smiled down at her. "She's very sorry."

"But then I saw Fremund was running towards us," Clover elaborated. "I'd nearly caught her myself. I would have done it on my own."

"Your hand was on her collar. I really did nothing at all," Fremund joined in. "I probably just got in the way!"

"I'm sure you didn't," Eadlyn turned and grinned at him. They were almost back with Elder-Modor now and waved a greeting. She knew how encouraged Todd's mother would be to see Fremund helping and how well he fitted into their small family. Eadlyn had to admit, if only to herself, that it was fun when he visited. *But if he were to be my husband then would we move to Postling, or would he return to Lyminge, the place of his birth?* Eadlyn pondered over this as they reached Elder-Modor and Clover again told of how she had almost caught the goat.

Safe in the pen, and ready to be milked later in the afternoon, the goat was soon chewing on hay. With the animals secure, Eadlyn recalled her earlier fall and could feel the bruises forming on her thigh. She moved the wattle fence separating the home from the goats' pen and walked through to fetch a pot of cream. Lifting her dress, she smoothed a little on her skin, liking the cool sensation.

Back outside again, Eadlyn saw Clover was returning to the village and Fremund was speaking with Elder-Modor. "Perhaps there is some pottage to share if I were to stay a while?" he suggested.

"There's always pottage for you, Fremund," Elder-Modor was saying. "We can add more to the pot."

"Elder-Modor, I have tools left out in the field and more work to do before the day ends," Eadlyn protested. "Of course, you are welcome, Cousin, but there is work to be done first."

"I'll help you with both," he announced. "As long as I'm fed!"

Working side by side, Fremund and Eadlyn moved along her strip of land, digging the earth and breaking up the clods. It had not been used since the summer before and grass and weeds had soon set down their roots. There was an ever-growing pile of chickens' and goats' droppings at one end, and Eadlyn planned to dig them into the soil within the next day or two. They worked at a good pace and if Eadlyn sensed Fremund's gaze on her, when he should have been labouring, then she just smiled and continued. They reached the end of her land and Eadlyn turned to Fremund, her face glowing with satisfaction.

"You've saved me a day's work," she said. "Now the seeds shall be planted sooner."

"And the food in your bellies a day earlier!" he replied. Fremund's face had reddened as he laboured, and he wiped his brow with the sleeve of his tunic. He stepped towards her, "Would you offer a kiss for all my hard work?"

She glanced around and found the field to be empty. Reaching upwards, Eadlyn gave him a swift kiss, her lips barely grazing his. "Now let's wash this dirt off and see if Elder-Modor has the pottage warmed through."

"That wasn't a kiss." Fremund put the tips of his fingers under her chin and lifted her face to his. Bending down, he pressed his lips on hers.

Eadlyn allowed herself a few seconds of pleasure before pulling away and stepping back. Then scowling up at him, with her heart racing and her lips yearning for more, she snapped at him: "This isn't what I wanted. Let us go and eat before she sends the children to fetch us." And, having grabbed at her fork, Eadlyn strode off, stepping over the freshly turned earth and exposed flints as best she could.

Chapter Twenty-Six

A raised area of land beckoned the wandering monk. He had walked for many hours with no destination in mind, just trusting the meandering tracks would lead him to a place where he could feel happy to settle for the night. As he walked, Brother Edwen had taken his time to pause and reflect on the landscape. The dragonfly hovering above the reeds and the delicate flies balancing on the still waters in the ditches all held his attention. The breeze was gentle, the air warm and sometimes, if he stood very still and listened, the monk could hear the distant roar of the ocean on the shingle bank. He had seen no other man since he had bidden farewell to those good fishermen and settled for the night in a pit he had hollowed out of the sandy soil. This place, Romney Marsh, was more peaceful than any monastery he had known. He could look up at the vast sky or across the flat lands to the shingle ridge and feel closer to the Lord than ever before. The hills were there, although now less defined, and they gave him a sense of place; without them he knew he would be in danger of walking without having any idea of the distance he had travelled, or where he was in relation to the Sandtun or Lyminge on the hills.

The sun had passed its peak and the monk's direction had turned, so now he had his back to the sea, whereas before it had been to his left. A spur of dry land, darting into the water-logged marsh, seemed to end with a rise, and a huddle of stunted trees. Brother Edwen was compelled to follow it, but he still walked at a slow pace, not feeling any need to hurry. He had set out to learn about Romney Marsh and had no plan to rush. The monk had not forgotten his promise to pray for the fisherman's sick children and he did this in earnest, whether looking out across the waterways or closing his eyes and listening to the gentle whisper of the reeds.

Having seen no sign of farming, or man making use of the land, since leaving the Sandtun, Brother Edwen's curiosity was aroused as he neared the rise. Squares had been formed by the digging of mud to form low walls, not on the dry ground, but on the marsh running up to it. "Salt pans," the monk murmured. And as he said the words, he noted a trickle of water filling them. He was now some way from the sea or the tidal lagoon, but the saltwater was finding a path through the marsh and would leave its deposits for man to gather.

There was no sign of human habitation. The monk walked a few paces to the highest point on the spur of land. It was topped with half a dozen gnarled trees; their bodies and branches were twisted, and, amongst the small dark green leaves and tiny white blossoms, the branches displayed vicious spikes. Kneeling on the ground, Brother Edwen could see between the trunks; the ground was dry and littered with the dusty leaves of last autumn. If he were to crawl in there later, it would make a dry shelter in which he could sleep when dusk fell. He placed his sack amongst the trees and continued to explore the area.

Beyond the trees, the land fell away until it reached the marsh. A causeway snaked its way into the distance, perhaps linking this area with another rise or perhaps leading all the way to the distant hills. Salt pans butted up against the causeway, joining with those he had already seen. On an area of bare soil, there was a pit and some charred remains of wood. The monk ran his fingers through the burned wood; it was cold but still dry. "People have been here recently," he said to himself. And as he did so, Brother Edwen scanned the trackway, as if expecting to see a sign that the men of the salt pans were returning. There was no one. It was as if he were the only person on Romney Marsh and that thought filled him with wonder, not fear.

Those fishermen on the Sandtun had questioned the monk about how he would feed himself while roaming the marsh. Brother Edwen recalled gazing to the heavens and telling them that God would keep him safe and nourished. The fishermen had pondered upon this; they were in awe of the monk's faith but saw no harm in furnishing him with a straight stick. One of them had swiftly shaped the end to a point and, as he handed the stick to the bemused monk, he had said, "You can use this for catching eels; there's plenty of them slipping through the waters."

Now Brother Edwen eyed the water-filled ditches and thought of the stick he had left with his bag amongst the twisted trees. He returned to his meagre belongings and picked it up, then returned to the salt pans. Where was best to place himself? He scanned the area beyond the pans, but it was too marshy and the water too shallow, although he believed that eels would happily slither along in very little water and would slip their way into the soft mud if needed. The causeway appeared to have been made, or at least improved on, by humans. Its banks were both firm and steep, and the tough stems of the reeds gave his shoes something to grip on. A narrow waterway flowed alongside the raised path, before turning towards the sea, and Brother Edwen decided it seemed to be both a practical and pleasant spot to sit in the hope of catching an eel. The last of his bread and cheese had been eaten at noon, and the marsh had little to offer to satisfy his hunger.

As he slid his foot down the bank and prepared to settle in wait for an eel, Brother Edwen remembered the kindness shown by the fishermen. He had prayed for the children, as promised, but was struck by a fervour to do more for them. This place with its bridge of land leading to the east, had raised itself from the marsh and so it deserved some recognition. What tenacity this spur had shown, and people from the higher land clearly appreciated and used it to gather their precious salt.

"The Lord must be thanked for this place." The words erupted as a joyous, yet desperate, cry. He raced back to the clump of trees, and searched through them, before wrenching a strong branch away from the others, using both his strength and the knife he wore hanging from his belt. The monk then set about cutting off all the spikes and smaller branches. Satisfied with his work, he repeated the process with a shorter branch. Then, with the branches in his hands, he ran back to one of the waterways and gathered the longest of the bannered leaves sprouting from the reeds. Brother Edwen wound the leaves around the branches until he was satisfied with the cross he had created. "This wood is strong," he said, somehow knowing that it must be to thrive on this land which was open to the gales from the sea.

The monk then scanned the area, looking for the highest point, free from the trees and with the best view of the surrounding land. He studied the way the trees bent from the wind and chose a place where they would shelter his cross, then pushed it into the ground. As he did so, Brother Edwen was filled with a sense of elation. This was no stone church or minster, but he had placed it on this barren land, and here he would pray for those fishermen and their families, if only for a day or two before he continued on his journey.

Chapter Twenty-Seven

"Sister," Eadlyn stood beside Janna as she kneaded the bread. How thankful she was to be able to do these jobs again, to be free of the leather-making. "I saw the wise woman of the copse a few days ago."

"What took you there?" Janna asked. She turned towards Eadlyn, although her hands never faltered in their kneading of the dough.

"I was going to Postling, but suddenly I was not so sure of what was best to do."

"And did she welcome you to her place in the copse? Were you fearful of her?" Janna whispered.

"When I saw her, I was not fearful," Eadlyn replied. "She was gentle and..." She faltered, not quite sure what the woman was, only knowing that she felt at ease with her.

"And was she wise?"

"Aye, I think she was. I need to return. I want to take her some eggs and milk. I wondered if you would like to come... perchance she has a potion for you?"

"For me?" There was no need for Janna to ask the reason why she would need such a thing. She was consumed with her need for a child. She pressed the dough into a soft round and marked a deep cross on the top. "Aye, I'll come with you when we've eaten our midday meal and as we walk you can tell me what reason you have to seek the wisdom of this woman."

It was not long before the sisters met again, this time at one of the bridges crossing the Nailbourne. They each carried a basket with a small gift for Mildrithe and left without speaking of their intent to anyone else. They talked of mundane matters until they were free of the settlement and the ears of the villagers, which were ever open to a piece of news. The sun was bright, clouds high, and if the wind was a little brisk, then it carried them along the sunken lane. The trees, now fully in leaf, huddled close, their branches forming a tunnel through which the young women passed. Then the scene changed again as the trees thinned and there were views of pastureland. By the time they had reached the turning to Postling, Eadlyn's confusion over her feelings for Fremund had been thoroughly explored by the sisters.

"I thought you had a distaste for Todd's cousin," Janna said. "But I have seen how he appears to care for you."

"Aye, I found him to be a little care-free. To make too much of a joke about everything," Eadlyn admitted. "But now he shows a protective nature."

"He has a fine figure..."

Eadlyn coloured. "Aye, he does."

"I trust you to do what is for the best, sister. If the wise woman says to wait, then I believe she is right. But he is a lusty man, I am sure of it, and if you wait too long, he will have another woman in his bed."

Thinking of their kisses and his persuasive hands on her body, Eadlyn replied, "I'll decide before the summer has passed."

"I wonder if he'll wait that long," Janna mused.

The copse came into view and, as they neared it, Eadlyn pointed to the track running through the grass, leading to the trees. They stopped talking, both a little in awe of Mildrithe, the wise woman, and wanting to show respect to her home surrounded by nature. On reaching the edge of the trees, Janna faltered and Eadlyn took the lead, pressing her way through the branches and entering the copse. As their eyes adjusted to the dim light, Mildrithe's humble shack took shape and they saw she was standing before it, plucking feathers from a bird.

"You brought your sister with you," Mildrithe said, as they neared her. "She has a look of you, despite her hair being darker."

"I hope you don't mind," Eadlyn said, placing her hand in the crook of her sister's arm. "This is Janna."

Mildrithe nodded her head slowly, as if to show her approval. "She has a need to be here and I welcome her."

"I thank you," Janna murmured.

"I brought you some eggs," Eadlyn said. Showing four brown eggs nestled in hay at the bottom of her basket. "We collected them this morning."

"You have so little and you thought to share with me." Mildrithe gave a slow smile.

"May we sit?" Eadlyn looked towards the fallen log serving as a seat.

"Of course," Mildrithe replied. She returned her attention to the bird, holding it down with one hand and plucking with the other.

Eadlyn and Janna sat watching the wise woman, understanding she would speak when ready. In the copse, the air was warm, scented with damp earth, the smoke from the fire and a hint of fresh leaves. The breeze they had felt earlier was now cushioned by the trees, but up high in the canopy leaves danced, while in the sky above birds wheeled and swooped.

"You are more at peace," Mildrithe stated looking at Eadlyn. "You are waiting for your path to become clear.

"Aye, I'll wait," Eadlyn agreed.

"But Janna, you are waiting too, and your wait is a different one. You have been patient."

"It's been two years," Janna responded.

"And still your husband's seed does not grow in you." Mildrithe had moved away from the dead bird now. She was seated on her bench and leaning forward; all her attention was on the sisters.

"All around me babies are being born," Janna said, her voice almost a whisper.

"You will be a good mother; you are gentle and able to guide the young ones," Mildrithe told her. "I see you with a small boy. But he is the child of your sister here."

"Aye, and my heart is warmed to be with him."

Mildrithe stood, and they saw that although she was not old, her back was badly bent. She said nothing but turned and walked into her tiny home, ducking as she went through the doorway. Janna looked at Eadlyn; her teeth bit gently on her lower lip and there was hope in her eyes. Eadlyn reached out and put her hand on Janna's arm. Mildrithe wasn't gone long and on her return, there was a small clay pot in her hand. She sat on the bench, cradling the pot in both hands. Her lips moved, although nothing but a whisper came from them, and that so faint her words could not be heard.

Several minutes passed and Mildrithe stood, then beckoned Janna to come towards her. Janna walked those few paces on her own and stood before the wise woman. "Brew these leaves in hot water three times a day," Mildrithe told her. "Just a pinch of them between

233

your fingers and by the time the leaves turn golden on these trees, you'll feel the flutter of new life within you."

"I thank you," Janna whispered. She took the pot and raised it to her lips. "You have given me hope." She returned to Eadlyn and took a bag of beans from her basket, which she offered to Mildrithe who took them and bowed her thanks.

"It's been a week since we spoke," Mildrithe now turned her attention to Eadlyn. "It will take time for your paths to reveal themselves."

"I'm happy to wait," Eadlyn said.

"People will offer you opportunities and you will take them, but not forgetting your true path awaits you."

"I won't forget," Eadlyn agreed. "And I thank you for your wisdom."

Mildrithe nodded slowly and it seemed she had said all that needed to be told. Her attention turned to the fire and she stood to add a couple of logs. Eadlyn and Janna sat in silence for a moment, with Janna gazing down at the precious pot of unknown leaves. Then they said their goodbyes to the wise woman but, as before, she seemed to have lost interest in them and was busying herself with prodding the fire into life. With Eadlyn leading the way, the sisters left the copse, parting the branches and stepping out into the light.

"There are pigs for sale in Postling," Eadlyn announced as they reached the road, and were about to turn back to Lyminge. "Fremund told me."

"To have a pig would be a fine thing," Janna replied. "But you can't buy a pig with a few eggs or a jug of milk."

"Nay, but I can buy one with a silver sceat!" Eadlyn put her hand over the purse hanging from her belt.

"A sceat!"

"Aye, Cedric gave me one when he said there was no more work for me." Eadlyn turned her back to Lyminge and continued, "It would take no time at all if we were to go and take a look at these pigs."

Janna, putting aside all thoughts of making her brew with Mildrithe's leaves, walked alongside her sister. "To have the meat to see you through the winter months would be a wonderful thing. I'll come with you to see these pigs and if we happen to see Fremund, then it will do no harm!"

"We must see Fremund," Eadlyn said, knowing she was satisfying her sister's interest in him. "It was he who told me about the pigs and will show me where to go."

They soon reached the village of Postling, a humble settlement, sheltered from the north-east by a ridge of hills. The homes, a collection of neat wood and thatch cottages, followed the course of a stream. The thane's hall was not half the size of that belonging to the Thane of Lyminge, but he was said to be a fair man and generous to those who worked on his land. The church in Lyminge was so small that most of the people gathered outside it to celebrate mass, but here in Postling there was no church to offer shelter. Instead a sturdy cross stood on a slight rise within the village and served as the place from where the mass was celebrated.

"Could you live in this place?" Janna wondered.

Eadlyn, who had been pondering on that very question herself, replied: "Aye, I could. The people are friendly, and it is no distance from Lyminge. I'd be glad to move away from Todd's brothers."

"And Elder-Modor?"

Eadlyn felt her spirits slump a little. "I can't leave the old woman. She would have to come with me." Then she turned and grinned at Janna, "But what are we talking of? There is no point in going milk-soft over me leaving my family behind. I am going to buy a pig and our family fends well for itself. We have no need for me to marry Fremund. He is an attractive man, and sometimes I have feelings I do not want to have when he is near me. It is nothing but lustfulness and I am going to put those thoughts aside." Eadlyn picked up her pace, determined to leave this talk behind her.

Fremund lived near the stream, to the south of the village. His workshop was beside his home and, as they approached, the sound of metal on metal could be heard ringing out. Smoke curled upwards through the hole in the roof; he was clearly busy forging iron into shape. Even as the sisters peeped around the corner of the open doorway, the heat from the fire hit them. Double doors were pushed wide open, allowing cool air to come in; it was the same summer and winter when the fire was burning fiercely, the logs blazing and air stifling.

As he turned to hold the metal to the light, Fremund saw them and lifted his free hand in a greeting. He put the metal and his hammer down, then walked towards the doorway, pulling off his leather gloves. Standing in the sunlight, Fremund's hair around his forehead was wet with perspiration and, when he removed his apron, his tunic was damp both on his chest and under his arms. His face and forearms had layers of smudged dirt over freckled skin.

"I would have made some effort to be a little cleaner, had I known you were coming," he said.

236

"You have work to do," Eadlyn replied. "I never believed metal-work was easy!"

"It's a filthy craft!" Fremund grinned. "Now I've a thirst for some ale; will you share some in my home with me?"

Eadlyn looked at Janna before replying: "Aye, we'd like that. But we came to look at these pigs you spoke of."

"Ah, you'll find them just beyond the thane's hall." Fremund gestured to the west, as he led the way to his home. "Shall we sit outside? It's a fine sunny day. You can tell me how you both fare. How is your husband, Janna?"

Before long Eadlyn and Janna were following Fremund's directions in order to find the elderly couple who had young pigs for sale. They passed the thane's hall and crossed the stream before approaching a small home. The thatch looked to be newly repaired and the nearby chicken coops and pig shelter were all in good order. They walked over to an enclosure where a sow was feeding her piglets. Flopped on her side, the mother pig seemed to be half asleep on the dry ground. "They look as if they should have moved on to new homes by now," Janna commented. "How many are there? Six, no seven!"

"There were three more!" a voice came from behind them. "Gone to homes in the village now. Are you looking for a pig? They're a healthy brood."

"Aye, we are," Eadlyn replied. "We've come from Lyminge and had been told you had some for sale. I only want one though."

"I'm wanting a sceat for one. Unless you're a woodworker and able to repair my doors?" The old man nodded towards his home and gave a broad smile.

"Nay, I do many jobs but not that!" Eadlyn replied. "I can give you a sceat for a pig."

"You won't regret it," he said, pushing the gate open and walking in amongst the pig and her piglets.

"How will we choose one?" Janna whispered to Eadlyn. The piglets were all the same: pink skin, covered in short russet-coloured hair; their legs were long and bodies like little barrels. Their snouts were wet on the end. Each one seemed as lively as the next.

"I think I'd be happy with any one of them." Eadlyn was leaning over the fence, watching them detach themselves from the sow as the old man moved within the pen. He pushed them off the toes of his boots and one ran to the fence, pressing its nose towards Eadlyn and Janna. "I'll take this one!" Eadlyn exclaimed. "Will it walk beside me?"

"It won't walk to Lyminge," the man replied, as he scooped up the piglet. "But you can carry her under your arm like this and she'll be happy enough. You have chosen a girl and you will not be sorry. I'll give you a sack of acorns with her and she'll soon settle in."

And so, the piglet was exchanged for Eadlyn's last sceat; in the late autumn she would be slaughtered then hung from the roof above the fire to smoke. The family would have meat to nourish them throughout the coldest days and be able to trade it for other foods.

The piglet, not knowing her fate, snuggled up in the crook of Eadlyn's arm. The sisters retraced their steps, following the track beside the stream. Eadlyn, satisfied with her piglet, was picturing the animal settled in her pen, alongside the goats and chickens. She saw the children gathering acorns in the woods and throwing scraps of vegetables in the pen. But then a new idea began to form in Eadlyn's mind, and it absorbed her completely. Janna's words went unheard and if she noticed her sister was no longer listening, then she said nothing. At first Eadlyn dismissed her thoughts as foolish, but no sooner had she done so than they began to grow again, nurtured by her mind which was so eager to grasp at any new opportunity. They crossed the stream and she admonished herself for her foolhardy ideas, but within the short time it took to walk to Fremund's home, the plan was so well established in her thoughts that she blurted it out before any other greetings were exchanged or the piglet admired.

"I was thinking of going to the Sandtun this year."

"The Sandtun?" Both Janna and Fremund repeated, equally surprised by this announcement.

"Aye, if you, Fremund, could take my tent in your cart, then I can walk with the children and the milking goats."

"But you have nothing to trade," Janna pointed out.

"She can come as my cousin and cook for us, just as Megan travelled there with Arlo." Fremund grasped at the idea, no doubt eager to spend more time with Eadlyn.

"Nay... I mean, I will cook for you, of course I will. But I'll also go there to trade, if only you'll take my tent as I have no horse and cart and nothing to offer the thane or anyone in exchange for one."

"You're not going to trade the goats?" Janna said, the disapproval strong in her voice.

"Nay, sister. I'll milk them and offer a jug of milk to those who need it. And...and I will take some chickens

239

in wicker baskets, so we have eggs." Eadlyn could not contain the joy she felt, and as she spoke another idea came to her: "We'll gather mussels and sell them cooked."

"I saw you in the spring, working on the leather," Fremund said. "Now you have a pig, goats, chickens and a strip of land. What do you think, Janna? I say she can do it!"

"I think she can," Janna agreed. "But Eadlyn this will take a lot of planning. You have the animals left at home to think of; Elder-Modor cannot care for them. And the children are still young."

"We can talk about it on the way home," Eadlyn told her. "I'm sure we can make it work and I'll only go if I can fend for myself. But before we go, we must show you our pig." She held the animal out, with one hand under the pig's chest and the other beneath her rump. "What do you think, Fremund? Isn't she fine?"

Chapter Twenty-Eight

"Word has come," Janna was breathless, having run from the Nailbourne, where she was washing blankets, and up the gentle slope to where Eadlyn lived. She found her sister chopping vegetables for the pottage.

"At last!" Eadlyn grinned, feeling the excitement run through her.

"Are you sure of this?" Janna questioned. "Can you do this on your own, with Clover?"

"I don't know."

"You're taking two goats and some of the chickens!" Janna reminded her.

"Clover is almost a young woman," Eadlyn replied, as she pressed the knife through the white flesh of a turnip.

"She is seven! Still a child."

"Aye, but she is a great help to me." Eadlyn thought of the children, busy with their chores in the village. It was time to fetch Clover and prepare to leave. "I'll have to tell them," she said. "They are at the bake-house."

"Then you must wait until the bread is baked," Janna said. "I'll look for them and tell them to return as soon as the bread is cool enough to carry. There is plenty of time; don't go without your bread and a bellyful of pottage."

"Aye, we won't go without food in us," Eadlyn agreed, even though she had every thought of going immediately. She felt as if even a spoonful of pottage would lie heavy in her stomach. But the vegetables were now ready for the pot, so she threw them in and stirred the mixture, having added more water from a jug. "We'll eat at noon with Elder-Modor and leave afterwards."

"And I'll check on the animals morning and evening," Janna confirmed. The pregnant nanny goat had given birth to twins just two weeks beforehand. They were all too energetic for Elder-Modor to handle safely, and now the young pig added to the chores.

"I thank you," Eadlyn gave her sister a quick hug as they stood in the doorway of her home.

"Eadlyn..." Janna paused before walking away. "Eadlyn if you need anything then you know to ask Fremund. He'll be pleased to help and if you grow closer, then it would bring happiness, I'm sure of it."

"He's taking our tent, and we'll camp near him." Eadlyn repeated what had already been told since she made the plan to journey to the Sandtun.

"I wish..."

"Nay, sister. I'll find my own path in time."

The sun was still at its highest in the sky when Eadlyn tugged at the rope handle and the wheels of the small cart began to turn. It would trail along behind her, with Clover at the rear, ready to give a push if needed. The path along the edge of Lyminge was no more than a mud track, narrow and rutted. "It will be easier once we are on the road," Eadlyn said to Clover. She had one goat's lead securely in her hand, while the second was held by the girl. They had bidden their farewells to

Elder-Modor and now the old woman watched them leave.

They walked slowly, knowing it was a long road for a seven-year-old girl, and unsure of how the goats would fare when expected to walk mile after mile. The two milkers were strong and full of energy, pulling at their ropes, but to take them so far could be a challenge. Eadlyn had packed as little as possible, relying on Fremund to bring a tent, fire-making and cooking equipment. If needed, she could push their bedding aside and make space for one goat at a time in the cart.

Although they stopped for a short time when Tolsford Hill came close, and later near a copse with views to the distant sea, Clover remained keen to keep walking and the goats showed themselves to be resilient. There were wildflowers and grass to snatch at as the animals trotted along, and plenty to talk about: old memories to recall and the prospect of new ones to be made. They spoke of Todd, but only of the happy times, not of his death.

It was with mixed emotions Eadlyn looked down upon Romney Marsh. All the old feelings of adventure were with her, yet she stood on the spot where Todd had been killed.

"Faeder died here," Clover said, in the way a child states the truth. She placed her small hand on Eadlyn's arm.

"Aye he did, my sweeting."

Yet the marsh still beckoned her: those flat lands with great pools of water and tidal creeks winding this way and that. The view was clear at that moment, but Romney Marsh changed with the weather and when the mists hung about at dawn, it was the place of mysteries and mythical beings. Eadlyn could almost believe that the pagan gods still lurked in this place which was half-land and half-sea. Christianity had chased them out of England, but did they skulk in places where humans had barely settled? An image of Mildrithe, the wise woman, flashed into Eadlyn's mind and she wondered if she had ever been to Romney Marsh. Here, a witch may well be tucked away under a group of willows or in the band of trees lining the very edge of the marsh.

"Help me hold the cart steady." Eadlyn shook away her romantic notions and considered how best to descend the Shipway. "This road is steep." She turned the cart, so now she held it back by the rope, rather than pulling it along. Its own weight would give it the power needed to move down the hill. "Clover, take my goat, please." The animals were flagging now and would give Clover no bother.

They moved down the Shipway, all views of Romney Marsh lost, for the lane was a deep cutting in the hillside and trees framed either side of it. Having crossed the wide plank bridge under which the water flowed inland with each incoming tide, Eadlyn and Clover paused at the edge of the Sandtun, the beach to their left and the area of raised dry land before them. It was the same as before, except Todd no longer stood at their side and Cym remained at home with his aunt. But the sun shone, as it always seemed to do when they arrived here, and the Sandtun itself was dry with the debris of the winter's high tides strewn across it and ragged weeds hanging on by tenacious roots. The breeze came straight off the lagoon, and the air was seasoned with salt and seaweed. Behind Eadlyn, the hillside rose steeply and was dark with trees, but before her the land continued as flat marshland until it merged with the sky, the two of them linked in a distant heat haze.

Breathing deeply, appreciating the tang of the sea air, Eadlyn turned to Clover. "It feels good to be here, doesn't it my sweeting?"

"Aye, Modor, it does." Clover stood close to her mother, looking up at her.

"Come on, let's find Cousin Fremund and set up our tent," Eadlyn said, as she tugged on the rope and the cart lurched forward. "We'll see our old friends and go home with so many stories to tell!"

As they walked, Eadlyn scanned the area for Fremund. Memories of his arriving late, and of late nights drinking mead, came to her mind. *What if he forgets his promise to arrive in time for us to set up the tent and I am struggling with both a child and the animals to look after?* Eadlyn felt her limbs tense as she became anxious. *I don't know if I can trust him to be here as he said he would.* Already there were about a dozen tents pitched and as many carts; the Sandtun was a hive of activity, but there was no sign of Fremund's distinctive head of red hair. Eadlyn slowed down, unsure of where to go.

"There he is," Clover screeched, as their cousin appeared from behind a tent. He carried a mallet in one hand and was knocking pegs into place, then checking the tension on the ropes. Clover began to run, hauling the weary goat behind her.

Fremund looked up and waved. "Here you are! Just in time to set up home in our Sandtun camp."

"I would have put up the tent," Eadlyn said.

"Eadlyn, you don't have to do everything," Fremund admonished. "You do not always have to be modor and faeder. Let me help sometimes."

Grinning back at him, Eadlyn was well aware of her need to prove she could care for the family alone. "I thank you, Cousin. We're lucky to have you."

"I won't do everything though," Fremund winked at Clover. "We need water and fuel. Let us tie those goats up and finish our camp."

It was not long before the goats were causing interest amongst the people on the Sandtun, and as the summer traders came to greet Eadlyn, they spotted the chickens in their baskets.

"With Todd gone, I had to find my own reason to come to the Sandtun," Eadlyn explained to a pot-maker and his wife. "I have two goats and six chickens with me. I can give you a jug of milk and two eggs for the five days we expect to be here, in exchange for one of your clay dishes. What do you say?"

"I'd say that we'd be very happy with that," the pot-maker replied.

"You're a hard worker, Eadlyn," his wife said. "Come and choose your dish now and we'll be glad of the eggs."

Eadlyn's plan was working and she felt satisfied. Now she must hope the journey had not unsettled the milk or egg production and she could keep her first customers happy. She followed the pot-maker to his cart and selected a dish. "I'll fill a jug with your milk every morning and when I leave, I'll have earned this dish," she suggested.

"Aye, you do that," the pot-maker agreed.

As the sun lowered in the sky, the colours of land and sea became more intense: the sea a glorious turquoise, the sand a deep golden brown and the marshland all shades of green. The camp was set up for the family. Not the family known by the Sandtun of the past, but a young woman, her daughter and her cousin by marriage. The moon had completed twelve cycles since their last visit and in that time life had evolved for the people who visited the Sandtun. As news was exchanged, the families learned of new lives born, old lives ending or cut short before their time was due. That was the pattern of their time on this earth, but whatever else happened, every year traders gathered on the Sandtun. Whether they sold leather or metalwork, it was admired by the men of Francia.

The fire was taking a hold on the logs, having spread through kindling, and Clover was mixing flour with water to make flat-breads on the pan. Eadlyn had milked the goats, who were resigned to being tethered to the handcart, and had produced a lesser amount than usual. "I'm not surprised," Eadlyn had said to Clover. "They've had quite a trek. Tomorrow we'll gather some fresh grass from the hillside and hopefully they'll choose to be more generous with their milk!"

And so Eadlyn settled into the first evening of a new type of Sandtun life: the camp grew with more people descending the Shipway, setting up tents and making themselves at home, albeit for just a few days. Eadlyn was looking towards the hillside track when she saw her friend Megan with the children. She was accompanied by her brother-in-law, Arlo, as she had been the year before. "I'm glad she could come," Eadlyn said. "You never know how life can change in a year."

"What did you say, Modor?" Clover asked, looking up from the dough which she was now stretching into shape.

"Megan is here with the children!" Eadlyn said, standing and pointing to the family gathered on the beach track.

"Is she with their faeder or his brother?"

"She is with Arlo," Eadlyn responded. "Penton was injured and can't travel to the Sandtun."

"I hoped he was better," Clover replied. "It's so sad he can't be at the Sandtun when we all like to be here."

"Let's go to meet them," Eadlyn said.

Within minutes, Clover was running to the sea with the children and the women were flinging their arms around each other, then standing back to see the changes in each other's faces, looking to judge if life had been kind. In Eadlyn's eyes, her friend appeared weary. Perhaps Penton still suffered and the burden of running the home fell on Megan. Then she saw how Megan's stomach was rounded and knew there was another reason for her to feel jaded.

"You are with child!" Eadlyn smiled but wondered if this was more burden than pleasure.

"Aye, it has been three years since our daughter, Alfreda, was born. I wonder if we will be blessed with a boy or a girl this time."

"And Penton – how is he?"

"A little stronger," Megan replied. "He cannot walk far, but he seems to manage a little better. Arlo is particularly good to us, and gives him as much work as he can, so Penton feels useful."

Eadlyn waved to Arlo, who had allowed the women time to exchange their news, and was taking the horse and cart towards an area where they could make their camp. She saw Fremund walk over to him, and the men reaching out to shake hands. Turning her attention back to Megan, Eadlyn felt her body go cold at her friend's words.

"I see Fremund, but where is Todd?"

"Megan, I thought... I thought you would have heard. I don't know how, but word travels about and especially when it is something..." Eadlyn paused, not knowing how to express the words, struggling to find the right way. "It was as you left us, only minutes after..."

"I've heard nothing," Megan reached out, putting both her hands on her friend's arms. "Don't tell me..."

"They went back to help, Todd and Fremund..." Eadlyn began. "They helped that man, I can't say his name – I just can't. They went to help him with his cart on the hill and he was so angry; it was always Todd – why was he so angry at Todd, who did nothing but try to help? He hit out and felled him. He killed him, Megan. He killed my Todd, there at the top of the Shipway."

"I didn't know," Megan whispered. "The news didn't travel to Aldington. If it had done, then I would have come to you."

They stood there and as they turned towards the men, they saw Fremund and Arlo looking back and knew Arlo had heard the news as well.

The two families gathered around their shared fire, while the sky created a blaze of its own with streaks of orange and red cast over the sky to the west. Clover was curled up next to Eadlyn, with Megan's son, Eadric, beside her; his young sister was already asleep in the tent. They sat on blankets, reminiscing, and speaking of the days to come. Sometimes there was silence within their group, with each one of them reflecting on their own thoughts. Comfortable with each other's company, the evening had passed quickly, and they were all reluctant for it to end.

"Time to go to bed, I think," Eadlyn said, knowing they would soon be chilled if they sat out any longer. She stood and offered her hand to Clover, "Let's settle in the tent before we fall asleep here."

Megan stood as well and began to usher her son to their tent. Arlo and Fremund would sleep beneath their carts-loads of metalwork. But as Arlo began to move, Fremund stopped him. "I have some mead," he said. "Let us drink to good trading this year."

"I'd enjoy a noggin-full, my friend, but that will be enough for me. I'm ready for my sleep," Arlo replied. "I know your mead will be a good one."

"It is!' Fremund said, moving away to fetch it from his cart. "But just one noggin? I swear you'll be wanting more when it has passed your lips."

"Nay, it will be just the one," Arlo said. "Sleep well, Eadlyn...Megan."

Fremund lifted the bottle of mead. "I tell you this is a fine one and I'll enjoy more than a noggin before I'm sleeping on the hard earth of the Sandtun."

"You do as you wish," Arlo gave a grin and shrugged his shoulders. "I have a thick blanket and will be comfortable enough without my head fuzzed."

"Eadlyn, my sweet," Fremund called out. "Tell him to keep me company. It would be ill-mannered not to."

Looking across at the pair of them, Eadlyn shook her head, "Nay Fremund, let Arlo do as he chooses for we all have busy days tomorrow and it would do you no harm to settle down to sleep." She crawled into the tent but could still hear the banter between the two men. This was the Fremund of the past; Eadlyn did not forget his kindness to her, but knew she was right to wait until her path became clear.

Chapter Twenty-Nine

On the first morning the sky was streaked with pink as the sun rose over the hills to the east of the Sandtun. The mist was lying low over the marshland and in the tidal lagoon four boats swayed on gently rolling waves. It was a peaceful scene, and if it were not for the goats bleating and pulling at the ropes tethering them, then there would have been no sound other than the rushes moving in the breeze and the tide running up the sandy beach. When Eadlyn crawled out of the tent and looked around the camp, it seemed as if she were the first out of bed. It would not be long before the men were up and pulling their carts to the sand; the tide was at its highest and as it dropped away, the boats would be beached, and the trading would begin. She looked at the fire, which needed wood, and the goats who demanded attention. Turning back to the tent, Eadlyn knelt and reached for the sack of grain for the goats; she took a handful and scattered it before the animals. "That will keep you busy for a while," she murmured.

Reaching under her cart, Eadlyn took a length of dry wood. She dragged it to the fire and snapped it several times before arranging the wood amongst the smouldering ashes. It was not enough; they would need some dry moss, leaves or twigs. Movement behind her caused Eadlyn to smile as she stood up. "Good morning!" She smiled at Megan's son, Eadric, then gestured towards the cart. "We need something very dry to start the fire with. Would you take the bucket from the cart and gather some twigs, please? I want to milk the goats and try to sell the milk; everyone will be awake soon. Have you seen the boats? The men are here to trade."

"Of course." Eadric took the bucket. He looked towards the sea. "Aye, I see the boats. I'm going to the beach with Arlo; I'll be working with him."

Eadlyn smiled, but for a moment her heart felt heavy to know her own son would not be learning from his father. The sadness faded as soon Clover was crawling out of the tent, and then Arlo was emerging from where he slept under his cart and calling out a cheery 'good morning'. The Sandtun was coming to life and she was glad of it. She would remember Todd and feel sad but still enjoy her time there.

Kneeling on the ground beside one of the goats, Eadlyn watched as people came from their tents and prepared to start trading. Fremund's mop of red hair appeared after he pushed his blanket aside and rolled out from under the cart. His eyes were heavy, and he barely waved a greeting to Eadlyn before heading towards the tidal inlet used as both a latrine and somewhere to wash. *I wonder how much mead he drank last night?* Eadlyn thought, before admonishing herself with, *he is a grown man and it's none of my concern.*

But when Fremund returned, his hands were full of fresh grass. "I brought fodder for the goats," he said, offering it. "You'll be so busy with the milking and making breakfast, and these goats are used to feasting on better than this, don't you agree?" He waved his hand, indicating how dry and ragged the grass on the Sandtun was.

"Wonderful," Eadlyn replied. *How kind he is; he looks better already. Perchance he only had a noggin or two.* "I'm going with this jug of milk for the woodcarver. The goats seem to have settled and I have two more jugs to sell, and that leaves one for us."

"I wasn't sure if they'd give you milk." Fremund gave a smile. "But I should have known your plan would work!" He had turned to his pony and was stroking her chestnut neck, then rubbing her forelock. She was snatching at grass from his other hand. "I'm about to harness this one and take the cart to the beach. I have spoken to the fishermen about giving us some fish. Come along when you can and choose some for our midday meal."

"Aye, I'll do that."

Three eggs had been produced that morning. Eadlyn took two and delivered them with the milk to the pot-maker and his wife. They took them with pleasure. "You've made the Sandtun feel more like home," they said. "Now if you go over there to the woodcarver, he'll be happy for some milk if you have some spare. No doubt he'd like an egg too."

"I'll do that," Eadlyn said. "I've only got one more egg, but I'm sure he'll be happy with it."

The woodcarver was happy to exchange two bowls for milk and an egg every day, as well as whatever Eadlyn could gather towards a meal. "We are going to search for mussels," she informed him.

By the time she returned to cook breakfast, Eadlyn had arranged to deliver milk to more Sandtun traders when she milked the goats later in the day. She had exchanged milk and cooked shellfish for a pretty circular brooch with inlaid copper for Clover, and milk for wooden plates from another woodworker. Her step was light and Eadlyn could not keep the smile from her face when she returned to the area around her own tent. The fire was now burning well and there was milk to spare for their porridge. Eadlyn set about adding oats and dried berries to sweeten it. When it thickened, she spooned some porridge into wooden bowls.

Long before breakfast, the men had taken the carts down to the beach and the boats were pulled up on the sand. Eadric had joined his uncle and Clover asked if she could be with Fremund on the beach. Both men were metalworkers, although Arlo worked on the more delicate items, such as small boxes, buckles and delicate hinges, whereas Fremund made tools, frames to hang over fires, pots and bolts. They were known for the good quality of their work and enjoyed discussing it with each other.

When Eadlyn handed the bowls of porridge to Fremund and Clover, the fishermen were on the beach. They had been out in a small boat and had a couple of baskets of fish with them. "Go and choose our fish," Fremund reminded her.

There were now five boats from Francia beached on the sands, waiting for the tide to turn and then rise in order to take them back to the *Oceanus Britannicus*. The men had plenty of time to move amongst the traders and on the first day the best of the Anglo-Saxon wares were available to choose from. Eadlyn loved to watch the men of both nationalities gesturing with their hands and using the few words they knew of each other's language. Words she could not understand rolled off the tongues of these men from across the water; their eyes and skin were a little darker than those of the Anglo-Saxons. This moment, when there were still five or six days of trading ahead of them, and it was all still new to her, was her favourite time on the Sandtun. Eadlyn had missed it that morning: she had been too busy with the goats. But to see the boats beach as the tide retreated and the men jumping down from them was an exhilarating sight. They were stranded here on foreign soil, or sand, until the next incoming tide released them, and often shared a meal with the Sandtun traders, sitting around the fires relaxing and filling the air with words which held mystery for the people of Kent.

"I'll go and choose some fish," Eadlyn confirmed. Afterwards she would make some dough and they would feast on fish and flat-breads at midday. She wandered along to the two fishermen whose catch was displayed in baskets at their feet.

"Good morning," one of them said. "I've got a nice pot-stand to collect from your cousin with flame-coloured hair. He says I'm to give you a couple of fish every day in exchange for it."

"Aye, that's right," Eadlyn agreed. "Let's hope the fish keep biting as there's plenty of us to feed."

"Have no fear of that," the second fisherman said. "There's more than enough to fill our bellies in this lagoon."

"How strange for you to come here fishing every day and have only the people of Lympne, up there on the hill, to think of, and now here we all are and wanting fish," Eadlyn looked back at the men on the beach and the tents on the raised ground beyond it.

"We could go for weeks and no other person would come here, just the women searching for shellfish and the men setting up the kettle nets or out on a little boat," the first fisherman said.

255

"There was that monk," the second reminded him. "Now he came as a surprise and let's hope he keeps God close to him, for he set off to walk across the marsh, and that's not something you should do lightly."

"You never know when she could take you," the other fisherman continued, lowering his voice.

"She?" Eadlyn queried.

"She...the marsh. She could suck a man into her depths or have him wandering about looking for a way out and him turning funny in the mind, not knowing which is east and which is west."

Eadlyn gazed towards the west, seeing nothing but the flatness stretching outwards until the land was nothing but a haze blending with the sky. "You can see the distant hills, if you stand at the Shipway," she mused. "But from here there are no hills unless you choose to turn and go back where you've come from. I wouldn't want to venture further."

"You've got sense in your head," the second man said. "But that monk, I can't say what will happen to him.

"He didn't come back though," the first said.

"He didn't come back," the second confirmed.

Eadlyn took her fish and walked back to the Sandtun. It was a glorious day, with the sky a rich blue and the sun warming her. Gulls soared above, riding the light breeze and voices rang out, many of the words coming from unknown tongues. But the young woman was frowning as something played on her mind: a half-remembered conversation. It was about the monk, and she couldn't quite place it. *It will come to me later, I'm sure of it. There was someone talking about a monk recently, but where was it and why?*

Midday had passed and the trading finished, but still there was work to do in the camp. The tide had retreated fully and the men from Francia waited for it to lap around their boats until they re-floated and they were able to leave the haven, returning to their own country with their fine Anglo-Saxon leatherwork, metalwork and wooden items.

With their feet slowly sinking into the sand, and water gathering in pools around their toes, Eadlyn and Megan were bent low, scanning the area for mussels. They ran their fingers through the sodden sand, searching for where the sea creatures gathered, usually in clusters. The sun was beating down on their backs and to have the cool water around their feet was a soothing reprieve from the heat.

Clover and Eadric had worked their way along to the west of the beach, also on the hunt for mussels. Young Alfreda was at their heels and Eadlyn felt, not for the first time, a pang of regret that she had left Cym at home with her sister.

"Modor, here! Here!" Clover shrieked, holding the glistening shells up high. Seawater and sand dripped from them, running down the girl's arms.

The women straightened their backs and walked towards the children, Eadlyn slowing herself to allow for Megan's pregnancy. As they reached the place where the shellfish had been found, Clover and Eadric already had their hands full and they dropped the gleaming treasures into Eadlyn's basket. They had found an area rich with mussels, and the children chatted constantly as they gathered them. They moved further to the west, to the point where the beach ended and there was a low outcrop of rocks. The basket grew heavy and it was time to return to the dry ground where Sandtun and beach met.

"Now let's tip them here on the grass and if any are open, you must give them a tap," Eadlyn advised.

"Why, Modor?" Clover asked, eagerly snatching at an open shell.

"Because if the mussel is alive, it will close its shell," Eadric told her, brandishing his own open shell.

"A dead mussel will make your belly ache or worse," Megan continued.

"Oh, this one is dead." Clover said. "I'll leave it over here."

"We'll throw them back into the sea later," Megan told her.

The shellfish were sorted, and the children ran back to the sea with the dead ones, throwing them in the shallow waters. The basket of fresh mussels was beginning to dry out and lose their glossy shine. Some were home to barnacles, rough grey encrustations which attracted strands of hairy seaweed, and straggly beards were captured between the tightly shut mouths of the shells.

"Time to clean them." Eadlyn handed Megan a sharp flint. They settled down on the edge of the ridge between the beach and Sandtun, their legs dangling down and feet still bare, with a dusting of sand over them. The young ones raced in the shallow waters, calling out and splashing each other. They collected pebbles and threw them into the water, exclaiming over the splashes they made, and the distance thrown. Eadlyn felt a sense of well-being wash through her. "I didn't know I could feel such happiness again," she said. "Clover has to work so hard and now she is able to laugh with her friends."

"It's wonderful you were able to come, and to enjoy your time here," Megan replied.

"Will you be here next year?" Eadlyn asked, her smile fading.

Megan put her hand to her stomach and shook her head. "It wouldn't be fair on Arlo. I won't be here, not if I cannot help him as I do now. To bring a baby to the Sandtun is not easy, as we know."

"I'll miss you."

"Mayhap Arlo will have a wife by then," Megan suggested.

"I expected to find him married," Eadlyn admitted. "He is such a good man, a hard worker and steady."

"He would make a fine husband and father." Megan tugged as a wisp of seaweed caught within the clamped jaws of the shell. "I should encourage him to marry, but what will happen to my family if he brings a wife to our home? We live together happily now, but he left his own house to live with us when Penton had his accident. If he marries everything will change."

"Does he think of this and choose not to marry?" Eadlyn pondered.

"I don't know, but it's not fair," Megan admitted. "He needs a woman in his life, and I am only thinking of myself. I see the way he looks at you and know he has all the needs of a young man."

"Looks at me?" Eadlyn turned her attention from the stubborn barnacle she was trying to prise from the shell. "Nay, you are wrong." She felt the blush rise through her neck; Arlo was a handsome man, and she had her own needs, which battled with her desire to provide for her family without help from a man.

Megan shrugged. "I shouldn't speak of it, perchance I was wrong."

"Now we need water," Eadlyn announced. "From the spring, to cleanse the salt away." She stood up, lifting the basket, satisfied with the work they had already done in preparing the mussels for eating.

They walked back to the camp and left the shellfish in the shade under the cart. The men, from both Kent and Francia, were sitting with their ale; their trading was done for the day. Fires smouldered, horses dozed, and the goats fretted at their tethers.

Arlo looked up and called out, "Did you collect many?"

"Aye, the children found a good cluster of them," Megan replied.

"I'll collect some wood soon," he suggested. "Enough for the evening and tomorrow morning."

"That would be wonderful," Eadlyn responded. "I can help, and the children too. Megan must not work too hard; the baby tires her. But first we're going to fetch water from the spring."

"Would you like...?"

"Nay," Eadlyn was quick to reply. "We can do it." She took a good-sized jug from her cart and waited for Megan to collect hers, then they walked along the track back towards the hillside.

It was cool once they stepped into the shade of the trees and began to walk the short way up the Shipway before turning to step through a gap in the hedgerow. Then they were in the sunlight again and the grass here was lush, not sparse as it was on the Sandtun. Cushioned from the noise coming from the camp and beach, it seemed as if they were the only two people for miles around. The fresh water sprang from a rocky outcrop; the ground around it was wet and weeds grew thick and green. Eadlyn knelt and filled both jugs, then let the water gather in her hands and drank deeply. Megan did the same and, as she straightened herself, she paused to hold her stomach.

"The baby turned," she said. "He's an active little thing." Her face was white and fine lines showed around her eyes.

"Take a rest for a while?" Eadlyn said.

"Aye, I'll do that when we're back at the tents."

They turned their backs on the field and were about to enter the shadowed area under the trees, when Eadlyn sensed a movement within the wooded area. She thought nothing of it. It would be a bird or small animal, or even someone else coming for water; the incomers walked the track all day to collect water from springs on either side of it. But when a figure stepped out of the shadows, Eadlyn gasped, her body stiffening and heart slamming against her chest.

"I had to come," the old woman said. Her wizened features could barely be seen between the drapes of her headscarf, but Eadlyn knew her voice and recognised her black eyes and brown skin as wrinkled as a walnut. "I had to come… Will you spare an old woman a few minutes?"

Chapter Thirty

"I thought if I waited here, you'd pass by," Hlappa said. Her hands were held before her: brown fingers were twisted, and agitation showed in the way she fretted with the ragged material of her apron. "I need to talk to you; there's things on my mind and they won't pass."

"Yesterday I learned how your son killed her husband; do you think Eadlyn's mind is at ease?" Megan stepped forward, one hand cradling her unborn child. "Leave us to move by and don't think of following us to the Sandtun."

"I mean no harm. I suffer too." Hlappa cowered, moving back towards the shelter of the trees.

"Your suffering comes from the hands of your own son," Megan snapped back at her. "I won't let you cause more hurt. Just go... go back wherever you came from."

"I understand your words," Hlappa replied. Whereas before, when she spoke at the Sandtun, there had been pleasure in her taunts and predictions, now her voice was hesitant.

Looking down at the ragged hem of the old woman's skirt, Eadlyn saw her feet were bare and, like her fingers, her toes were also twisted, the nails black and gnarled. Her hands still clasped at the stained apron and her headscarf fell back a little, revealing thin tufts of grey-brown hair. Hlappa's eyes, once so bright and probing, were dulled. Eadlyn looked at

262

Megan, who was still poised to defend her, but was weary from the child growing within her. "Go back to the children, Megan. I'll talk to Hlappa; she means no harm and I know she dare not follow us to the Sandtun."

"I'll go, but I'll be speaking with Fremund," Megan said. She looked directly at Hlappa and continued, "Say what you need to say, and leave. Her cousin will be here as soon as I tell him of this."

"I thank you." Eadlyn placed her hand on Megan's arm and attempted a smile, then she turned back to Hlappa, "You heard her, now speak quickly and go."

"I watched him hang, my Bradwin, my son," the old woman began. "He can do you no harm, nor anyone else."

"The harm he has done lives on with me and my family," Eadlyn said. "And in you... I can see that. You are hungry and ragged, but do not come to me and ask for help. It is more than I can do for you. Go to the village on top of the hill and beg them for some food or a place to sleep. I have suffered greatly and have nothing to give you."

"I do not ask for food," Hlappa said. For the first time her eyes came to life, as she defended herself. "I needed to see you, to know if you and the children have survived. It is not easy when you are left with no husband. My own died when my Bradwin was young."

"It has been hard, but we are growing stronger," Eadlyn said.

"I know that. I know more than words can tell," Hlappa replied; she took a step towards Eadlyn, but the young woman recoiled. "The Sandtun, which brought such tragedy also brings happiness to you."

"It was not the Sandtun which killed my husband."

"Nay, but the event was here, or near enough." Hlappa glanced up the hill, in the direction of the Shipway crossroads. "I had such strong messages coming to me when we were here at the Sandtun. I saw people moving by night and I felt there was death hanging over us. I saw gold too…gold on the Sandtun, but where it was, I could not tell. If I knew, then I'd have shoes on my feet and a home to go to."

"But you didn't know it was your son who would cause the death?" Eadlyn asked.

"I didn't know," the old woman confirmed. "I think there was another death, nothing to do with the traders. I get these feelings coming to me, but I cannot tell the whole story. It's a blessing and a curse all as one."

The sound of voices came drifting up the hillside and wafted through the trees. Eadlyn looked in the direction of the Shipway and her throat tightened; she did not want the women of the Sandtun to be looking on as she spoke with Hlappa. It was time to slip amongst the trees and run back along the shaded track and out onto the beach.

"There's still gold on the Sandtun," Hlappa's voice broke into Eadlyn's thoughts. "It's come back."

Eadlyn thought of the pendant cross, with its polished stone at the centre and scrolls of golden patterning. *The gold is gone: you are wrong.* She kept her reply to herself. *My Todd had it and I wish you could tell me why, but your thoughts are unclear, and you still believe it to be here. It is lost and most likely still in Lyminge.* She thought again of the beach and the warm sand underfoot and the sun on her skin and took a step towards the Shipway. *It would do no harm to ask about the gold.*

264

"Where did the gold come from?" Eadlyn asked, her curiosity aroused. "Not from Francia?"

"Nay, the gold I see has travelled far, but not across the sea. It came from Middle England. I believe it to be holy, but now it is lost." Hlappa narrowed her eyes, and her tone became sharp: "Do you know of the gold, Eadlyn?"

"Nay," Eadlyn scoffed. The lie came easily to her. "If I am lucky, I have a silver sceat. I know nothing of gold."

"You will know of it," Hlappa declared. "I see you with it, and I'm thankful for that." Now she moved into the trees. She had learned all she needed to. When her time to die came, and she knew the shadow of death was at her heels, she would be at ease. She could pass to the next world knowing all was well with Eadlyn. "Your path will soon come clear to you. When you see the pendant cross, all will be clear." The wizened old hag took her feeble body through the line of trees and stepped out onto the Shipway. The last Eadlyn saw of her was the corner of her shawl becoming snagged on a tree; it fanned outwards before the branch released it. Then she was gone.

Eadlyn stood, feeling slightly sick. Hlappa's last words screamed in her head: "When you see the pendant cross, all will be clear... your path will be clear." *Who said it was a pendant cross here on the Sandtun? I did not tell her that it was a golden pendant that Todd found. She only said gold before, but now she says it is a pendant. And she speaks of paths, just as Mildrithe did. What does she mean by it?* Conscious her heart was pounding, Eadlyn knew she must hear more, that Hlappa must explain herself better. *And if she refuses to, then I will offer her food, or clothes. I must understand these riddles she throws at me.* Her body, which had been rigid with horror just a moment before, flew through the trees, away from the field and the spring, and to the shaded Shipway.

The track was dark, and empty of people. *Yet, I heard voices just moments ago,* Eadlyn puzzled. But there were other springs and other narrow paths off the Shipway which the Sandtun women could have used. There was no figure, small and bent, hurrying up the hill. Eadlyn glanced downhill but knew the old woman would not face the people at the Sandtun. The news of Todd's death at the hands of Bradwin of Saltwood was known to most people there, and they would feel protective of Todd's widow.

Eadlyn took a few steps up the hillside, her eyes adjusting to the gloom, but there was no sign of Hlappa. *There it is – the path through to another spring!* Eadlyn dashed through the trees and onto a further area of open hillside. There were women collecting spring water in jugs, but no sign of the old hag. She retreated. The Shipway still looked to be deserted. It was no good, the old woman had vanished. *It is almost as if she was never here at all,* Eadlyn thought. *She looked barely alive.*

Shivering, Eadlyn recalled the warmth from the sun and all the people gathered on the beach and within the camp. She turned to walk down the hill. There was someone there. Not Hlappa. This was a man, and he was striding up the track. *Of course, Megan was going to tell Fremund and he is coming to keep me safe from the old woman.* Eadlyn's heart calmed. *If it is Fremund coming to make sure I am free from the words which flow from Hlappa, then perhaps my path is clear?*

But Fremund was tall and slender, and his hair would shine red, even in this dull place. The man approaching Eadlyn, almost at a run, was a little shorter and stockier.

"Has she gone?" he asked, looking around. "She shouldn't have come."

"Aye, she's gone," Eadlyn confirmed. "I thought Fremund..." She stood before Arlo feeling rather small and awkward. For a moment, she had imagined running into Fremund's arms, and now she was unsure of how to behave in front of this man, who was gentle and kind, but he was not her cousin, nor her lover.

"Has she scared you?" Arlo reached out and drew Eadlyn to him, pulling her against him. She stepped forward and rested her head on his chest.

"A little," she admitted, mumbling into his tunic. She moved back, "But why did you come? Megan was to fetch my cousin."

They started walking down the hill. Arlo had taken the heavy jug of water from Eadlyn and he held it in both hands. "Megan came looking for Fremund, but he was busy. She asked me to come to you."

"That was kind of her."

"She's a good woman," Arlo said. "Their life is hard, hers and Penton's. I do what I can..."

"You do," Eadlyn replied. "You are very good to them."

"You said she scared you?" The conversation returned to Hlappa, and Arlo's voice deepened a little, "Why did she come? I can hardly believe she would dare to."

"She came to find out if I was well and managing without Todd," Eadlyn began. "But then she started saying strange things. Like she used to talk..." She looked up at Arlo, "Nothing she says makes sense, but I feel it should."

"Would you like me to listen and perchance I can help?"

"I need time to think and I feel it will come clearer..." Eadlyn paused.

"Of course. Whenever you feel ready."

They crossed the bridge. The water flowing out to the sea was a mere trickle; the tide was now low and no longer forcing itself inland. Then Eadlyn felt her body relax as they stepped out onto the edge of the Sandtun and she felt the sun's rays soak through her tunic. It seemed like days had passed since she and Megan had been gathering mussels on the beach, but the shellfish were still waiting to be washed and cooked. To sit on the sand, washing the grit from them would be relaxing.

"The tide is rising." Arlo's words broke into her thoughts.

"Aye, they'll be gone soon." She spoke of the men of Francia who were walking back to the beach with the traders.

"I'll go to say farewell and help push their boats out when the sea is deep enough." He looked towards the beach.

"You must do that." Eadlyn reached out for the jug. "I thank you, Arlo. It was good of you to come to me."

"I was glad to be able to."

Megan was resting in her tent when Eadlyn returned to the camp which felt strangely deserted. Their own menfolk, and those from across the sea, had come to the Sandtun for the midday meal and had sat about relaxing for a while afterwards, but now it was just the women amongst the tents and fires. Even the children were running around on the beach or exploring the paths and pastureland to the west. She retrieved the bucketful of mussels from under the cart and returned for the second jug of water, placed there by Megan. Then, sitting on a log beside the slumbering fire, Eadlyn poured the first jug of water over the mussels and stirred them about with her hands.

The gentle clatter of shell upon shell was mesmerising, and Eadlyn became lost in the moment. The protective cases of deep blue, dulled by the heat of the sun, became dark shining jewels again. The movement of the mussels against her fingers as she pushed them about was strangely soothing. They gave up their grit to the water and in time Eadlyn moved them to the pan, rinsed out the bucket and repeated the process.

By the time the mussels had been washed for the second time, Eadlyn found her confusion was beginning to wane. Hlappa had spoken of gold on the Sandtun, and she spoke the truth, for Todd had found it and carried it with him. Like Mildrithe, Hlappa had a gift of seeing things in her mind and spoke of what she saw. The old hag had been given a vision of the pendant cross, and now she saw it again back on the Sandtun. Hlappa was frail, no doubt she was confused and still thinking of last summer when the cross was indeed somewhere nearby. She spoke also of paths and if Eadlyn's sister, Janna, was near then she would have reasoned, "All wise women speak of paths. Do not think too deeply or give her too much thought. Your future will become clear in its own good time and no quicker for you fretting over it."

Eadlyn stood, lifted the bucket, and placed the clean shellfish back in the cool under the cart. She had been considering how to cook the mussels since they had set out to gather them earlier in the afternoon. Now she began to walk back to the bridge and the wooded area running along the very edge of Romney Marsh. The narrow track took her away from the beach area and although Eadlyn was still on the low-lying land, all views of the marsh were obscured by the strong upright trunks of oak, ash and beech trees, and their canopy of this season's leaves. The smell of wild garlic was strong here and its leaves grew in blankets of rich green, each one a fragile spear. Amongst them delicate stars of white flowers grew in clusters. Eadlyn bent down to gather bunches of the garlic leaves.

When she stood up and turned to retrace her steps, Eadlyn saw the figure of a tall man coming towards her. A shaft of light came through the trees. It was Fremund. Eadlyn, not realising she had tensed, breathed a sigh of relief.

"I saw you come this way," he said. Placing a finger under her chin, Fremund lifted Eadlyn's face and kissed her firmly on the lips.

"Fremund!" She scowled and stepped back.

"You looked so pretty gathering the leaves. But should you be alone in the woods? I've just heard the old woman, Hlappa, has been bothering you." His voice became a little rougher as he continued, "What brought her here? How dare she bother you."

"I'm not alone," Eadlyn responded. "I'm no distance at all from the Sandtun and you are here."

"What did she want?"

"She wanted to be certain I was well," Eadlyn replied. "Fremund, she is very frail. I don't think she is any threat to me."

"You must stay close to me, or Megan, or at least not be alone." Fremund stepped forward. He reached for Eadlyn's hand and took the wild garlic from it, then placed it in her basket. Now her hands were free, and he took both in his own. "Have you decided to marry me yet, Eadlyn?"

"I have not decided."

"Let's take some pleasure here in the woods while it's quiet," he suggested. "Perchance you'll realise that we both have passions that need releasing?"

"Here, where anyone could walk past?"

Fremund shrugged his shoulders. "What does that matter? But I know of somewhere more secluded."

Eadlyn shook her hands from his and looked away; she could see the reeds and the wading birds through a gap in the trees. Should she accept his offer and follow this path which was open to her? Eadlyn looked back at him and knew, although she liked him more than she had thought possible, something stopped her from becoming his wife. "Nay, Fremund."

"It's what everyone expects. We are both young enough to find contentment with a new companion. What would be wrong with us having some pleasure?"

"What everyone expects?" Eadlyn snapped back at him. "Nay, you're wrong. I know you are. You are my cousin and people see you as nothing else." Thoughts ran through her head, barely taking shape before she blurted them out, "Do they see Arlo and Megan and think she comes here to lie with her husband's brother? No, they don't. And I did not come here to lie with you in the woods. I came here to sell my eggs and milk and to cook for my cousin."

Fremund waited until she had finished, then he reached down and handed Eadlyn her basket. "I'm not your cousin," he said. "Let's not fight."

Chapter Thirty-One

In his bid to learn about Romney Marsh, Brother Edwen had spent several days trying to cross it. Although much of the area was dry, he had been hindered by waterways cutting through the land. He walked one way, then another, sometimes jumping across a narrow ditch if the mood took him, sometimes passing over by a plank bridge. At times he had been given no choice but to turn back when a waterway could not be crossed, or the ground became too marshy. It was the height of summer and the banner reeds were strong and lush at the sides of the ditches, hindering his view so he could not look ahead and see the rambling turns of the waterways.

There was much to contemplate as the monk meandered to and fro, gradually moving towards the west. He thought about his vocation and wondered if he could spread the word of God more easily if he served the Him within a settlement, rather than the grounds of a monastery. With the sun as his guide, the monk kept to his hours of prayer "seven times a day I praise you," he would murmur as he looked to the sky in an effort to know if it was time to pray again.

Many of his thoughts concerned the Romney Marsh and Brother Edwen wondered about the men who walked over this land. For those days when he wandered about on the open landscape, he saw no other human being, but there were the signs that they did come. There were the ditches which had been cleared out in order for the water to run freely in them, and the piles of mud on one side or both of these waterways. Once he found a broken shovel propped up against a pile of dried mud; how that labourer must have cursed himself to have left a precious tool behind, albeit broken. It could have easily been repaired. The monk picked it up and took it with him. *Perchance it can be exchanged for a meal when I reach a settlement,* he thought. Another time he found several bundles of reeds at the side of a ditch. *Of course, they come here to harvest reeds for thatch, but how careless of someone to forget to return for these.*

The monk had expected to find a settlement, or at least a cottage or two, out on the Romney Marsh, but there were none. He saw just an occasional shelter, and it seemed that a farmer may spend a night or two out on his land, but his home was on the distant hills.

Much as Brother Edwen was in awe of the barren landscape, man's attempt to tame it and keep the sea at bay, it was hunger which drove him to the coast. Forced to eat the roots of grass, and the bitter leaves from the weeds, along with the occasional eel he managed to spike, his stomach gnawed with hunger. The water in the ditches had become stagnant as it lazed under the warm sun. Puddles of rainwater were more palatable, but scarce. And so, after ten nights, Brother Edwen returned to the shingle spit of land, a natural barrier keeping the sea from covering Romney Marsh.

When the monk first stood on the shingle and gazed across the wide golden sands, he was in a place where a settlement would later grow and be named Demechurch, then Dymchurch. But for now, there were low cottages of mud and reed thatch scattered in small numbers on the highest points of ground beyond the beach. These were inhabited by fishermen who were both cautious of the newcomer but willing to feed him. Sometimes he laboured for them, offering to clear a ditch near their home or cut reeds for their thatch. Other times a promise of prayers every day for a week was of more worth than anything else this holy man could offer.

Looking back along the coast towards the Sandtun, Brother Edwen could see what little distance he had travelled. Had he walked from the Sandtun to the coast, he would have reached these humble fishermen within a day. But he knew his time on the marsh had not been wasted. He had wanted to learn about this land and now he had gained some understanding. He had watched the water move along the channels and saw how man was taming Romney Marsh. He gained pleasure from the wildlife – the birds soaring up high and the insects darting about above the waterways. But more than anything Brother Edwen felt the great peace of this desolate land seep into him and he found he could forgive himself for fleeing Lyminge and thwarting the Lady Abbess' plans for bringing wealth in the form of relics to her minster.

Two weeks after leaving Lyminge, the roaming monk reached another community of fisherman's shacks and small boats pulled up on the beach. The tide was retreating, and he looked on as fishermen prepared to haul in the kettle nets which were set up to snare the fish, and women stood by with wooden crates ready to stow the catch. As he neared, Brother Edwen noted a group of men working on a boat and a couple of women bent over a sail which was spread out on the dark gold sand. They turned their heads and watched him approach, "God bless you all," he murmured as he neared them, and the people of this coastal settlement bowed their heads in respect for the holy man. They said nothing in reply.

A flat pan hung from the strap of the monk's shoulder bag; he had exchanged the broken shovel for it when he had first reached the coast a few days beforehand. "God has sent me here at the right time to help these men," he murmured, as he approached the fishermen. Then he spoke aloud, raising his voice so he could be heard over the tumbling waves. "It looks as if you would welcome some help with pulling the net in. I am young and strong and will help you in return for a couple of fish which I could fry in my pan."

They turned and assessed the monk's strength before one of the fishermen answered, "Aye, go on then."

Still unused to speaking for the sake of exchanging words for no good reason, Brother Edwen stood near the fishermen and waited, as they did, for the tide to fall back a little more. When they stepped forward, he moved with them, and pulled the net onto the sleek wet sand. The women moved forward with the crates and, as the net was peeled back, the writhing fish were placed within the crates. It was the women who carried the fish to the top of the beach and sorted the catch, killing the fish with a sharp blow to the head with a rock. One of them picked up a couple by their tails and walked back to the monk, offering him the fish.

"I thank you," he said.

"I have a fire burning; you may use it," she offered.

"That is good of you," Brother Edwen replied. His fish were soon cooked, and he ate them from the pan, picking flesh from the bones with relish.

Long before the sun began to set, the monk planned to continue his walk. But to his confusion he discovered he had reached the end of the coastline, at least it continued, but he could not carry on without crossing an estuary. A river was flowing out to the sea, seemingly without any urgency, and the mud-banks either side of it were wide. So, he was forced to turn inland and follow the course of the river. After several days wandering along the beach, he reluctantly turned his back on the sea and the bountiful supply of fish which had served him well.

Chapter Thirty-Two

It was on their second full day at the Sandtun when Eadlyn felt ready to share her thoughts with Arlo. He had been patient, never demanding that she try to explain what was on her mind. But after a supper of fried fish, when the work was done for the day, Eadlyn found herself with just the two men, while Megan tended her young daughter, and the older children paddled in the shallow water on the beach.

"Do you remember how Hlappa used to speak?" Eadlyn asked. "It was as if she knew things we didn't. As if she could see things in her mind she hadn't witnessed."

"I thought she was looking to cause upset," Fremund said.

"It seemed like that," Eadlyn admitted. "But I know she spoke the truth about one thing. There was gold on the Sandtun."

"Gold?" Fremund and Arlo repeated in unison.

"Aye, I don't know where it came from, but Todd had it." She turned to Fremund, "Do you remember on that day…on the day he died, you took his pouch and poured the sceattas into my hand? Then you took most of the coins and returned them to his pouch; you knew his brothers would want them, but you said I should take some for myself."

"I had a feeling they would give you none," Fremund replied.

"You were right; they offered me nothing. In fact, they took my animals from me and made me work for them."

"How could they do that?" Arlo exclaimed. He did not know the story of Eadlyn's survival over the past year.

"They did, yet I fought back, with some help from my good cousin here," Eadlyn told him. "But that is a story for another time. Let us go back to when Fremund thought to give me the sceattas; there was a small package with them, and it fell into my hand. At that time, I thought nothing of it and put it into my own purse. Inside the ragged piece of cloth was a gold cross, with a red stone at the centre. I knew then it was something special and I hid it away in my mattress. What it was doing here on the Sandtun, we will never know, but Todd must have found it and I kept it as my own."

"It's strange to think that anyone who had something of such value would wear it here and be so careless as to lose it," Arlo said. "Todd said nothing to me about finding it. What about you, Fremund?"

"I knew nothing of it," Fremund replied. "It seems that he kept it as his secret. But Eadlyn, since you have this precious cross, surely it can be sold, and the money used to bring comfort to you and the children?"

"I didn't know how to sell it without arousing questions which couldn't be answered," Eadlyn admitted. "But now it's too late."

"Too late?" he repeated, his freckled brow creased in a frown.

"Elder-Modor changed the straw in the mattresses..."

Eadlyn was quiet for a moment, reliving the scene, remembering the horror she had felt. She thought of

278

that dear woman, who felt her distress but did not understand what was causing it. Elder-Modor had gone to the nuns and asked for something to soothe Eadlyn, and the younger woman smiled as she thought of that scented sachet hanging near her bed at home. The men were silent, as they too pictured the elderly woman doing her best to be of some help and losing something so precious to the family.

"Hlappa said something very strange and I can't understand how this could be true..." Eadlyn spoke again. "She said that the gold was on the Sandtun, that it had come back."

"Perchance she is right and it came with you, caught up in a blanket or a piece of clothing?" Arlo suggested.

"Or does she just want to cause upset in your mind?" Fremund's tone was dismissive. "You must think nothing of it, Eadlyn. She came to see if you were well but couldn't resist troubling you again. If there is gold, you'll find it in Lyminge, in the grass outside your doorway or in a dark corner of your home." He stood up and Eadlyn's gaze followed him as he stretched and took a couple of steps towards his cart. "Let the three of us drink a noggin of mead and forget about that old witch."

They watched him go and reach into the cart, retrieve the flagon, and pull the stopper from the top. He rummaged about for some small clay noggins and filled them all, then handed one to Arlo and one to Eadlyn, who both smiled their thanks.

Fremund placed his own on the ground and announced, "I'm going to relieve myself at the creek and I'll get some wood for the fire." In a few long strides, he was on the beach track and heading towards the bridge.

Arlo and Eadlyn sat in silence for a while, both looking out across to the beach and the lagoon. Frustrated by Fremund's not listening to her, Eadlyn said, "He's wrong. I don't understand it, but Hlappa knows about my gold. She called it a pendant, and that's what Todd found here – a gold pendant cross."

"There's some people who know..." Arlo began. "We have a woman in Aldington who makes potions and seems to be able to read minds."

"There's a woman in Postling, where Fremund lives, she is the same," Eadlyn was eager to offer this, but stopped herself from telling that she had been to visit Mildrithe. "But she's kind, not like Hlappa." She paused for a moment, "Oh, I don't know... I'm not sure if Hlappa means to be so strange."

"I can't make her out," Arlo offered. "I found it difficult when she was amongst us last year."

Eadlyn took a sip of the mead. It burned her throat, but afterwards the taste in her mouth was pleasant. "She spoke of the cross being holy and it had travelled here from Middle England. Sometimes I think her words have no meaning at all, and now I wonder. It was special; I am sure of it."

"Holy?" Arlo repeated. Where his voice had been low and gentle, now that one word was spoken with rare urgency.

"Aye, holy, she said."

"Eadlyn, I need to speak with Fremund." Arlo stood abruptly, he drank the mead in one gulp and placed the noggin on the ground beside Fremund's.

Eadlyn drained her noggin of mead and stirred herself to check on the goats. They needed to be kept provided with fresh grass and were taken for walks several times a day. The milk supply had been good, and her customers were happy. She walked to the west of the Sandtun, where the grass was lush, and pulled up several handfuls of it. On her return the men were back sitting by the fire, and it was clear they had something to share with her.

Fremund told the story of their first evening on the Sandtun the previous year. He recalled the time when Todd and he had walked along to the tidal inlet and had heard people approaching the Sandtun at night, yet they never crossed the bridge. Curious, the cousins had taken the track inland towards the Roman fort and had crept up behind a group of men. He told Eadlyn how the cousins had looked on and seen the tonsured heads of four monks in the moonlight and then how they had noted the monks had something slung between them.

"Monks," Eadlyn repeated. "But we saw monks the next day, didn't we? They walked through the Sandtun and later they were at the spring. I remember they had tools to sell."

"Aye, they did," Fremund replied, his voice dark. "They had tools to sell and no body to carry. It seems as if the body was gone. Buried on the marsh."

"It was that evening, when you and the children went to bed, Todd and Fremund told me what they had seen," Arlo picked up the story.

Now both Fremund and Arlo told of the three of them following the track and this time going further than the wooded area. They followed a causeway and then a track across the open land and discovered a grave. There must have been an agreement between the men before they disclosed this to Eadlyn, as they omitted to mention a fourth man who had been out on the marsh that night, and had been seen digging at the grave of the unknown person, whom they presumed to be a monk.

"At that moment, there was a great storm," Fremund said. "The rain was torrential; do you remember?"

"Aye," Eadlyn recalled. "The land was badly flooded."

"And later all sign of the grave was gone," Arlo added.

"Perchance Todd picked up the cross that evening, or he returned another time and saw it?" Eadlyn suggested.

"It seems likely," Fremund agreed.

"Will you take me there?" The idea came to Eadlyn in a flash. Although evening was setting in, there were still a couple more hours of daylight.

"Why not?" Fremund agreed. He refilled his noggin with mead and took a long sip before rising to his feet. "We'll walk the way the monks travelled a year ago."

They entered the area shaded by trees and followed the track, past where Eadlyn had gathered garlic the previous day, and only pausing when they reached the ruins of the Roman fort midway up the hillside.

"This is where we first saw them," Fremund told her. "Although we knew they were ahead of us and had been following them for some time. Eadlyn closed her eyes and tried to imagine the scene: four monks standing there, perhaps gazing up at the pale grey stones of the Roman walls. *It must have been cumbersome*, she reflected, *to carry the weight of a man and tread these uneven tracks by night. I wonder where they journeyed from.* The tree branches grew low in places and brambles sent out their shoots across the track. By daylight, they could be pushed aside, by moonlight they were constant risks to the safety of anyone walking these paths.

The men led the way from the wooded area and back onto the open marshland. Here the sea still streamed in along the tidal creek and spilled out onto an area of thin spiky reeds, soft mud, and pools of water. The air was thick with swarming insects and they covered their faces as they walked in single file along a raised causeway.

The land dried out and the causeway became a track; sheep grazed on the pasture and raised their heads to watch the progress of the three strangers.

"I can see a bridge over there," Arlo pointed towards the end of the track. "A good one too." It was the place where the mystical light had shone from the sky, guiding the way for the four monks. But the three who crossed it today knew nothing of that.

The drainage ditch they had just crossed snaked its way towards the three willows marking the grave of the Abbot Botolph.

"He lies there," Fremund murmured, pointing in the direction of the grave.

Moments later, Fremund, Arlo and Eadlyn stood with their backs to the pastureland, facing the patch of ground before the willows and the ditch. The ground was even, a little dry from the summer sun, and with a layer of grass growing across it.

"It was washed smooth by the flooding after the storm," Arlo reminded them.

Eadlyn nodded, recalling the torrential rain that night and how close the high waters had come to flooding the vulnerable Sandtun. She had woken to find herself almost on an island, with their campfires swept away on the seaward side and the marshland flooded behind them. She knelt before the grave, her head bowed a little and hands clasped on her lap. "There's a body buried here," Eadlyn murmured. "It doesn't seem right, does it? To leave a person all alone."

"There must be a reason for it," Arlo said. "I can't say why but I feel it isn't sinister. I wonder if the monks brought the body here to do good."

"I'd like to think they did," Eadlyn looked at Arlo and gave a small smile. She was feeling so serious. Almost overwhelmed by the enormity of learning this. She had been given an insight into the last days of Todd's life and wanted to thank his friends. But somehow Eadlyn could not express her thoughts. *Sometimes it must be right to say nothing and wait until the words come more easily,* she decided.

"We thought it must be another monk," Fremund said. "That's what the three of us decided. But of course, we have no way of knowing."

The evening sun cast its soft golden light on the ground in front of the three willow trees. There was nothing at all to show what had happened here. The men had told their story and there was little more to add. They could only stand, each of them absorbed in their own thoughts, and reflect on the possible reasons why four monks would have buried someone here on the remote Romney Marsh.

"Before we leave, shall we pray for him?" Eadlyn asked. The men murmured their agreement, and so Eadlyn began her short prayer, sometimes struggling to know how to form it, but knowing the importance of her words. "Dear God in heaven, please look down on this...on this man and treat him with mercy. He lies in unconsecrated land, but he still needs you to hear his sins and think kindly of him, so he may rise to heaven and rest in peace. Please bless this man, or woman. Bless whoever lies here and listen to the prayers we three will send for him and know wherever we are, we will think of him beneath the willows and implore you to be lenient with him. Amen." She looked at Fremund and then Arlo, who knelt on either side of her. "Was that enough? Can you think of anything else?"

"It was enough," Fremund said, as he rose to his feet.

But Arlo was preoccupied; something hard was half-buried amongst the roots of the grass, it pressed into his knee and he pulled back to explore the area. He could feel it with his fingertips and was tugging it free. Then he stood, and as he did so he was pulling the grass free and studying the golden cross he had retrieved. With his sleeve, Arlo rubbed the smooth red garnet.

Eadlyn, standing before him, felt a chill run through her body and her mouth went dry.

Arlo held the cross out before him. "Perchance God has sent us our answer," he said. "This cross looks to be holy to me. If it belonged to the dead man, then I'd say he was a monk and someone of great dignity – an abbot or a prior?" Then his attention fell upon Eadlyn, he saw her face was white and the confusion in her eyes. He reached out a hand and placed it on her arm. "What is it?"

She did not know how to say it; her throat was so constricted, and she hardly knew how to explain. She wanted to tell him that it was her pendant cross; at least it had come from Todd and it had become hers. But the words stayed held within Eadlyn and in her mind came Hlappa's words "There's gold on the Sandtun," rang out over and over.

"Have you seen this before?" Arlo asked. His voice was gentle, and she knew he was a patient man who would wait until she was able to tell her story more fully. "Have a look." He took her hand, then placed the pendant cross in her palm.

Eadlyn's fingers closed around the cross; she held it tight within her hand, feeling the sharp corners and the coldness of the precious metal. Then another voice came to her; this one was full of loving kindness and care. It replaced the taunts of the old woman with its own gentle reminder: "There are two paths ahead of you. When you see the red stone, the answer will come to you. It will show you your future." Eadlyn closed her eyes; someone was standing close behind her. She believed it to be Fremund. She opened her palm; the stone took the light of the evening sun and glowed. The gold, with its carved swirls became warm from her hand and the sun. She looked up from the cross and straight at Arlo who still stood, looking down at her and Eadlyn knew she had been right to wait for the cross to lead her to her future.

Epilogue 683 AD

Brother Edwen knelt on the dry earth in front of a stone cross on a plinth. Nurtured by the warmth of the sun on his skin, he found a sense of peace from the familiar rhythm of the psalms led by the priest at his side. Then he rose to say the final doxology:

"Glory be to the Father and to the Son
And to the Holy Spirit
As it was in the beginning,
Is now, and ever shall be,
World without end.
Amen."

It was satisfying to be following the monastic rules alongside the itinerant priest who had wandered into Edwen's new life the previous winter. Together they had brought some order to the lives of the people who lived in this remote settlement surrounded by fertile farmland and the tidal estuary. The wooden cross had been replaced by one of stone, and mass was celebrated regularly. Edwen's brown hair, no longer tonsured, was ruffled by the light breeze. To his right three willows lined the gentle arc of a drainage ditch. Their leaves were pale green, newly unfurled in the springtime. He felt blessed by the presence of the three trees; they reminded him of those near where

Abbot Botolph lay in his own desolate patch of Romney Marsh.

"Let us praise the Lord," the priest's voice rose as he completed the office of Sext.

"Thanks be to God," Edwen said. He rose to his feet and straightened his tunic. The two men nodded to each other and moved away in different directions. Edwen walked towards the river and paused as he reached a slight rise in the land. He took a deep breath and exhaled slowly, a feeling of satisfaction running through his body.

"Is it high enough?" a man asked, as he approached and stood beside Edwen. The shovel in his hand rested on the muddy ground.

"Aye, it's a fair height. You've done a good job."

"I've never known the river to flood this far," the labourer offered reassurance.

"But if it was to, then this area will be spared, and we'll thank God that we thought to build the land up."

"Aye we will," the labourer nodded. He left Edwen and returned to his job of clearing the nearby ditch.

It had taken nearly two years for Edwen's dream to begin to take shape and now he was on the brink of seeing the next stage of his plan grow before him. He had always loved working on the land; the activity made him strong and helped him sleep well at night. It was due to his endurance that he had been given the privilege of fulfilling Abbot Botolph's last wishes. His thoughts digressed to the long journey he had taken nearly three years beforehand; Edwen shook himself and returned to the present.

Whereas in the monasteries his labours had been in the form of working the land to grow grains and vegetables, Edwen now worked with nature in a different way. He was one of a gang of men who dredged the silt from the riverbank and strengthened the sides with upright planks. Over time, a long stretch of the river had been prepared to accept ships. Not fishing boats, although they were welcome, but they were small enough to pull up anywhere on the mudflats. It would be ships from faraway lands which would moor up, bow to stern, at the place now named Langport by the local men. Dredging the shallows had been filthy work but would bring wealth to the settlement growing beside the river. The fertile flat lands to the north and east were already producing good crops and the grass was lush for hardy sheep and cattle. A port would be an excellent addition to the settlement.

The silt dragged from the riverbed had been put to good use, placed on an area of land in the heart of the village, not far from the track leading to the coast. Edwen scanned the raised area again and repeated, "It's high enough. This place will serve us very well."

He turned from his view of the countryside and the reed-thatched village homes and continued to move towards the river. It was wide, with treacherous mudflats which would suck in any person who dared to step on them. The river was tidal, and it was only at high tide that a boat could leave Langport, sail over the water-covered mudflats and land on the opposite bank. Somewhere over there, a settlement named Lydd was rising from the marshland on a shingle ridge. Edwen shielded his eyes and squinted a little. It was no good; sometimes he fancied he could see the cottages of Lydd, but not today and it was most likely in his imagination. Closer still, a middle island rose between saltwater channels; it was said that just a handful of hardy fishermen lived there in low shacks.

"One day I'll go there," he said to himself. "The people of Lydd and Middle Island will want to know of this place, Langport, and the glorious house of prayer I have created here." The estranged monk was naturally modest, but on that day his mood was jubilant and rightfully so.

Time passed, with Edwen lost in these thoughts, and another man came to stand beside him. This man had become a natural leader within the settlement, and it was he who had instigated the shoring up of the riverbank, providing the mud needed to fulfil Edwen's dream. He had seen the ships passing by for towns inland and believed that if a port could be created, then all manner of foreign goods could come to his village. A loyal servant of God, Bertwald of Romney had welcomed Edwen, whom he saw as deeply religious, despite the newcomer's reticence to speak of his time before he came to Romney Marsh.

"I had a vision last night," Edwen said, partly to himself. "I saw a church on a rise overlooking the river and the Romney Marsh. It had a tower standing beside it, and within the tower there was a bell to call the villagers to worship the Lord."

Bertwald of Romney had heard this talk before and Edwen's words usually sailed past his ears, but one caught his attention and he replied. "A tower? What is this tower you speak of?"

"Did I say tower?" Edwen responded. He frowned a little, trying to recall the dream. "Of course, it came to me in my sleep, tall and square with pointed roof, like a knife blade. We will not see it here in our lifetime. Our oratory is to be built in wood from the Weald. But I believe one day there will be a church of stone here at Langport. The community will grow and there will be a demand for it."

"Ah, in your dream," Bertwald repeated, and he turned away. He straightened himself as something caught his eye, and stepping forward he looked towards the north-west, from where the river flowed. "Edwen," he called. "They are here! Two, mayhap three, boats. Our wood is coming. Soon the men will be unloading it and carpenters will work all the hours they can give until your oratory is built!"

Edwen ran to the riverside. It was true, three boats in full sail were moving down the river. The tide was high, with the currents of river and sea battling against each other. But these boats were large and the mooring posts strong. He looked back at the rise of land; he had dreamed of this moment for so long and could picture the wooden house of prayer standing proud between river and settlement.

"Soon our priest will be leading us in prayer, and people from foreign lands will see our veneration of the Lord when they moor at our harbour and see our oratory raised above us all."

"They will." Bertwald of Romney was looking down at the mooring posts; this would be the first test of their strength. "But our good priest will move to other places; he is driven to serve the Lord throughout our land. Whereas you, I believe, are settled here at Langport."

"I am."

"You speak little of your past, but I hope you will lead us all in prayer if we are to lose our priest."

"If the good Lord wishes it to be, then I will serve the best I can," Edwen conceded. He closed his eyes and imagined himself ensconced within the wooden walls of his house of prayer.

A warm sense of well-being washed over him and he recalled that time when he had asked Brother Halig, "What sort of place is this Romney Marsh?" and the older monk had replied, "There's nothing to speak of." That was the first he had ever heard of the place and even then he had been curious about the low-lying land.

"Wherever you are now..." he murmured, thinking of the older monk, "...you are wrong. There would have been plenty to tell, if only you had looked."

The End

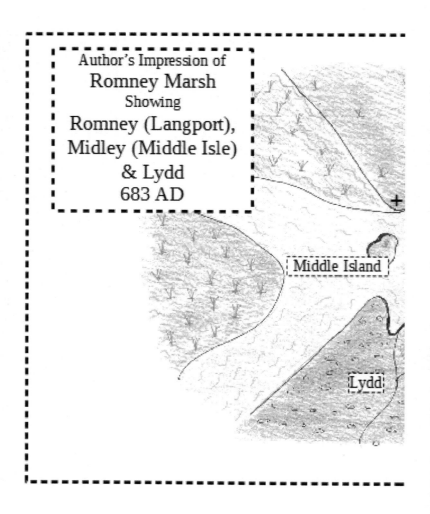

Author's Impression of
Romney Marsh
Showing
**Romney (Langport),
Midley (Middle Isle)
& Lydd
683 AD**

Middle Island

Lydd

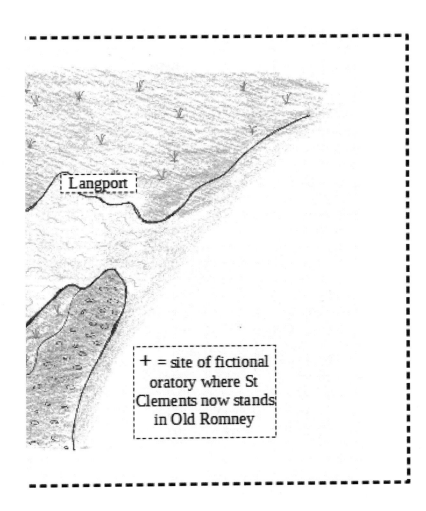

Langport

+ = site of fictional oratory where St Clements now stands in Old Romney

About the Author

Romney Marsh writer, Emma Batten, loves to combine her interest in local history with creative writing. It is important to her that historical details are accurate so as to give readers an authentic insight into life on Romney Marsh. She enjoys giving author talks about her journey as a writer, planning unique writing workshops and meeting her local readers.

The Pendant Cross is Emma's seventh novel.

Her first, *A Place Called Hope*, is set in the 16th century and tells the story of the lives of two young women living through the decline of the remote settlement of Hope on Romney Marsh.

Her second novel, *Secrets of the Shingle, is* a mystery set on the wild, windswept wastes of the Dungeness peninsula in the 19th century and seen through the eyes of a naive young teacher.

Her third, *What the Monk Didn't See,* is the story of New Romney and the 1287 storm which changed the fortunes of the town forever.

But First Maintain the Wall is set in Georgian Dymchurch. Harry is passing through the village when the seawall breaches and events force him to stay. As an outsider, he struggles to be accepted and a tentative friendship is forged with a young woman who seeks answers to her past.

Stranger on the Point, a sequel to *Secrets of the Shingle,* is the story of a young woman's quest to fulfil her worth as the shadows of WW1 live on. Set in Dungeness and Ashford.

The Artist's Gift tells the story of a fictional character living amongst real life events during the Second World War. Set in Lydd and Dungeness. A sequel to *Secrets of the Shingle* and *Stranger on the Point.*

Still Shining Bright, a prequel to *Secrets of the Shingle*, again features Dungeness and Ashford. Cora and her daughter are brought ashore by lifeboat. With no home or possessions, they rely on the kindness of strangers and Cora must use her wit to survive.

For more details take a look at Emma's website:
www.emmabattenauthor.com